THE BIG MAN UPSTAIRS

A DCI JACK LOGAN THRILLER

J.D. KIRK

ZERTEX CRIME

THE BIG MAN UPSTAIRS
ISBN: 978-1-912767-24-3

Published worldwide by Zertex Crime, an imprint of Zertex Media Ltd. This edition published in 2020.

www.jdkirk.com
www.zertexmedia.com

For Lindsay Jarret, whose strength knows no bounds.

CHAPTER ONE

THE PATH WAS NOT A PATH. NOT THIS EVENING. IT WAS an inhospitable desert. A vast Arctic ice floe. The Valley of Death itself. It would take him hours to cross it. Days. Weeks.

He hoped so, at least. He wanted to delay it, to push it away to some far-off date, to someplace and sometime he wouldn't have to think about too much. Not now, at least. Not yet.

But it was too late for that. There was no delaying it, no holding it back, no escaping it. He no longer had that choice.

He creaked open the gate, but didn't yet take a step. Instead, he just stood there, the drizzle matting his hair to his head. The high winds that had battered him on his walk back to the house had died away, like the night itself was holding its breath.

Waiting. Watching him. Damning him with its silence.

The path was not a path. It was the Gaza Strip. A World War I trench. A river of molten lava. Crossing it would be the end of him. By the time he reached the front door, the old him—this him—would be dead, and whatever version of himself still existed would have to live forever with what he'd done.

The wind returned. The hand of God Himself, pushing him on. Urging him to get it over with. To face up to his sins.

His legs moved. He didn't want them to, but they did it anyway. One foot, then the other, plodded him up the impossibly long path to the cottage way, way off in the distance.

There were lights on, despite the relative earliness of the evening. The rainclouds had cast a shadow over him, and the house, and the town around. The gloom was entirely appropriate. All it needed was a flash of lightning and a boom of thunder to fully set the stage.

He'd seen the house a thousand times. More. It was different now, knowing what he knew. Knowing what awaited him inside. And what would await him after he had done it. After he had rent the world asunder with his next awful act.

There would be a lot of questions. A lot of accusations. He would have an endless amount of explaining to do.

Despite the impossible distance he had to cover, he arrived at the front step after just a few seconds. His heartbeat was thumping in his head, and his legs, and his stomach, and his throat. His chest, strangely, felt empty. Hollow. A void, filled with nothing at all. No air. No heart. No soul.

His keys rattled in his shaking hand, the metal scratching and scraping around the lock as he struggled to insert the front door key in the dim light of the porch.

A car passed, the beam of its headlights moving through the gaps in the hedge like dancing fairies. He took the opportunity to slot the key into the lock, but otherwise didn't move until the vehicle had continued on along the street and around the corner at the far end.

Even when it was gone, he didn't turn the key. Not yet. He wasn't ready.

Instead, he placed a hand on the door, like he could feel through it to the rooms on the other side. He ran his fingers across the smooth wood, caressing it and savouring the moment. Right here and now, it was still his house. Still his home.

When he opened it, that would all change.

Everything would change.

He took a breath. He choked back a sob.

And then, the Reverend Gareth Mann opened his front door and stepped inside to face the raw, awful horror of what he was about to do.

CHAPTER TWO

THE ONCE-DETECTIVE CHIEF INSPECTOR JACK LOGAN
had cracked the case less than five minutes after the ferry had
left the terminal. The ex-wife had done it. Caved her former
husband's head in with a garden gnome, then had it fixed up
and repainted.

The gnome, that was. Not the head.

It was obvious. Far too obvious. All the clues were there
in the folder he'd been given back at the pub. He'd been out
of the polis for the better part of a year, but he'd been able to
spot the killer a mile-off on a skim read of the first few pages.
Anyone who couldn't, had no bloody business issuing
parking tickets, much less being involved in murder investigations.

Logan dropped the folder on the table Sinead Bell was
sitting at. The weather had taken a turn for the worse while
they'd waited for the boat to come in, and everyone in the
lounge—including himself—was leaning left and right to
compensate for the choppiness of the water.

Sinead had recently moved to the Major Investigations

Team from Uniform and was now a fully-fledged Detective Constable. Logan had pegged her as one-to-watch from the moment he'd met her. She was smart. Competent. Thought outside the box, and quickly, too.

He saw from the way her eyes went to the folder that she understood. She knew the plan was a bust. They'd been well and truly rumbled.

"I'm assuming she confessed?" Logan grunted, lowering himself onto the hard plastic chair across the table from Sinead.

"Who?" she asked, her brow creasing into a frown. He saw through the look of confusion right away.

"It's a good job you're a decent copper, Detective Constable, because you'd make a shite actress," Logan told her. "You know full bloody well who."

For a moment, it looked like Sinead was going to maintain the pretence, but then she smiled sheepishly at him and gave a little shrug. "She did, sir, aye. Couple of days after the body was found. Admitted to the whole thing. Turned out she'd thought she'd get the life insurance. We had her down as the culprit from the get-go."

Logan nodded, then sat back in his chair. The floor undulated beneath him, and he shifted his weight to compensate. "Aye, well I should bloody hope so. You'd have to be blind not to see what she was up to," he said. "And I told you, don't call me 'sir.' I'm not your boss. I'm no' even on the Force."

Sinead nodded while fighting to stay straight-faced. "Right. Aye. Whatever you say."

"This Ben's idea, was it?" Logan asked, tapping the folder. "Tell me there's some big mystery, try to tempt me back in with it?"

Sinead picked up the folder and slipped it into her briefcase.

"Kind of a joint team decision," she said, giving nothing away. She chewed her lip for a moment as she buckled the bag closed. "You're not angry, are you?"

"What, that my former colleagues all got together and conspired to deceive me?" Logan asked. It came out more harshly than he'd intended, and he offered a thin, lopsided smile by way of an apology. "No. I'm not angry. Truth be told, I've been thinking about coming back. For a while now, actually. The job... it gets its hooks into you, I suppose, and..." He sighed. "God. I don't know."

"Admit it, sir. You missed us."

Logan gave a dry chuckle. "Aye, like a hole in the head."

He looked around the small passenger lounge. It was busier than he'd expect for a Wednesday. There were a dozen or so people spread out around the tables. Most of them were reading newspapers or had their noses buried in books.

A young couple sitting together near one of the windows had their phones raised, searching for a signal. To the best of Logan's knowledge, they hadn't spoken a word to each other since stepping aboard.

There was a small arcade area down a corridor. He could see Sinead's brother, Harris, shooting wildly at a screen with a bright blue plastic revolver.

"Speaking of holes, where's Tyler?" Logan asked.

"He's out on deck for some fresh air," Sinead said, indicating a door that led outside. "He gets seasick."

"Jesus Christ, is there any mode of transport that boy doesn't have some bloody issue with?" Logan asked. "Still, least it's no' my upholstery that's in the firing line, this time."

"He says it's an inner-ear problem," Sinead explained.

"Fair enough. I'm not sure what kind of inner-ear problem makes you nearly shite yourself in a helicopter, mind you. But then, I'm no' a doctor," Logan said.

"Sinead! Have you got any more money?"

Logan turned in his chair to see Harris come stumbling across the rolling lounge, wild-eyed with excitement.

"I gave you all my change already," Sinead told him, and the boy flinched like he'd been struck.

"Aw, but I've nearly got the bad guy!" Harris groaned, bouncing up and down with excited frustration. "I'm so close, but I've died. I've only got sixty seconds to put more money in. I've had to leave the gun sitting on the floor so it doesn't reset!"

"You cleaned me out," Sinead told him. "Sorry."

"*Sorry* doesn't stop the bad guys, Detective Constable. Have they taught you nothing?" Logan said, getting to his feet. He shot her a reproachful look as he fished in his trouser pockets. "Come on, son. Let's you and me go show this bugger who's boss."

WHEN THEY DISEMBARKED AT SCRABSTER, DC Tyler Neish was the first down the ramp onto dry land. He stumbled the last few steps, staggered as he adjusted to the motionless solidity of the ground beneath his feet, then clung to a lamp post until everything stopped spinning.

"I'm fine. I'm fine," he insisted, although the colour of his face—or rather, the complete lack of it—said otherwise. "Just give me a second, and I'll be right as rain."

It was a fitting choice of words. The rain was coming

down in sheets now, making the small settlement of Scrabster look even greyer and more miserable than usual, which was no mean feat.

Up above, seagulls called their screeching laments, keeping their beady eyes peeled for any poor, hapless bastards emerging from the ferry with a bag of chips in hand.

"I'm freezing," Harris said, pulling his thin jacket around himself. "Can we go to the car?"

Logan stepped aside to let the smattering of other passengers disembark. Vehicles were trundling down a separate ramp beside them, their drivers dry and warm inside.

"Aye, get your finger out, and pull yourself together, son," Logan scolded. "We're getting soaked to the knickers here."

"Sorry, Boss," Tyler said. He gulped down some salty air, and tentatively released his grip on the lamp post.

They all watched him swaying on the spot for a few seconds, before he smiled, nodded, and gave a thumbs up. "Right, that's me," he announced.

And then, he turned away, coughed, and what little was left of his stomach contents splattered onto the ground at his feet.

"No. Tell a lie," he managed to wheeze before the next heave trembled through him, and the hungry seagulls cried out with glee.

Logan sighed. The two-and-a-half-hour drive to Inverness suddenly seemed like a very daunting prospect.

Four hours and multiple pitstops later, Sinead pulled into the Burnett Road Station car park, cut off the engine, and pressed the buttons that wound up all four windows.

The journey had been a cold and wet one, but it was better that than the smell.

It had also been arse-numbingly uncomfortable. Technically, Sinead and Tyler were not on official polis business, so they'd taken Sinead's car.

Logan didn't think he'd ever been in a Vauxhall Corsa before, and he hoped to Christ he was never in one again. Or, if he was, he was going to make a point of not being in the back seat.

Tyler had insisted that he'd feel better if he was sitting up front. If that was the case, Logan thought, he'd have hated to see what the bastard would've been like in the back.

Logan had squeezed in there next to Harris, his knees jammed up against the back of Tyler's seat, his head at an angle so it wasn't sticking up through the roof.

Harris had fallen asleep a few minutes into the drive. Logan didn't think he'd ever been more jealous of anyone in his life and had contemplated nudging the boy awake multiple times throughout the drive, if only so he had someone else to share his misery with.

As she'd driven, Sinead had filled Logan in on what he'd missed since he'd left. For the most part, this involved her complaining about DCI Sam Grant—Snecky, as he was more commonly known—who had come running back from the Central Belt with his tail between his legs just as soon as his old job had become available.

Tyler had chimed in with his own remarks about Snecky, as and when his rigorous vomiting schedule had allowed. It was safe to say neither Detective Constable liked the man. This came as no surprise. Logan had not yet met anyone on the Force with a kind word to say about Snecky, beyond someone once remarking that they quite liked his new shoes.

A job had opened up with CID in Aberdeen, and Snecky was keen to make the transfer out east. First, they needed to find his replacement, and the new Detective Superintendent overseeing the MIT team was keen for it to be 'someone familiar with the role,' and 'a safe pair of hands.'

Logan was certainly the first of those things. He wasn't so sure about the second.

"She, eh, wants you to go in as soon as you're here," Sinead said. "Detective Superintendent Mitchell, I mean." She turned in her chair and looked around at him, all squashed up and crooked-necked. "She said to say that if you don't go and see her, you can forget the whole thing. So... yeah. You should probably go see her, eh? You think?" She looked to Tyler for support. "He should probably go and see her."

With some effort, Tyler turned in his seat. Logan hissed and drew back at the sight of his bleary red eyes and green-tinged skin.

"Holy shite, son," Logan said. "Are you sure you survived that journey? You look like a bloody zombie."

"I'm actually feeling much better now, Boss," Tyler said, although this was not supported by how he looked, or the way his voice rasped through his dry, aching throat. He smiled weakly. "But, aye. You should go talk to her, pronto. Take it from me, she does *not* like to be kept waiting."

CHAPTER THREE

It was a strange feeling for Logan to walk into Hoon's old office and not find himself on the receiving end of a torrent of abuse, or some creatively offensive personal insult.

Detective Superintendent Chuki Mitchell sat behind the same desk Hoon had used for years, and yet it was barely recognisable. It looked bigger, for one thing. This was partly because the person sitting behind it was considerably smaller, but also because the desktop wasn't hidden beneath teetering stacks of paperwork, notebooks, mould-infested coffee cups, and the general clutter that Hoon had been happy to live with.

Now, Logan could see the actual top of the desk itself, which was something of a first. The Out Tray was almost as full as the In Tray. Hoon had rarely, if ever, used the Out Tray, other than as a makeshift bin when the cleaner hadn't come round to empty his wastepaper basket.

Logan had met the new DSup a handful of times over the years, but had never really got the measure of her beyond the very basics. She was a good five or six years older than he was, he estimated, and she was a clear foot shorter.

But then, most people were.

She'd risen through the ranks pretty quickly, which had led to a fair amount of gossip. He'd done his best to ignore it, but hadn't been able to avoid hearing occasional snatches of it over the years.

Her mother was Kenyan. Maybe Ugandan, depending on who you asked. Her father had either been a Glasgow lad serving in the Royal Navy, or a Fife boy serving in the Merchant. Their paths had crossed somewhere between here and there, and they'd wound up in a council house in the Gorbals a few years later, with four kids, three dogs, and no garden.

Like most long-serving members of the polis, she'd had her share of nicknames over the years. The only difference was that repeating most of them would now be a sackable offence.

Her friends called her, 'Chook,' apparently, although Logan had never met any of them to be able to confirm this.

She was writing on an A4 notepad and didn't seem to have noticed him. The door had been open—something Hoon had tried to avoid at all costs, in case it gave the impression that he was available. The last thing he'd wanted was for any Tom, Dick, or Harry to come wandering in with a question.

"They're grown fucking adults," he'd once barked at Logan, after a Uniform sergeant had stopped by with a question. "Can they no' figure this shite out for themselves?"

"You, eh, wanted to—" Logan began, but a sharp raising of the Detective Superintendent's pen stopped him. She flicked her gaze in his direction for a fraction longer than a nanosecond, and pointed with the pen to the empty chair on his side of the desk.

"One minute," she said, turning her attention back to her notepad.

Logan pulled the chair out and took a seat. It complained at the sudden weight it was being forced to bear, drawing a slightly concerned look from the Detective Superintendent that was there one moment, gone the next.

He'd gained weight working in the pub. Nine months of standing around with unlimited access to bar snacks and fountain soft drinks had taken its toll. It was part of the reason he'd grown the beard, to disguise his additional chins.

There had been two extra when he'd last looked. He dreaded to think how many were under there now.

"Right, then," Mitchell muttered, finishing her note with a flourished signature which seemed oddly flamboyant for someone with a reputation for being wound so tight. She set the pen down, stood up sharply, and thrust out a hand for Logan to shake. "Detective Superintendent Mitchell."

Logan didn't stand, but took the offered hand and shook it. "Aye. We've met."

"Have we?" Mitchell asked, returning to her chair. "I mean, I've heard of you by reputation, of course..." She said this like it was not, by any stretch of the imagination, a good thing. "...but I didn't think we'd met."

"Aye, well, it was a wee while back," Logan said. "Some training thing across in Edinburgh, I think."

The woman across the table studied his face for a few seconds, then a flicker of recognition crossed it. "The beard's new?"

Logan gave his facial hair a stroke. "It is."

"Right. Well, that'll have to go, of course," Mitchell said, in a way that made it clear it wasn't a suggestion. "You are coming back, yes?"

Logan mulled over his response for a few seconds. The Detective Superintendent tapped a finger on her desk, the short, neatly-trimmed nail *tick-tick-ticking* on the wood like she was giving him a countdown.

"I'm considering my options," he said. "Wouldn't want to rush into anything."

The DSup sat back in her chair, interlocked her fingers, and laid them across her stomach. The dark skin of her hands made her crisp white shirt appear even brighter than it was.

"Hoon spoke very highly of you during the Professional Standards inquiry. Very highly for him, at least, in that he wasn't completely disparaging about you and your performance. You clearly made an impression."

"Aye. Well. He's known me a long time," Logan said. He looked around the office. It was the same size and shape as Hoon's, located on the same corridor, but there was almost nothing left to connect the place with its former occupant. It even smelled different.

Not just different. Better. Much better. Unlike Hoon, Mitchell obviously didn't object to opening the windows from time to time.

"What happened to him?" Logan asked. "Hoon."

"Dismissed, obviously," Mitchell said. "Pension's looking substantially less healthy, too."

Logan raised an eyebrow. "That's it? No' the jail?"

Detective Superintendent Mitchell flexed her fingers, then drummed them on her stomach. "It was felt that this would only serve to undermine the public's trust," she said, as if reading it verbatim from a prepared statement. "He handed over all the money Bosco had given him, and provided evidence that helped ensure Mr Maximuke won't be back out on the street anytime soon."

"Aye, but—"

"Much of the information Maximuke had on you and your team did not come from Hoon," Mitchell continued. She didn't raise her voice to speak over him, or rush to cut him off. She just spoke, and there was an assumption there that he'd shut up and listen. "The actual information he provided was substantial in terms of quantity, but of negligible use to an organisation such as the one Maximuke was running. And so, for better or worse, no prosecution took place."

Logan had sat forward, ready to voice his objections, but there was no point. Hoon's fate, whether he agreed with it or not, had been decided in his absence by powers far greater than his own.

Would slinging the bastard in prison have done any good? Probably not. Losing his job, and the power and respect that went with it, would have to be punishment enough.

"Before you decide if you're coming back, I want to tell you what I told the others when I first arrived," Mitchell said. "I know what people think of me. The assumptions. Gay black woman in a high-powered job? Got to be affirmative action at work, right? Only explanation. Goodness, throw me in a wheelchair—make it the hat-trick—and I'd probably have made Chief Constable already. Oh, which reminds me."

She scribbled a note on her pad, then set her pen down and looked back at Logan again. "The cold hard fact of the matter is that I am in this job *despite* those things," she told him. "Not because of them. I got here because I worked harder than anyone else for it, and because I'm good at what I do. And that's precisely what I expect of everyone in this station, whether they're in uniform or out of it.

"Detective Superintendent Hoon was loud. Brash. He was all bark. You'll find I'm quite the opposite," she continued, trapping Logan with a piercing glare that made him want to edge his seat back an inch or two. "There'll be no turning a blind eye to anything with me. I expect things done properly, and I expect them done to the best of everyone's ability. That will, of course, include you, should you decide to grace us with your presence. Especially you, in fact. You more so than anyone else. Do I make myself clear on that?"

Logan confirmed that she'd made herself very clear indeed, which seemed to satisfy her, at least temporarily. She picked up her pen and gave a curt nod in the direction of the door.

"Go talk to the team. I'll expect your decision by close of play tomorrow," she said, already turning to another page and starting to write.

Logan stood up and pushed the chair back to where it had been in front of her desk. He hung off there for a few moments, like a child waiting to be excused, then made for the door.

"Oh, and Jack?"

Logan stopped in the doorway. Mitchell made a vague up and down gesture at him with the end of her pen.

"I seem to remember you were thinner."

Glancing down, Logan subtly sucked in his gut, but the DSup was fixated on her notepad now, and he got the feeling that she'd already chosen to forget he was even there.

"Detective Sergeant Khaled," Logan beamed, shaking Hamza by the hand. "Moving up in the world, eh?"

"Apparently, sir, aye," Hamza replied. "Nobody told me about all the extra bloody paperwork, though."

"Here's a tip, son," Logan advised, leaning in closer. "You've got two perfectly good Detective Constables..." He regarded Sinead and Tyler, who sat watching him from their neighbouring desks. They still had their jackets on, and had left Harris in the car. The poor bugger was going to be fair confused when he woke up. "Well, you've got one perfectly good Detective Constable, and Tyler," Logan clarified. "Delegation is a wonderful thing."

"I'll keep that in mind, sir. Thanks," Hamza said, grinning.

"You don't have to call me 'sir,'" Logan told him.

Tyler sat bolt upright like a startled meerkat. "Eh? You mean you're not coming back, boss?"

"Course he bloody is."

The voice came from the doorway of the inner office that had once been Logan's. He turned and felt a twinge of pain, or maybe guilt, deep in the centre of his chest.

"Benjamin," he said, tilting his head in the direction of Detective Inspector Ben Forde.

"Jack," Ben replied, mirroring the head movement. He stepped aside, indicating the open door behind him. "Mind if I have a word?"

Logan leaned his weight onto one foot and peered past the older officer into the small office. The blinds were drawn, making the doorway the only means of seeing inside. "Snecky's no' in there, is he?"

"He's on sick leave," said Sinead. "Stress."

"We reckon he'll get miraculously better if he gets his

transfer to Aberdeen, though," Tyler added. "I've got twenty quid on it."

Ben cleared his throat, and even Tyler took the hint. He gave Sinead the nod, and they both stood up.

"We'd better be getting off," Sinead said. "We'll, eh…" She looked from Logan to the others, then back again. "We'll hopefully see you tomorrow."

They headed for the door while Logan made his way through the maze of tightly-packed desks towards Ben.

"No interruptions unless it's urgent," the DI instructed, then he followed Logan into the office and very firmly closed the door.

Logan noted that he was not the only one whose appearance had changed over the last nine months. Unlike his own outward spread, however, Ben had shrunk. He was definitely thinner, and seemed shorter, too. The lines of his face were deeper than before, like the passing of time had carved them further and further in. Possibly with some kind of power tool.

His greying hair was thin, and wispy, and white. He was a man who had always enjoyed complaining about something or other. He'd enjoyed a good rant about parking, or littering, or how kids these days didn't know they were bloody born.

But, there had always been a lightness to him, even during the darkest of times and the angriest of rants. He'd had an air of mischief about him that made you constantly suspect that he might be on the wind-up.

The lightness was gone now. A great weight had replaced it, stooping the DI's shoulders and making him look tired and old.

"What's with the beard?" Ben asked. He leaned against the desk so he was half-sitting on it, half-standing.

"Fancied a change," Logan said. "Been clean-shaven all my days, thought I'd give it a go and see how it looked."

Ben gripped the edge of the desk, leaned some of his weight on them, and waited.

"And it's good for hiding the double chin," Logan confessed after a few moments.

"Ah. Right. I'd imagine it would be." Ben nodded at Logan's midriff. "Mind you, it'll have to grow some to hide the gut."

Logan gave a chuckle, but it was a self-conscious one. "Aye. Tell me about it," he said. He ran a hand across his stomach, gave it a pat, then asked the question he'd been dreading. "How are you doing?"

Ben shrugged. "Oh. Getting there," he said. "You know me. Just getting on. I mean, obviously it's been... an adjust-ment. I won't lie. But what can you do?"

"You're looking well," Logan said, but Ben saw through the lie right away and dismissed it with a snort and a shake of his head.

"Aye, well, I'd best get a repairman in, then, because my mirror's obviously broken."

He looked down at the floor for a few seconds, and Logan knew he was building up to saying something. He braced himself, fearing the worst.

Ben would have every right to blame him for what had happened to Alice. He'd have every right to hold Logan responsible for her death. Was that what was coming? Nine months was a lot of time for resentment to build.

"You didn't phone, Jack," Ben said, which caught Logan off guard. "Not once since the funeral. Not a call, not a letter, not an email, not... I don't know... a bloody postcard."

Logan winced. "I, eh, I wasn't sure anyone would want to

hear... You know. After..." He blew out his cheeks and exhaled. "Sorry. I should've. Of course, I should. I was..."

"A selfish prick?" Ben suggested. "A self-centred, thoughtless bastard?"

For a moment—a brief one—Logan saw the old mischief flashing in the DI's eyes.

"That about sums it up, aye," he agreed.

"A self-absorbed, heartless piece of—"

"I think we get the idea, Benjamin!" Logan protested.

"And now you think you can just waltz back in and pick up like before?" Ben said, the mischief departing as quickly as it had arrived. "Carry on where we all left off?"

Logan blinked, taken aback by the harshness of Ben's tone.

"Eh, no, that's not... I wasn't..."

Ben stepped in closer, grabbed hold of Logan by the upper arms, and stared up at him. "You'd bloody better do," he said, breaking into a thin smile. "Another minute working under Snecky and I'll be seeing a murder investigation from the other side."

He squeezed Logan's arms, then released his grip.

"It's good to see you, Jack," he said. "All of you."

"You, too."

"Because, you know, there's so much more of you to see."

"Aye."

"I mean with all the weight you've—"

"I got it. Aye. Very good," Logan said, cutting him off. He turned sideways and ran a hand down his front. "It's no' that bad, is it?"

"Depends what trimester you're in, I suppose," Ben said, then he chuckled and shook his head. "No. It's not that bad. You look good. I mean, if I was you I'd lose the beard. It does you no favours. But, you look like all the fresh air agreed with you."

He left the compliment hanging there just long enough before following up.

"And all the cake."

There was a sharp knock at the door. Hamza didn't wait to be told before opening it.

"Sorry to interrupt," he said. He sounded grave. Or as grave as he could with his dense Aberdonian accent, which tended to take the edge off even the most sombre of announcements. "We've had a shout. Bad one by the looks of it. Woman and a kiddie down in Fort Augustus. Uniform's secured the house, SOC are on the way."

"Shite. Well, let's get organised and head down, then," Ben said. The DI shifted his gaze from the door to the giant of a man standing beside him. "Ready to get back in the saddle, Jack?"

Logan glanced around the office. *His* office, not so long ago. "Aye," he said. "I'll maybe tag along and keep you company."

"Good man," Ben said, gesturing for Logan to go ahead through the door. "It'll need to be some size of saddle, though," he added, fighting back a grin. "And I don't envy the poor bloody horse."

CHAPTER FOUR

By the time Logan, Ben, and Hamza arrived at the crime scene, Geoff Palmer's team were already in attendance. They filed in and out in their paper suits and hats, barely saying a word. Their expressions were usually hard to read behind their masks, but there was a sombre air to them today that was hard to miss.

Uniform had secured the entrance to the cul-de-sac leading to the house, and there were no immediate neighbours overlooking the property. It made it easier to control the scene, but meant witnesses may well be thin on the ground.

As soon as they were out of the car, Ben sent a couple of Uniforms to go door-to-door at the closest addresses, with orders not to say anything specific. A quick check to ask if anyone had seen or heard anything unusual at the house in the last few days. Anyone snooping around. That sort of thing.

When they were gone, the DI stopped one of the white paper suits and asked them to send Palmer out when he was free. Logan let out an almost imperceptible groan. He wasn't even officially back on the job, and already he'd have to contend with Geoff 'Sex Pest' Palmer. Not the start he'd been hoping for.

A uniformed sergeant waited for the SOC investigator to head inside before making a bee-line for Logan and the others. He gave Ben a curt, respectful nod, glanced briefly at Logan and Hamza, then answered the question he knew the DI had been about to ask.

"Woman in her late thirties and a girl aged six," he said. "We believe the woman is Lois Mann, and the girl is her daughter, Ruby. The call came from a Postie, who saw Lois's body through the living room window. Local lad. He's given a statement. We've taken his details and sent him home."

"Did he go inside?" Logan asked.

The sergeant frowned, unsure of who this bearded giant was. DI Forde was staring expectantly at him, though, so he thought it best to answer.

"No. Called from outside."

"He didn't go in to try and help her?" Ben asked. "Make sure she was OK?"

The sergeant shook his head. "No, sir," he replied, and from his tone it was clear that she'd been well beyond any possibility of help by the time she'd been found. "Looks like she's been there for a few days. Paramedics went in with me. Smell told us what we needed to know, and—"

"Jesus Christ Almighty! What happened to you?" Gasped a slightly muffled voice from behind them, struggling to contain its laughter.

Logan felt his heart sink and his arse tighten, and turned to find Geoff Palmer striding out of the garden, his bright-red face encircled by the elasticated cuff around the hood of his paper suit.

Palmer stopped in Logan's shadow and looked the former DCI up and down. "I have to say, I bloody loved you in the *Harry Potter* films." He pulled a shocked face and covered his mouth with a gloved hand. "Hang on. You're no' here to tell me I'm a wizard, are you?"

Logan shot Hamza a sideways glance, clearly hoping for an explanation.

"I think he's saying you look like Hagrid, sir," the DS explained.

Logan grunted. "Which one's he?"

It was the sergeant in uniform who replied, jumping in first while the other two officers were taking more time to carefully choose their words.

"The big fat lad with the beard," he explained. "Robbie Coltrane played him."

Ben bit his lip and looked away. Hamza, to his credit, stood stock still, his face remaining almost completely immobile aside from the faintest curving at the corners of his mouth.

"Detective Inspector," Logan said, his gaze fixed on the man in uniform. "Permission to tell this fine officer to fuck off."

Something about the look in Logan's eyes jogged the sergeant's memory, and he realised who he was talking to. He didn't wait for Ben to grant permission, and instead hastily offered an apology, and told them he'd be over by the cordon if they needed him.

"Geoff," Logan said, once the sergeant had cleared off. "Always a pleasure. Or lack thereof."

"I thought you'd left?" Palmer said. "You know, after that business where you nearly got everyone killed."

"I did. I have," Logan said. "I'm here as an observer."

"Oh, so we've got observers at murder scenes now, have we?" Palmer asked, flicking his gaze to Ben. "Why not stick it on Ticketmaster and see if we can make a bob or two while we're at it?"

DI Forde sighed. Clearly, his opinion of the head of the SOC team was not a million miles away from Logan's own. "Just tell us what we've got, Geoff."

"It's early days," Palmer said. "We've barely finished photographing, and the pathologist is still doing an initial examination."

Logan's gaze went to the front of the house. "Pathologist?" he asked, subconsciously sucking in his gut.

"Aye. Dr Maguire. I believe you used to know her?" Geoff said, stressing the past tense of it all. "That new Detective Superintendent of yours insists on Pathology attending every scene. Proper by-the-book approach. Not that you'd know too much about that."

Hamza had his notepad open with his pen poised to write. He'd been standing that way since Palmer had started talking, and was growing impatient.

"So, what do we have?" he urged.

Palmer gave a sigh, like he resented even this most basic aspect of his job. Logan had often thought the man would've been much happier in some other career. Traffic Warden, maybe. Or airport security staff. Some job where being an obnoxious bastard was a help, rather than a hindrance.

"It's an educated guess and subject to change," he began. "But it looks like the daughter's throat was cut upstairs while she was in bed. The mother then returned downstairs and slit her wrists with the same knife."

"The mother? Jesus," Ben whispered, looking along the path to the house. The sun was edging towards the horizon behind it, painting the sky in pinks and purples. With that background, the cottage would've made a lovely postcard image, were it not for the cordon tape and forensics team currently combing through the garden.

"What about the father? Is there one?" Logan asked.

Palmer tutted. "Well, short of a virgin birth, one can only assume so," he said.

"You know what I bloody mean," Logan snapped back. "Is he around?"

Palmer very deliberately turned away from Logan and addressed Ben. "Chatty for an observer, isn't he? And putting together the family tree isn't my department, is it? If there's a dad around, he isn't in the house, that's all I can tell you."

He put his hands on his hips and looked across all three faces. "Is that it? Can I get back to it now? Or are we going to stand here wasting light?"

"On you go," Ben said, dismissing him with a wave. "I want kept informed, though. Any new developments, I'm first to know."

Palmer curtsied sarcastically, then turned and went marching back along the path towards the house without another word.

"He's still an arsehole, then," Logan remarked.

"Oh God, aye," Ben confirmed. They both watched him until he'd vanished back into the house. "Grade A. Annoyingly good at his job, though."

Infuriatingly, Ben was right. For all his faults—which

were legion—Geoff Palmer knew his way around a crime scene better than almost anyone Logan had ever worked with.

"Hamza, find out about the father, will you?" Ben asked. "If he's around, we need to find him."

"You think he's involved, sir?" Hamza asked, folding closed his notebook and slipping it into his jacket pocket. "From what Palmer said, sounds like it was the mother."

Ben gave a non-committal shrug. "We'll see."

"Not that unusual though, is it?" Hamza asked. "Parent killing their kid. I mean, it's not normal, obviously, but not unheard of."

"It's usually the father. Much rarer with mothers," Logan said. "Not unheard of, obviously, but even in cases where the mother ends up prosecuted, there's usually a man involved, too, goading her on."

"Right. Aye, makes sense," Hamza said. He shook his head sadly. "Men are bastards."

"I'd also get onto Social Services and the school. See if there's any history of abuse, or if anyone suspected anything untoward was going on at home," Logan continued. He caught himself, and looked across at Ben. "I mean, assuming I'm not stepping on anyone's toes...?"

"You go ahead and step away, Jack," Ben told him. "Aye, metaphorically, I mean. I'm no' wanting your weight coming down on my foot. I'd be lucky to walk again."

Logan rolled his eyes and gestured to the pocket where Hamza had stowed his notebook. "If I'm going to be hanging around, remind me to sign up for a gym membership, will you? Or I'll never hear the bloody end of it."

Ben made a sudden grab for Hamza's arm. The DI

smiled, but it was an unconvincing mask that did nothing to disguise his wide-eyed look of panic.

"Actually, Hamza, I'll come with you and help with those phone calls."

Hamza frowned. "What? It's fine, sir, I can—"

But Ben wasn't hanging around. With a tug of the Detective Sergeant's arm and a hurried, "Let's go," he set off at pace towards his car.

For a moment, Logan stood there, wondering what the bloody hell that was all about.

And then, he heard the creaking of the gate behind him, and the *clack* as the rusty spring mechanism pulled it closed again.

"Sorry, excuse me."

Logan froze as a woman sidled past him. He smelled her before he saw her. Her perfume had always been unique. Disinfectant and embalming fluid made up the core scent, but this was usually infused around the edges with subtle notes of pickled onion-flavour *Monster Munch,* or something from the *Pot Noodle* range of fragrances.

She glanced up and smiled as she passed, walked on three more steps, then stopped dead as if her feet had been magnetised to the ground.

The process of her turning involved a series of stunned, shuffled steps. Logan pulled in his stomach and smoothed down his beard as her gaze fell on him. He tried to smile but realised he'd completely forgotten how, and ended up pulling a pained sort of sneer that he imagined made him look like he was suffering from a painful and unpleasant bowel complaint.

"Jack?" she said, whispering his name like she was

worried saying it too loudly might startle him and scare him off.

"Shona," Logan said. "Aye. Hi. Hello."

She lunged at him, closing the gap in two big steps. A finger prodded him in the stomach, an inch or so above his belly button. Sharp. Painful.

"Ow," he said, in the hope that it would defuse things, although he could see that this was unlikely. Her eyebrows had come together until they met in the middle, and a flush of red was spreading up her neck and across her cheeks. If looks could kill, she'd already be weighing his internal organs and sending tissue samples off for toxicology testing.

She jabbed him again, harder this time.

"And just where the bloody hell have you been?"

CHAPTER FIVE

Shona Maguire was not happy. That much was obvious.

If the look on her face wasn't enough to give that fact away, then her body language made it very clear. She stood with her arms folded, one foot tapping the ground as she waited for Logan to answer the question.

"Well?" she demanded when he hadn't replied after four or five seconds. "Where were you?"

He wasn't quite sure what to say, so opted for the bare truth of it.

"Orkney," he said.

Shona's mood was not improved one bit by this response.

"Orkney?" she said. Her voice, which usually lilted with an Irish twang, was flat and dry. "That's it? Orkney?"

Logan was skating on some very thin ice here, he knew. The bloom of red that had crept up Shona's neck had turned her face the colour of beetroot now, and he could see that she wasn't just angry. It'd be fine if she was just angry. Just angry, he could deal with.

But she was hurt, too. His disappearing act had wounded her.

What else had he expected?

"I, eh, I had to get away," he said.

"Get away? From what? Me?" she demanded.

Logan was quick to shake his head. "No. No, God. From... After everything that happened."

"Everything that happened? You mean like me getting a bomb strapped to me?"

Logan winced. "Aye. That. And Ben. And... My daughter, she's not speaking to me. Nor's my ex-wife, although that's more of a blessing than..."

The look in her eyes told him now was not the time to start joking around about past romantic relationships. He cleared his throat and continued. "I just... I had to get away. Clear the head."

"Sounds lovely. You know what I've been doing since you left?" Shona asked, her voice rising a little like she was losing the battle to keep her emotions in check. "I've been hanging out with a fucking twelve-year-old. Every week, without fail, the batshit crazy daughter of a Russian drug lord turns up at my house to watch DVDs. Every week. She brings popcorn. Eats the lot herself."

It was at this point that Logan made what could've turned out to be the worst mistake he'd ever made. He laughed.

He tried to hold it in, but the idea of Olivia Maximuke rocking up to Shona's house every week to hang out and watch movies was so ridiculous that he couldn't contain it.

"You think it's funny, do you?" Shona asked.

"Maybe a wee bit," Logan admitted.

Shona sighed and shook her head, but the exhalation

seemed to take the edge off her anger. "We're doing the Bond movies at the minute," she said. "It's *A View to A Kill* this week."

Logan wrinkled his nose in distaste. "Roger Moore? Aye, that'd be one way to get rid of her, right enough."

"I tried calling you. Like, God, I don't know. A dozen times," she told him. "Often while drunk. Didn't you get the messages?"

Logan gave a single shake of his head. "No," he lied.

"I started to think you were dead. Bloody hoped it at some points. At least that'd be a decent excuse. I'd have let you off if you were dead."

"Very generous of you," Logan told her.

"Oh, stop, Jack. Just..." Shona tutted and shook her head again like she was as angry at herself as she was at him. She gestured to her car with a jerk of a thumb. "I have to go prep for the post-mortem."

She turned away, then carried on until she'd done a full circle.

"Is this you back, then?"

"I... Maybe," Logan said. "They've asked me to. Come back, I mean."

"So, what's stopping you?"

Logan shrugged. "Not sure how welcome I'd be."

Shona nodded, as if agreeing with this sentiment.

"Aye, I get that," she said, to his dismay. "But when has that ever stopped you?"

Before he could reply, she gave him an abrupt little wave, turned away, and went scurrying off to her car.

Ben Forde sidled up while Logan watched Shona's car drive over to the cordon and wait to be waved through.

"That went better than I expected," the DI remarked.

"Did it? Christ, what were you expecting?"

"She didn't chin you, so that's something."

"True," Logan said, tearing his eyes away from the pathologist's car.

"And she'd be well within her rights to," Ben continued. "You left her high and dry."

"Yes, thank you, Benjamin. I'm well aware of that," Logan said.

"Did she tell you anything about the bodies?"

"Shite," Logan muttered. "I forgot to ask."

Forensics were still swarming over the cottage like worker ants, all following the same lines to limit the chances of compromising the scene. The focus would be on the area around the bodies to start with, then would move outwards to encompass the rest of the house. Everything would be photographed, recorded, and catalogued—a process that would almost certainly take hours.

Under normal circumstances, Logan would've donned his protective gear and gone inside to check it out for himself, but he wasn't running the show now, and Ben was happy to give Scene of Crime the time and space it needed to do its job.

This would've left the detectives at something of a loose end, had Hamza not come hurrying over to them with his notebook open.

"Got some info about Ruby's father. Lois's husband," he announced a few paces before he'd reached them. "Gareth Mann. Local Minister. Lives at the same address."

"So where is he now?" Ben asked.

"Don't know, sir. His church isn't far away, though. I could send Uniform to scope it out."

Ben looked back at the bungalow, then checked his

watch. "Or you two could take a look," he suggested. He puffed up his chest and drew Logan a look that somehow managed to be both smug and self-deprecating at the same time. "I'd better hang off here. Senior Investigating Officer, and all that. Nothing much likely to happen here for the foreseeable. You might as well keep busy."

Hamza looked to Logan, as if seeking permission.

"Here, I'm just an observer, son," Logan reminded him. "You're the boss. I'm happy to tag along, though."

"Right, then," Hamza said, after a moment's consideration. He flipped his notebook closed. "Let's go check it out."

FORT AUGUSTUS PARISH Church was an unremarkable enough old stone building situated a stone's throw from where the Caledonian Canal flowed into Loch Ness. As Logan and Hamza made their way across the car park, the masts of a tall ship were visible above the roofs of neighbouring houses, and they could hear the thunder of water pouring through the sluice gates, lowering the boat for its onward journey.

A woman in her sixties sat on a bench across from the church's front door. She read on a Kindle, which she glanced up from just long enough to watch Logan and Hamza approaching the entrance.

"It's locked," she remarked.

"Oh. Is it?" Hamza asked.

Logan tried the handle for himself, and gave the double doors a quick rattle. They held fast.

"See? Locked. Told you," the woman said, a little smugly.

"Would it normally be shut at this time?" Logan asked her.

"Would I be sitting here if it was?" she asked with a roll of her eyes.

"I have no idea," Logan said. "For all I know, you live there."

Judging by the look on her face as she lowered her Kindle, the woman had already come to the conclusion that she didn't like the big bearded fella.

"Yes, it should be open. It's open every day. But not today. I'm assuming the Reverend is running late."

"Aye, well, I suspect he's running somewhere, right enough," Logan muttered.

"I'm sorry?"

Hamza smiled warmly. "Nothing. Do you know if anyone else has a key? A cleaner, or...?"

"His wife. Lois. She usually helps with the cleaning. You could ask her."

Hamza didn't miss a beat. "Anyone else?"

The woman set her Kindle down on the bench beside her, but pinned a hand on top of it like she was worried one of the men was going to make a grab for it. Her gaze tick-tocked between them, sizing them up.

"Why do you want to know? Who are you exactly?" She paid special attention to Hamza. "You don't look like you're Church of Scotland."

"Detective Sergeant Hamza Khaled. Police Scotland," Hamza said, producing his ID.

The woman beckoned for him to hand it over, took it, then studied it for several seconds from various distances, like she couldn't quite bring it into focus.

Eventually, she handed it back over and gestured to

Logan. "And who's he?"

"He's—"

"Civilian observer," Logan said, before Hamza could respond. He caught the DS's eye, then motioned to the back of the church. "I'm going to take a look around. You see what you can find out from this lady."

"You can't go bossing him around, son," the woman said. "He's police. He tells you what to do. There's no respect for the law these days. None."

Logan smiled so thinly his lips all but disappeared. "Fair point," he conceded. "Detective Sergeant Khaled, what would you like me to do?"

"Maybe check out around the back?" Hamza suggested.

"Sounds like a plan," Logan replied. "Couldn't have come up with better myself."

He beat a retreat around the side of the building, leaving Hamza to question the busybody on the bench.

Logan didn't know much about architecture. Or churches. If he had to guess, he'd put the building at a couple of hundred years old, although it was a wild guess that he knew could be way off. Had someone told him the church was built five years ago, he wouldn't have been all that surprised. It was a stone rectangle with an apex roof, and was timeless in its blandness.

A bellcote stood at the front of the roof, the bell within it hanging silent and still. There was a tiny spire of some description in the middle of the roof, too, although he had absolutely no idea what purpose it possibly served beyond decoration. A weather vane was fixed to the top of it, but the Highland weather had buckled and rusted it so that it always said the wind was blowing downwards at a forty-five degree angle, and consistently from the same direction.

There was a fire exit around the back, which was presumably a reasonably recent addition. Like the front door, it was shut tight. The only way inside the building would be by breaking one of the windows, and he had no reason to do that. Yet.

Besides, the windows were all tall and narrow. Even if he was the one who did the breaking, the entering would be up to Hamza, or someone else of a similar-sized frame. Even in his prime, Logan would be hard-pressed to squeeze through the gap. Now, it would take either a miracle, or an industrial-sized tub of Vaseline and some sort of blunt instrument.

The glass was dusty, making it hard to see much of the church's darkened insides. Definitely no sign of movement, though. If anyone was in there, they were well-hidden.

By the time Logan completed the circuit around the church, the woman had packed up her Kindle and was walking away.

"Was it something we said?" Logan asked Hamza.

"Hmm? Oh. Haha. Aye, maybe, sir."

"Still not your boss, son," Logan pointed out.

Hamza flinched. "Right. Sorry."

Logan gestured after the woman. "Get anything useful?"

"Elizabeth Strand. She's been sitting here all day, more or less, waiting to get in," Hamza said. "She comes most days and just sits, apparently. Reckon's she's pretty lonely."

"Can't think why, charmer like that."

"She last saw Reverend Mann on Sunday evening. Early on," Hamza continued. "She said she'd see him on Monday, he said he was looking forward to it, and would have the kettle on, then nothing. He didn't show to open up."

"Why was she coming to see him on a Monday?"

"She comes every day, apparently. Has done since her husband died. The Rev hasn't showed face all week."

"Has he failed to show before?"

"I asked that," Hamza said. "And she said no, although she did say he's been a bit 'less dependable' lately. Turned up late, left early, shut for a few hours in the afternoon without notice. That sort of thing."

"And that's new?" asked Logan. "That's not normal?"

"Not according to her, no. Started a few months back. Not major, but enough for her to notice it."

Logan regarded the front of the church for a few seconds, logging all this new information and filing it away. "You got her details, I assume?"

Hamza confirmed that he had, and Logan made a clicking sound against the back of his teeth.

"Good. Fine," he said. He motioned with a wave at the buildings standing around the edges of the car park. "Let's get Uniform going door-to-door to these houses. See if anyone call tell us when they last saw him here."

He leaned back and looked up at the street lights, searching for cameras, but finding none. "No CCTV. Is there any between here and his house?"

"Not sure, sir. But I can check," Hamza said, scribbling a note in his pad. "You think he's involved?"

"Almost certain of it," Logan said. "Either he's dead, or he's played some part in the murders at the house. Or both. For all we know, he's swinging from a rope in the church there. We need to find that key and check it out."

He fired a final glance at the church's front doors, then buried his hands in his pockets. "He's involved one way or another, though. I'd stake my career on it." He shrugged. "You know, if I still had one."

CHAPTER SIX

By the time Logan and Hamza made it back to the cottage, spotlights had been set up in the garden, their beams pointing down at the grass as three white-clad figures conducted fingertip searches.

Rain had started to fall on their walk back. It was the sort of vague, half-hearted drizzle that characterised summer in the Highlands—heavy enough to soak you to the skin in five to ten minutes, but not heavy enough to drive away the midges. If anything, it only encouraged the vicious little bastards, and Logan had spent most of the walk back to the cottage fending them off and scratching.

Ben gave a beep of his horn when he spotted them ducking under the cordon tape, then wound down a steamed-up window and beckoned them over to the car.

"Jump in. I've got chips," he said, although he needn't have bothered. The smell of the chips—and the lashings of salt and vinegar—had come wafting towards them as soon as the window had rolled down.

Logan's stomach rumbled hungrily. The last thing

he'd eaten had been that morning, and even then it had been a twin-pack of miniature pork pies that were two days past their use-by date. They were now well into the late evening, and now that a big bag of chips was on the go, his hunger was quick to make its presence felt.

"Don't mind if I do," Logan said, reaching through the window and helping himself to a handful from the bag in Ben's lap. He munched on them as he walked around to the other side, and climbed into the front passenger seat.

Hamza was already in the back by the time Logan sat down. The Detective Sergeant had reached into the front and plucked a couple of chips from the bag before he'd even shut the door, and had just popped the first one in his mouth when Logan closed his door.

"Good call," Logan said, taking another chip from the offered bag. "Where'd you get these?"

"Chippy down by the petrol station," Ben said. "I was going to wait until you got back, but..." He shrugged. "I didn't."

Logan used a chip as a pointer and indicated the house. "Any word?"

"They're getting there," Ben said. "Bodies have been taken up the road. We'll be able to get in soon."

Hamza stretched over from the back and pinched another chip. "Anything from the door-to-door?" he asked.

"Nothing useful yet, no. Nobody saw or heard anything. Not a big surprise, though, the house is pretty isolated from the neighbours," Ben replied. "We've identified a relative, though. Victim's sister. Lives down south. Shropshire, or somewhere. Uniform down that way's going to go break the news."

"No family locally?" Logan asked between blowing on a chip and eating it.

"Not that we've been able to find, no. How did you get on at the church?"

"Reverend Mann hasn't been seen since Sunday, apparently," said Logan. "Meant to have opened the place up Monday, but he didn't show."

"And he's not inside?"

"Not that we can see. Place is locked up, though. There's meant to be at least one key in the house. Thought better to find that, than to kick the door in."

"Aye, well, you don't want to get on God's bad side, I suppose," Ben said.

Logan chuckled but stopped when he realised Ben wasn't laughing.

"No," he said, with a shake of his head. "No, I suppose that wouldn't be ideal."

The rain was getting heavier now. Ben flicked on the windscreen wipers, but the condensation caused by the steamy chips meant everything outside the car was in the process of being swallowed by a thick white fog.

"Thoughts, Hamza?" Ben asked, after wiping the steam from his rear-view mirror.

"Thoughts, sir?"

"Whodunnit?"

"Bit early to say, sir."

"Aye, but you can have a gut instinct. No' saying it's right yet, but what's it telling you?" Ben urged.

Hamza took a tissue from his pocket and wiped chip grease from his fingers. "Well, if we're assuming it wasn't a murder-suicide."

"Which it might be," Logan said. "But let's assume not."

"Then got to be the husband, hasn't it?" Hamza said. "The dad, I mean. The minister fella. He's picked a shocker of a time to go AWOL if not. Unless he's dead somewhere, of course, in which case... I mean, I suppose it could still be him."

Logan and Ben both nodded in near-unison. "Aye, don't think you'll be far off the mark with that," Ben said.

It was usually the husband. Or the boyfriend. Or the brother-in-law. Logan had investigated a lot of murders over the years—so many he was ashamed to admit he'd lost count —and in the majority of those cases, there was very little actual investigation involved.

Often, the killer would still be on the scene, blood both literally and metaphorically on their hands. In many cases, they'd already confessed to the emergency services operator when calling it in, and the polis's job was just about making the arrest and doing the paperwork for the Procurator Fiscal.

In those cases, the *why* was more important than the *who*. The *why* could decide if someone got five years or life. In some instances, the *why* could see the killer let off entirely.

He hadn't stepped inside the house yet, but Logan's hunch was that this would turn out to be one of those cases where the *who* wasn't in question. Right now, though, the *why* wasn't important, either. Right now, all that mattered was the *where*.

"You going to put out a shout on the minister?" he asked, eyeing up Ben's chips. The DI only had a few left in the styrofoam tray. Hard bits, mostly, currently wallowing in a puddle of vinegar. "Sooner we track him down, the sooner we can get this cleared up."

"Already done," Ben replied. To Logan's dismay, he screwed up the greasy paper that had been wrapped around the chips, squashing the tray and the vinegar-soaked crispy bits inside.

"Here, I'd have had them," Logan protested.

"I know you would've," Ben said. He opened the door with one hand, while patting Logan on the stomach with the other. "You can thank me later."

It was an hour or more later before they were finally allowed into the house. Geoff Palmer had tried to insist that, as Logan wasn't currently under the employ of Police Scotland, he shouldn't be allowed into the crime scene, but DI Forde had expertly countered his objections by telling him to piss off.

The house was almost the very definition of the word 'quaint,' with floral-patterned wallpaper, mismatched antique furniture, and a blackened metal bucket that held logs for the old stone fireplace.

Bookshelves lined two walls, crammed to overflowing with hardbacks and paperbacks of every possible taste and genre. There were a lot of religious texts in there, but an almost equal number of books on science and technology.

These were kept well apart in separate bookcases, Logan noted, with a rack of *Dan Brown*s and *Stephen King*s jammed on another set of shelves between them in case anything should kick off.

Next to one of the bookshelves, angled to face the fire, was the most ridiculously comfortable-looking chair Logan had ever seen. It was made of red leather and what he thought was probably walnut wood, and had a bucket-shaped seat that had no doubt been moulded over years to fit the contours of the owner.

The leather was faded and worn to white at the arms, and an empty glass water jug sat balanced on one of them. There was a patch of a slightly different shade of red down at a bottom corner that suggested it had been damaged at some point, but these only made it look better, somehow. More distinguished, like the greying at the temples of some Hollywood heartthrob.

"They got a dog?" Logan asked.

Ben looked around, like he might see one scampering around at his feet.

"Don't think so, no. Why?"

Logan indicated the patch at the corner of the armchair. "Could be a chew spot. Right height for a pup."

Hamza made a note. "I'll check."

There was no TV, which was unusual. An old Hi-Fi system with wooden speakers and a dusty record turntable was set against the far wall, next to where an oak staircase led to the floor above.

There was a framed photograph on the top of each speaker. One showed a bride and groom in their twenties. The other showed a woman in her mid-thirties hugging a smiling little girl. They wore rain jackets with the hoods up, and the background suggested they were on a boat somewhere. Loch Ness, judging by the tree line along the shore in the middle-distance.

That was then, whenever *then* was. Now—or before she'd died, at least—Lois had been at the wine. There were two empty bottles on the floor beside the couch, one upright, one toppled over, and a similarly empty glass with a purple-red stain at the bottom.

She'd been drinking then. It was possible that both bottles weren't from the same time, or that she'd even touched them that night at all, but the rest of the room was fairly tidy, so he doubted two wine bottles were the kind of thing that would've been left lying around for days.

It was good to study the room. Useful. It was amazing the number of things even the most cursory glance of a murder scene could throw up.

But it was also a delaying tactic, Logan knew. The longer he looked at the furniture and the fireplace, the longer he could delay looking at the outline on the floor, and at the patch of dried crimson on the carpet.

It wasn't that it particularly bothered him. Not these days. It was that looking at it brought him one step closer to coming back. Looking at it felt like a commitment he wasn't quite ready to make yet.

He looked, regardless. Otherwise, what was the point in him even being here?

"Shite. Hamza. I forgot the thing," Ben said, pointing to his open left hand. "The doodah. The iPad. Go and grab it for me, will you?"

Hamza caught the car keys Ben tossed to him. "No worries, sir. Be right back."

Logan waited until Hamza had left before asking the question. "The iPad?"

Ben emitted a little groan. "Aye. Our new Detective Superintendent's bright idea to speed things up and... what was it she said? 'Enable ease of information sharing.' Some shite like that, anyway."

Logan grunted his disapproval and turned his attention back to the outline on the floor.

"What do you think?" Ben asked.

"Well, I'd need to see the post-mortem results," Logan replied. "But I'd say she's deid, right enough."

"You've no' lost the knack, then. Sharp as ever."

There was an oak staircase running up to the floor above at the far end of the room. Logan's eyes were drawn to it, then to the ceiling. "The wee one was in her room, right?"

Ben nodded. "Aye. In bed, I'm told." He joined Logan in gazing up at the ceiling. "We'll have to go and take a look."

They would, of course. There was no getting out of it. But not yet.

"So, the story we're meant to believe is that she went upstairs, killed her daughter, then came back down here and killed herself in the front room?"

"It's not impossible," Ben said, playing Devil's Advocate.

"No. Suppose not," Logan conceded. He walked to the area where the victim's feet had been, then crouched down and looked along the length of the outline. "Blood splatter's unusual, though."

"Aye," Ben agreed. He nodded for a few seconds, before adding, "In what way?"

"Well, there isn't much of it, is there? She slit her wrists, apparently, and if she'd just killed her daughter you've got to think her heart's going to be racing, so..." He gestured around the room. "The place should be covered in it. Only way this blood pattern makes sense is if she was lying face down on the carpet when she did it."

"Could've been grief-stricken after what she'd done. Came down the stairs, collapsed onto the carpet..." Ben suggested, but it was abundantly clear that he wasn't buying the words coming out of his own mouth, and he let the rest of the sentence peter out. "Held down, then?"

"Maybe, aye," Logan said. He groaned quietly as he stood

up, and gave his legs a shake, encouraging the blood to start flowing to them again. "Shona will be able to give us a better idea."

"Aye, if she's talking to us," Ben said. "Or, you, mostly."

The door opened and Hamza returned with the iPad. "Got it, sir."

"Cheers, son," Ben said, accepting the device with an air of reluctant resignation.

He poked at the darkened screen. When nothing happened, he poked it again.

"It's not working. Is the battery gone?" he asked of nobody in particular.

Hamza pointed to a small round button at the bottom of the screen. "You tap that, sir."

"Shite. Aye. I remember now," Ben muttered. "Stupid bloody thing."

He tapped the button and the screen illuminated. Logan and Hamza watched as he leaned his head back and peered down his nose at the now-wakened gadget. "Right," he said, in a way that suggested there was more to follow.

Nothing did.

"Fingerprint, sir," Hamza prompted.

"Fingerprint. Right." Ben looked the screen up and down. "Fingerprint. Fingerprint."

Logan side-eyed the Detective Sergeant. "Is he like this every time?"

"I heard that. And it's no' me, it's this stupid bloody gadget. I swear, the bastarding thing hates me," Ben grumbled. He remembered that the fingerprint scanner was housed in the same button he'd already pressed, and touched his index finger to it until the iPad gave an audible *click*.

"Nothing's happening," he said, after a moment. "It made the noise, didn't it? You heard it make the noise."

"You need to press the button again now that it's unlocked," Hamza pointed out.

The lad had the patience of a saint, Logan thought. He'd probably gone through this same rigmarole half a dozen times already. It was Logan's first time, and he already wanted to tear the thing out of Ben's hands and chuck it against the wall.

Ben rolled his eyes, tapped the button again, and then nodded his approval when the display finally changed. "Good. Right. We've got a body. All SOC's photos automatically download to this thing once they've saved them to the..." He looked to Hamza for confirmation. "...server?"

"Bingo. That's right, sir," Hamza replied, smiling like a teacher at a prize pupil.

"It's a right pain in the arse, but it's pretty handy, I suppose," Ben begrudgingly admitted.

He turned the screen around, and Logan was confronted with a high-angle view of the room they were standing in. Instead of the white tape outline, though, there was a woman's bloodied corpse.

Logan recognised her as the woman in the photograph with the child, although she now bore little more than a passing resemblance to that younger version of herself, terror and death having conspired to forever alter her features.

She was lying on her back, which he hadn't expected. Lying like that, even down on the floor, slitting her wrists would've caused far more spray around her than he was seeing now. She was wearing fluffy pale blue pyjamas that were relatively unmarked by bloodstains. Nowhere near enough to fit the picture someone had tried to paint, anyway.

The knife was clutched limply in her hand. Or, more accurately, resting on her open palm. He'd have expected her to drop it, had she made the cuts herself. Judging by the depth that the blade had gone in, the tendon damage would've made controlling her fingers impossible.

Definitely staged, then.

"There's a laptop," Logan observed. He turned to the spot in the picture where the computer was, but Palmer's team must've already taken it. "We'll want to know what's on there."

Reaching for the screen, he swiped to the next image. It showed the body from another angle, much lower than the one before. He looked from it to the expansive blood spot on the carpet at his feet, comparing the two.

"I think she was dead before her wrists were cut. Only way I can see to explain the blood pattern."

Ben turned the screen so he and Hamza could see it, and tilted his head as he looked it over. "I see what you mean," he said. "No heartbeat, so there wasn't the pressure to spray it around."

Logan nodded. The post-mortem would confirm it, of course. In fact, had he thought to ask, and not just stood there like an idiot talking about Roger Moore, Shona Maguire would almost certainly have been able to tell him all this already.

Ben swiped on through a few more photographs. Logan couldn't see the screen, but he could see from the DI's face when he'd gone all the way through the photographs of the mother and come across those of her child.

It never got easier. Not really.

Adults? Fine. You got used to those in no time. Male, female, black, white, fat, thin—they were all the same in the end. Puzzles to solve. Wrongs to right. If you let them affect you beyond that, let their names and faces worm their way into your head as anything more than that, then you were in the wrong job. They were victims to be avenged, and when you'd done that, when you'd brought them the peace they deserved, you pushed them aside and you moved on.

That was how you coped. That was how you survived.

It was different with children, though. You never really got used to seeing those.

And part of you hoped to God that you never would.

In the silence of the cottage, there was a soft *click* as Ben turned off the iPad screen. He cleared his throat, pulled a thin, grim smile, and looked from Hamza to Logan. "Right, then," he announced. His eyes crept all the way back to the ceiling. "I suppose we should go head upstairs."

CHAPTER SEVEN

UPSTAIRS HELD TWO BEDROOMS, A BATHROOM, AND A cupboard with a curtain instead of a door. The daughter's room was immediately obvious from the brightly-coloured nameplate that hung on a ribbon from a push-pin shoved into the wood.

'Ruby's Room.'

The carpet was strewn with scattered toys—a couple of dolls with oversized heads and attitude problems, assorted soft toys that bore no resemblance to any animals Logan had ever seen, and enough LEGO to make anyone think twice about venturing in barefooted.

The walls were adorned with posters of *My Little Pony*, *Moana*, and a rocket blasting off from a launchpad. There were eight or nine scribbled drawings pinned between them, some crayon, others done in marker pen. Most of them showed a girl and a woman. One or two included a man, although he stood apart from the others in the picture, Logan noted.

And then, of course, there was the bed. The quilt had

been removed, but a check of the iPad showed it half-covering Ruby's body, several bloody spots merging to form an uneven red stain on the patterned fabric.

The sheet was gone, too, so only the bare mattress remained. Blood had seeped into it, and had trickled in rivulets down the valance sheet that covered the bed's base and eventually dried in.

Logan had caught the smell as soon as he'd stepped into the house. It was an odour he hadn't smelled in months. He hadn't missed it. It had been bad downstairs, but up here it was worse. Up here, it seemed to permeate the pores of the room, like Death had come in and marked its territory.

The three detectives looked through the pictures on the iPad in sombre silence, the only sound the faint tap as DI Forde moved from one image to the next.

When they finally reached the end, they stood a moment longer without speaking, all three of them silently paying their respects to the girl who had once played here in this room.

"Thoughts?" Ben finally asked.

"Nothing yet I'd care to say out loud," Logan muttered, turning back to the bed without making eye contact with the others.

"Looked like she was stabbed through the covers," Hamza ventured. He had to swallow and take a breath before continuing. "Multiple times. Large blade. There are... The mattress has holes in it, suggesting..." He cleared his throat, exhaled sharply, then forced it all out at once. "Suggesting the knife went through her body and into the foam, meaning it was done with some force."

"Poor wee bugger," Ben said. "Must've been terrified."

Logan bent closer to the mattress and examined the

epicentre of the bloodstain. The holes in the mattress were almost certainly just what Hamza thought. They weren't deep, but they nicked in the material in five unevenly-spaced places, suggesting the attack had been frantic and frenzied rather than tightly focused on one area.

There were two much deeper slits, too. The killer had missed at least twice, then.

He turned away and found himself drawn back to the crayon and pen pictures on the wall. Each was attached with the same push-pin as the nameplate on the door had been. Nine in total, clustered in a tight pattern.

"There should be ten," Logan said.

"Eh?" Ben asked, paying attention to the drawings for the first time.

Logan tapped a gloved finger against an empty spot on the wall near the centre of the group of pictures. "This space is the same size as the other drawings."

Hamza and Ben both came over to join him. "Maybe she hadn't finished putting them up," DS Khaled suggested, but Logan shook his head.

"There's a pin hole. Something was here."

"Could've been blood on it. Maybe Palmer's lot took it," Ben said.

Logan took the iPad from him and swiped back through the pictures. One of the angles showed the wall, complete with the same bare spot in the artwork.

"No. It wasn't there when they arrived," he said, showing the others the image. "So, it's possible someone else took it. The killer, maybe."

"Or she might just've taken it down because she didn't like it," Ben reasoned.

"Aye, maybe," Logan conceded. He gestured to the

images. "But look at them. They improve. These aren't just random pictures, they're a progression. Those on the left are... Well, let's no' beat around the bush, they're shite. Moving right, they get better. More controlled, less scribbly. I think they've been picked out to show her art skills improving over the years."

"Like a retrospective," Hamza said.

Ben frowned. "A retrospective what?"

"An art retrospective, sir. Like, when an art gallery shows a range of work from an artist's life."

"Right. Right, aye," Ben said. "Never really been one for art galleries."

"Hamza, do me a favour? Go check with Palmer, see if he's found it."

"No bother, sir," Hamza said, heading for the door.

"We'll meet you out front," Logan told him. "We're nearly done here."

"You think the picture's important?" Ben asked, as Hamza went clunking down the wooden staircase.

"I do," Logan said. He turned away from the wall. "And Hamza's own wee girl isn't far off the age this one was. Thought he might appreciate the fresh air."

They left Ruby's bedroom, hung a right, and entered the room next door. It was a little larger than the other bedroom, but the double bed, bedside cabinets, and two mismatched chests of drawers made it look far more cramped.

The bed was made. The curtains were drawn. There was no lingering whiff of death in this room, just the cloying perfume of the glass dish of potpourri that sat atop one of the sets of drawers.

At first glance, the room looked like a perfectly ordinary

couple's room. Very quickly, though, incongruities began to jump out.

"There's no pillows on that side," Ben said, indicating the side of the bed furthest from the door.

"Nothing on the bedside cabinet, either," Logan remarked.

Ben looked from one cabinet to the other. The closer of the two had a book on it, a slate coaster to sit a hot mug on, and two different charging cables trailing over the top.

The upper part of the cabinet was open, and there were another couple of books in there, some newspapers, and at least two or three pens. Presumably the section below this, which had a closed door concealing the contents, would be full of stuff, too.

The cabinet on the other side was bare. Nothing on top, and nothing shoved into the upper shelf. The door to the cupboard part was open, showing that section empty, too.

Logan walked around the bed and started working his way through the chest of drawers from top to bottom. It was an old piece of furniture, and he had to wrestle a bit with the warped wood, but every drawer he looked in was the same.

"Empty," he said. "It's been cleared out."

Across the room, Ben checked the other drawers. Each was full of women's clothes—underwear and socks at the top, progressing down to heavy jumpers and fleeces in the drawer at the bottom.

"All his stuff's gone," Logan said. There was a built-in wardrobe that lined most of one wall. He slid the mirrored door aside, then carefully rifled through several dresses and skirts. "There's nothing of his in here."

"Looks like he's our man, then. Killed the family, grabbed his stuff, and did a runner."

Logan slid the wardrobe door closed. Ben could well be right, of course. There was definitely a narrative that could be built there. But taking *all* his stuff? Hardly conducive to a quick getaway, and not easy to explain away when he was caught.

Which he would be. Logan would make damn sure of it.

"Aye, very probably," he said. He glanced at his watch and winced. It was well after ten, and it had been a long day even before the double homicide. "We can leave Scene of Crime to it for now, and catch up in the morning. I've still to find a hotel."

"Hotel, my arse," Ben said, appearing offended by the very suggestion. "You'll stay with me until you've decided what you're doing."

"I can't ask you to do that," Logan replied. "Thank you, I mean, but I don't want to... You know. Impose."

"Oh, shut up!" Ben waved a hand dismissively. "You're staying with me, and that's that. I've a perfectly serviceable sofa-bed in the wee box room."

There was the briefest of pauses before Logan spoke again. "Box room? Since when did you have a box room?"

"Oh. Aye," Ben said. He glanced down and shuffled his weight from one foot to the other. "I didn't tell you, did I?"

"Tell me what?"

"I've, eh... I've made a few changes since you left."

CHAPTER EIGHT

IT MADE SENSE THAT HE'D MOVE, OF COURSE. BEN would've built up a lot of good memories in the house he'd shared with Alice for years, but her brutal murder there would've understandably dampened his enthusiasm for the place.

The new house was soulless by comparison. It had been built recently, but with enough stone cladding that, to the disinterested casual observer, it might pass for having a bit more age and gravitas than it actually did.

It was located in the Milton of Leys area of the city—or, as the non-native Logan tended to think of it, 'out past Mata-lan,'—and looked more or less identical to the dozens of other houses lined up in regimented ranks around it.

The garden was full of stone chips. A pile of brown weeds by the path suggested Ben had tried to keep on top of them for a while, but the multitude of greenery between the stones revealed he had long since given up.

The house was cold when they entered, both literally and metaphorically. Ben clicked on the lights, turned up the thermostat on the wall in the hallway, then gestured to the place with something that was equal parts pride and embarrassment.

"Well. This is me," he said. "The bachelor pad. What do you think?"

Logan looked around at the bare magnolia walls. The carpet was a featureless expanse of dark grey that ran through the hall, up the stairs, and into what Logan assumed was the living room.

His initial impression of the place was not of a home, but of a house left on its default setting.

"It's... nice, aye," Logan said. He grasped for something specific to say about the place, and settled on, "I like the doors," even though they looked more or less like any other door he'd ever seen.

Ben turned and studied the door to the living room, like he was seeing it for the first time. "Thanks. Aye, they're lovely, aren't they? Can't take credit, though, they came with the place."

Logan followed the older man through to the living room. It was equally as impersonal as the hallway, with a beige-coloured two-seater couch and matching armchair, a thirty-two-inch TV on a black glass stand, and a generously sized coffee table with a single coaster on it at the corner nearest the chair.

An electric fire stood in the hearth of a cheap-looking wooden fireplace that had almost certainly come flat-packed for under thirty quid. The mantelpiece was bare, aside from a thin layer of dust and a little bowl where Ben immediately dumped his car keys.

There was a single picture to break up the otherwise featureless magnolia-painted walls. Logan felt a flicker of concern as he looked at it, but would've said nothing had Ben not clocked him staring.

"It's Jesus."

"So I see," Logan remarked. "The beard and the halo there were both clues."

"Was never really my thing. Religion. More herself's cup of tea," Ben explained. "But... I don't know. It's helped. There's a church nearby. Lovely folk. Bit... odd, maybe, but... Aye. Some of the stuff they've said has been reassuring. Comforting, or what have you."

Logan nodded slowly, like he was half-expecting a punchline to follow. "That's good," he said, when it was clear that Ben had finished saying his piece. "If it helps..."

"It has. It does," Ben said. "You should come sometime. It's not like you'd expect. They're called... Shite. What is it? Newfrontiers? Aye. Think that's it. Newfrontiers."

"They're no' a cult, are they?" Logan asked.

Ben tutted. "I said they're a bit odd. They're no' shagging goats and sacrificing virgins. Too bloody closed-minded. That's your problem, Jack." He indicated his friend's stomach. "Well, that and the belly."

Logan ignored the jibe, turned away from the smiling picture of Jesus, and cast a glance across the other walls. "Could maybe do with some photos up, or something. Brighten the place up a bit."

"Aye. Aye, maybe," Ben said. He fixed a smile in place, but it was a shrivelled, poor excuse for a thing. "It was always more herself's department. She had an eye for it."

"You don't say her name."

Ben frowned. "Eh?"

"That's twice now you've said, 'herself.' Not Alice."

There was a pause. A silence that seemed to stretch on

forever, but was in reality only a second or two. "I can say her name," Ben said. "I can say her name anytime I like."

"Good," Logan said, and he didn't push it any further.

Instead, he turned and looked out through the front window. The house on the other side of the street was identical to this one, and Logan felt like he was looking in a big mirror.

"Not a bad spot this," he said. "Close to the twenty-four-hour Asda, aren't you?"

"Och, don't get me started on that bloody place," Ben said, his tone becoming clipped. "You ask me, that's what's wrong with the world these days."

"Christ, not this again," Logan muttered.

Ben took off his jacket and draped it over his arm. "Yes, this again. They're what do you call it, aren't they? Symptomatic. Of the world's problems," he explained. "It's that sense of expectation, isn't it? That entitlement. Once upon a time, you wanted a box of cornflakes, you had to wait until the shop opened next morning. Now? You just go in anytime you please. Want a Twix at 4AM? Aye, away you go, help yourself. Need a big bag of Wotsits at half past midnight? Not a problem, step right this way. Nobody has to wait for anything, so they expect everything right now."

"Aye, well, like I've told you before—" Logan began, but Ben wasn't finished.

"Same with that bloody... what's it called? Netflix and Chill."

"I think it's just Netflix."

"Whatever it's called, it's the same. In the olden days, if you liked a programme on the telly, it was an event. You watched it, then you waited until it was back on the following week, and you watched it again. Maybe you taped it on the video recorder, if you could figure it out. Whatever. There was an element of patience involved. A degree of bloody restraint."

Ben shook his head. His mouth was pulled up like he'd tasted something unpleasant.

"Now, it's all there on demand. It's all now, now, now. People *binge*. I mean, what was wrong with just watching something? Why do folk have to *binge* nowadays? I heard someone say the other day they were going to go home and binge *The One Show*. How do you binge the bloody *One Show*? There's a million episodes. It's never-ending. And why would you, more importantly? It's a heap of shite."

"Beats me," said Logan, not really wanting to get drawn into the discussion. He puffed out his cheeks and raised his eyebrows in what he hoped came across as a show of sympathetic agreement. "So, eh, are we close to the Asda or not?" he asked. "Because I could do with picking up a few things."

Ben gave a wave in the direction of the window. "Oh. Right, aye. It's just down the road."

"That's handy."

"Aye. Good for when I'm coming back from a late shift, I have to say," he admitted. "I was going to stick the kettle on, but I'll give you a run across first."

"You're fine. I'll find it," Logan said. He glanced at the bowl where Ben had deposited his keys. "Mind if I borrow your car?"

"Help yourself," Ben said. "But put the seat forward again when you're done. Last time you used it, I couldn't reach the bloody steering wheel."

Logan took the keys from the bowl. "Will do. And I shouldn't be too long."

"If you get lost, give me a ring," Ben said. "Oh, and Jack?"

Logan stopped halfway to the living room door.

"Have you decided? You sticking around?"

Logan passed the car keys from one hand to another, considering his reply. "I don't... I'm not sure yet. Still debating it," he said.

"What's to bloody debate? The team needs a good DCI. You're a good DCI. Problem solved."

"You could do it," Logan suggested. "You'd be ideal."

"Bollocks I would!" Ben countered. "Besides, I'm far too old. They'd never offer it to me. The team needs you back. You've been gone too long."

Or not long enough, Logan thought, but he just smiled and nodded, then twirled the keys around on his finger. "Be back in a bit," he said.

And with that, he was gone.

IT TOOK Logan less than ten minutes to get what he needed from the supermarket, and then another fifteen of driving around and consulting Google Maps until he found the house he was looking for. It would've been an epic trek right across the city until just a couple of years back, when the A8082 connecting trunk road was built, creating a shortcut to the A82 near the canal bridge.

The house was one of the smaller, less prestigious looking places out in Leachkin, arguably the city's leafiest of suburbs. Logan had never been to it before, but he'd had a note of the address for a while now, knowing that eventually he'd wind up here, on this step, knocking at this door.

He waited. The lights were on inside. He could hear a

TV blaring, too. Gunshots. Shouting. Some action movie or another.

He knocked again, louder this time, giving it some welly.

He waited again. This time, he could hear movement. Clattering and muttering. The *chinking* of glass.

Unhappy footsteps approached along the hallway.

Thud. Thud. Thud.

There was *clack* of a lock being undone. Logan drew himself up to his full impressive height as the door was pulled inwards with a sudden yank.

It was the light that hit him first, followed a moment later by the smell of alcohol and stale smoke that came wafting from inside.

A man in a curry-stained t-shirt and checked boxer shorts stood swaying in the doorway. His bloodshot eyes squinted at Logan's chest, clearly expecting someone much smaller, then moved up until they found his face. They narrowed for a moment, before widening in surprise.

"Well, fuck me red raw," spat the former Detective Superintendent Robert Hoon. "If it's no' Grizzly bastarding Adams."

CHAPTER NINE

HOON'S PLACE WAS A MESS. BUT THEN, SO WAS HOON himself, so it felt quite fitting.

The curtains were drawn, and the stale odour that permeated the whole house suggested they'd been that way for days, if not weeks.

There was a strata of dirty plates almost completely covering a coffee table, and a second layer of takeaway packaging topping it off. An array of mugs and glasses sat at various strategical points on the floor. At least two of the cups and one of the takeaway boxes had been repurposed as ashtrays, and were now overflowing with dog ends and spent matches.

Hoon shoved a stack of unironed clothes off an armchair and onto the floor, and gestured for Logan to take a seat.

"I'm alright, thanks. I won't be long."

"Sit your fat arse down," Hoon instructed. "Before you make the fucking place look untidy."

He snorted with laughter at that, erupted into a fit of

coughing, then hoiked up a mouthful of phlegm and spat it into a napkin bearing the *KFC logo.*

Reluctantly, Logan lowered himself onto the chair. It gave a sharp, sudden *creak,* like it had taken offence at this sudden weight being placed upon it.

"Ah, fucking shut up," Hoon grunted, apparently addressing the furniture.

"I like what you've done with the place," Logan remarked.

"Fucking... Aye, well. Fucking..." Hoon began, but the remainder of the sentence failed to appear. He began fishing down the side of one of the couch cushions like he was searching for them missing words. Then, with a little cry of triumph, he produced a half-bottle of Tesco own-brand Scotch. "You having one?" he asked, waving the bottle vaguely in Logan's direction.

"No. Thanks. I'm still off it."

Hoon swayed on the spot, his nostrils flaring with distaste. "Do you know the only bastard worse than a reformed alcoholic, Jack?"

Logan shook his head.

"No, nor me. Because I've never fucking met anyone," Hoon retorted.

He unscrewed the top of the bottle, glugged, winced, then twisted the cap back into place. His eyes swam for a moment, and he looked around the room like he couldn't quite remember where he was or what he was doing there.

"You alright, Bob?" Logan asked.

Hoon scoffed. "Alright? Me? Alright? Don't you worry about me. I'm fucking peachy, Jack. Peachy. I'm Princess Fucking Peachy of the fucking Peachy Palace. That's what I am. I'm A-O-fucking-kay. I'm A-O-fucking-kay with a fucking cherry on top." He jabbed a thumb in the direction of his chest, and somehow managed to miss. "See me? I'm ex-fucking Special Forces, I'll have you know. There's nothing I can't fucking deal with."

"Is that right?" Logan asked him.

"Aye! That's fucking right, alright!"

Hoon sniffed loudly, ran a hand through his hair, then his legs seemed to give up and he flopped down onto the couch. He burped loudly, drew his forearm across his mouth, then sized Logan up.

"What happened to you, by the way? You turn out to be allergic to a fucking wasp sting, or something?" he asked. "I mean, Jesus fuck, man. Look at you. You look like you've swallowed a birthday balloon. Or... no. One of them punch-ball things. On the elastic bands." He mimed punching a balloon over and over. "Boom, boom, boom. You know the things I mean? Fucking... big long elastic bands on them."

Logan adjusted himself in the chair a little self-consciously. "Aye. Well, a few too many fish suppers, I suppose."

"Fish suppers? What the fuck kind of fish was it? Blue whale?" Hoon asked.

"Listen, if we're going to have a competition here about who's let themselves go the most, I don't fancy your chances, Bob," Logan said. He indicated the rest of the room with a quick, cursory glance. "What's the matter? Cleaner on holiday?"

Hoon held Logan's gaze as he took the cap off his whisky and gulped down another mouthful.

"Funnily enough, I've had other things on my mind," he replied, once the amber liquid had burned its way down his throat.

"Like how you betrayed the team, you mean?"

"Oh, here it fucking comes," Hoon spat. "The big fucking lecture from the big fucking 'I Am.' Is that what this is, Jack? Is that why you've heaved your hairy, sweating fucking carcass over here? So you can lord it over me and tell me I'm the bad bastard? Is that the plan?"

Logan remained calm. In control. It wouldn't do to lose the head, no matter how much he might want to.

"You sold us out to Bosco Maximuke," he said.

"Fucking... Bosco. Sold you out? I did fuck all of the kind, Jack. I protected that fucking clown-car of halfwits and cretins you call a team. That's what I did. I put my own fucking job on the line to keep your people safe."

Logan sat forward sharply, but reined in his temper just in time. He fixed Hoon with a cold, dangerous stare, but figured that was better than grabbing him by the throat.

"And how do you figure that one out, Bob?" he asked. His voice was level, but there was an edge to it that said it wouldn't necessarily stay that way for long. "Because from what I understand, you were protecting your niece, and then your bank balance."

It was Hoon's turn to sit forward. His own temper was building, the lines of it drawing themselves like battle paint on his pale, unshaven face.

"You and I know full fucking well what Bosco was like. Us more than anyone. If he didn't get what he wanted from me, you think that'd be it over? You think he'd have just turned around and packed it all up? 'Nice fucking try, didn't work out, no harm done.' You seriously fucking think for one moment that that's what would've happened?"

Logan said nothing, but Hoon chose to pluck a reply out of the silence.

"No. Exactly. Would he fuck. He'd have found some other bastard to latch onto. Ben, maybe. Threatened Alice a bit. Got him scared. Or your... man with the hair. The fucking loudmouth. What's his name?"

"Tyler," Logan said.

"Aye. Him. You think he'd have coped wi' Bosco bastarding Maximuke coming at him wi' cock in hand? You think he wouldn't have flapped his fucking lips and spilled his guts when that Russian fuck applied the thumbscrews? Or one of the others?"

Hoon gave that a few moments to sink in, before continuing. "Do you honestly think that Bosco wouldn't have set his fucking sights on someone else, and done whatever the fuck he needed to do to get them to talk? That crooked shitestick wanted someone on the inside, and he would've gone through the whole fucking station until he found someone. "

Hoon shook his head, unscrewed the lid of the bottle like he was about to take another swig, then tightened it up again.

"So, I took the fucking bullet, Jack. Me." He slammed a hand down on the arm of the couch, throwing up a small cloud of dust. *"Bang!* Career-ending injury. Man down. Stretchered off the fucking park." He laughed bitterly. "But better me than some other clueless bastard. At least I knew how to deal with the tubby Russian fuck. Go check through the investigation. See what I told him. Fuck all, that's what. Nothing useful. Nothing he couldn't already find out without me."

He sat back in the chair, nursing the half-bottle to his chest. He'd been glaring at Logan through most of his outburst, but now looked at a spot on the wall that appeared to be completely unremarkable, but evidently held some sort of fascination for him.

"I didn't sell you out. I fucking protected you," he said. There was a glug as he took another drink. "And what thanks do I get?"

"Interesting perspective," Logan said. It was curt and dismissive, and yet there was nothing in what the other man had said that he could deny. Bosco wasn't one to take no for an answer. If he'd really wanted someone spying for him, he'd have found someone, even if he'd had to terrorise and torture his way through the whole department to do so.

Besides, Logan's own history with the Russian wasn't exactly squeaky-clean.

"We're no' that dissimilar, you and me," Hoon said, as if reading Logan's mind. "You'd have done exactly the same."

"Aye, you keep telling yourself that, Bob," Logan replied. He tried to laugh it off with a wry chuckle, but was he right? Would Logan have behaved in the same way? Done anything different?

One of the main reasons he'd come here had been to tell Hoon exactly what he thought of him, but maybe he needed to cut the man some slack. Or, at least beat a retreat until he'd thought it all through a bit more.

Logan stood up. The smell was becoming too much for him, anyway, and the sight of Hoon—the state of him—was turning his stomach. This was not the man he remembered. The man that he and every other officer he'd ever met had lived in a near-perpetual state of fear of. This was a ghost of that man. His shadow.

"Sorry," he said. "I shouldn't have come."

"Fucking sit down. Come on. Have a drink. Come on," Hoon urged. There was a pleading note to his voice that Logan had never heard before, and despised hearing now.

"Sorry. I can't," Logan said. "Another time, maybe." He

moved as if to turn, then stopped. "Can I ask you something, though, Bob?"

Hoon muttered something largely unintelligible, then jerked his shoulders in a sudden shrug. "What?"

"After everything you've seen. Everything you've done… Would you go back?" Logan asked. He watched his old boss carefully, studying his reaction. "If you could? Would you do it again?"

The former Detective Superintendent burped quietly, and blew the breath away. He motioned down at his dirty t-shirt and crumpled boxer shorts, and his face knotted up into something that was part-smile, part-sneer.

"What the fuck do you think?"

Logan nodded. He glanced around the room again, then gave Hoon one last look. "Take care of yourself, Bob," he said. "I'll see myself out."

"THE WANDERER RETURNS," Ben cheered, when Logan got back to the house. "I was about to report my car stolen. Thought you'd done a runner."

"Just… trying to clear the head," Logan told him.

Ben nodded. He crossed his arms and leaned against one of his many magnolia walls. "And did it help?"

"Eh… aye," Logan said. "Aye, I think it did, actually."

"That's good. Come to a decision, then?"

"I think so," Logan replied. "But first…" He held up the carrier bag of stuff he'd bought in Asda. Inside, metal clacked against plastic. "…you mind if I use your bathroom?"

CHAPTER TEN

DETECTIVE SUPERINTENDENT MITCHELL LOOKED UP from her paperwork, briefly regarded the clean-shaven man standing on the other side of her desk, then slid him a stack of forms.

"Read and sign these. Get them back to me before the end of the day," she instructed, scanning back over whatever it was she'd just been writing.

Logan picked up the forms, briefly wondered if he was making a mistake when he felt the weight of them, then tucked them under his arm.

He ran a hand over the bottom half of his face, marvelling at how different it felt. The skin was still red, blotchy, and tender to the touch, the shaving exercise having taken well over an hour the night before.

Ben had stepped in eventually, and had hacked away at the beard with a pair of scissors he'd taken from the kitchen drawer. Between his unsteady hand and the cheap disposable supermarket razors, Logan's face had felt like it was hanging in ribbons when the ordeal was finally over, and he'd been forced to sleep with a dozen or more wee bits of toilet paper stuck to his neck and chin to stop the bleeding.

"I've got you booked in for a meeting with Professional Standards at two," the DSup said.

The paperwork slipped from beneath Logan's arm and he sprackled to catch it. "Eh, Professional Standards, ma'am?" he asked, once he'd got a firm hold of the bundle.

Mitchell placed the lid on her fountain pen and looked up. "Yes. Professional Standards," she reiterated. "You broke all manner of rules, Jack. You encouraged... or, no. Let's be generous. Let's say you *inspired* others in your team to do the same, and to take unnecessary risks. So, to keep everything above board, you'll meet with Professional Standards."

"So... what? You brought me back in so you could fire me?" Logan demanded. "Is that it?"

"I brought you back in because Detective Inspector Forde recommended you for the DCI position after he turned it down," Mitchell said. "Quite insistent he was, too."

The bastard, Logan thought. *So much for 'too old.'*

"But, due to some poor decision-making on your part in the past, it would be remiss of me not to refer you to Professional Standards," Mitchell explained. "It's just for a chat. A reminder of what flies here and what doesn't."

The spot on the desk where he'd lifted the paperwork from suddenly looked awfully inviting, but he fought the urge and forced himself to keep a firm hold of the forms.

"Right, ma'am. I'll be there," he said.

"Good. Also..." She pointed the end of her pen at him and made a vague scribbling motion in his general direction. "There'll be a fitness test."

Somewhere, an alarm sounded. It took Logan a moment to realise that it was inside his head.

"Fitness test?"

"Yes. Standard procedure, as you know," Mitchell told him. "It'll be the usual bleep test. Do you want me to arrange it for today?"

"Christ, no!" Logan ejected, more forcefully than he'd intended. He smiled. "I mean, given what we're dealing with at the moment, maybe we could postpone it for another time. Like a couple of weeks from now? Or next month?"

Or never, he thought.

"Let's say Monday, then. That gives you the weekend to prepare."

"I'm not sure that's the best idea, given what—"

"Good. Monday it is," Mitchell said, scribbling a note on a Post-It and sticking it to her monitor.

Logan could tell that continuing to protest was not going to do him any favours. If anything, she'd only bring it forward. "Fine. Monday," he said. "Is there anything else?"

"No, nothing else. Just have those done for me by close of play," she said. She lowered her head, then brought it back up. "Oh, actually. There was one thing I wanted to discuss."

The top drawer of her desk slid out with a *thunk*. Reaching inside, she produced a single sheet of A4 paper and placed it on the desk in front of her.

"This came from the notes Assistant Chief Constable Haldane made about a discussion the two of you had about DCI Grant, and his... shortcomings. I asked for a copy."

"Snecky's shortcomings? Would've been a long conversation."

"You don't remember it?"

Logan blew out his cheeks. "Vaguely, why?"

"You said, and I quote, 'Snecky couldn't catch VD in an African brothel.'"

"I think that's a pretty fair description of him."

Detective Superintendent Mitchell interlocked her fingers lightly on the desk in front of her. "Why an African brothel?"

Logan blinked. "Sorry?"

"Why, specifically, an *African* brothel?" she asked. Her face was impassive, but there was an intensity in the stare that had locked onto him like a tractor beam. "Why not just 'a brothel'?"

"Well, I mean—"

"Is the implication that there is something inherently dirtier about a brothel in Africa as opposed to brothels anywhere else in the world?"

Logan's mouth moved up and down. Some sound came out, but nothing that could reasonably be construed to be words.

"Yes. That's what I thought," Mitchell said. She folded the paper neatly in half, then scrunched it up and dropped it into the waste paper basket down at her feet.

"I wasn't... I didn't mean anything by it."

"Of course you didn't. No one ever does. But—and I say this not for my benefit, but for yours, Jack—do better. *Be* better. You have a team who, for whatever reason, all think the sun shines out of your rear end. Do us all a favour. Don't prove them wrong."

"No. Aye. I mean... No. I won't," Logan replied. He felt himself straightening his shoulders just a fraction. "I won't."

"Good. I'm very glad to hear it. Now, go. Crack on. Dazzle me," Mitchell said. She reached into the desk drawer again. There was a *click* as she placed an ID card down on the desk. Logan's own face scowled up at him from the front. "And welcome back, Detective Chief Inspector."

"Alright, boss?"

Logan didn't acknowledge the question until the door to the Incident Room had swung closed behind him. Those two words were loaded with meaning. Even if he hadn't immediately understood that, the expectant looks on the faces of Hamza, Sinead, and Tyler would've caught him up on it pretty sharpish.

He nodded. "No' bad, son," he said. "But I'll be a lot better when you get your arse off that desk. There's a reason we provide you with chairs. Nice as they are, they're no' just for decoration."

"Right, boss," Tyler said, beaming from ear to ear despite the telling-off. Or, just as likely, because of it. He jumped up from where he'd been sitting on Sinead's desk, and took his seat. "Sorry, boss."

"You'll be making a speech, sir?" Sinead said, half-teasingly.

"Aye, that's traditional," Hamza said. "New man in charge, and all that. Snecky made a beautiful speech when he came back. Not a dry eye in the house, there was."

Logan gave a grunt. That didn't sound like Snecky. "What did he say?"

Hamza tapped his pen against his chin as he tried to recall the words that had so moved them all. "I mean, I won't be able to do it justice, sir, but pretty sure it was something like, 'What the fuck are you all staring at? Have you no' got work to be getting on with?'"

Tyler nodded enthusiastically. "It was powerful stuff, boss. But it was the finish that got me here." He thumped a fist against his heart, and sniffed, like he was becoming emotional. "'I'll be in my office. No interruptions under any circumstances.'"

"Say what you like about him, sir, the man has a way with words," Hamza concluded.

The door opened at Logan's back, and he had to take a hurried step forward to avoid being hit by it. Geoff Palmer recoiled in fright at finding the DCI looming over him, and hissed out a whispered, "Jesus!" below his breath.

"Palmer?" Logan said, regarding him like he might regard an errant smear of dog shite on a new carpet. "What do you want?"

"A word," Palmer replied, bouncing Logan's glare back at him with interest. He indicated Logan's office door with the briefest of glances. "In private."

Logan stepped aside and motioned for the SOC man to go ahead. He turned to the rest of the team and gave a shrug that managed to be both an apology and unmistakably sarcastic. "Looks like the speech will have to wait," he told them, then he followed Geoff Palmer into the office and closed the door.

"Take a seat," Logan said, gesturing to the empty chair nearest the door. Palmer didn't look at it before dismissing it with a shake of his head.

"This won't take long. I just wanted to give an update on the double homicide case," he said, then added, "From yesterday," in case Logan needed help narrowing it down.

"Aye, funnily enough I know the one. But what brings you here in person?" the DCI asked. "You usually just send in your report."

Logan would have preferred that. Sure, Geoff Palmer's summaries could be terse to the point of being personally offensive, but they were nothing compared to the man himself. They'd only been in the room together for a matter of seconds, but Logan already felt compelled to batter him across the side of the head with the bundle of paperwork the Detective Superintendent had given him.

He set it down on the desk, just to be on the safe side, and shoved his hands into his pockets.

"It's... I just..." Palmer sighed. Logan had never seen him this uncertain before. This vulnerable. "It feels a bit personal, this one, that's all."

"Personal how?"

"With the kiddie, and all that," Palmer said. He was looking at the desk, at the wall, at the floor—anywhere but at Logan's face. "My sister's the same age."

Logan frowned. "As who? The mother?"

"No. As the wee one."

The frown deepened considerably. Geoff Palmer was fifty if he was a day, and that was being generous. "The wee one? As in... the child? As in Ruby Mann? That wee one?"

"Aye."

"Your *sister*?"

"Technically my half-sister," Palmer said. "On my father's side."

"Well, I didn't think it was on your mother's side. No' unless she's got a place in the *Guinness Book of Records*," Logan said. "How old's your dad?"

"Seventy-two," Palmer said. He shuffled his weight from one foot to the other, clearly not relishing the conversation. "His wife's thirty-seven."

Logan blew out his cheeks and dropped into his chair. "Fair play to them, I suppose."

"Aye, well. I think it's fucking ridiculous, personally, but there you go. The point is, my sister, Alanna, is about the same age as Ruby. I know we're not supposed to let it get to us, that it shouldn't affect us, but seeing her there like that..."

He relented and sat down. There were bags under Palmer's eyes that hadn't been there the night before. Clearly, he'd had a sleepless one.

"It should get to us, Geoff," Logan told him. "I mean, aye, we pretend it doesn't. We kid ourselves on, but it should *always* get to us. Otherwise, what's the bloody point?"

Palmer raised his gaze enough to meet Logan's own, then nodded. "Maybe. Aye," he conceded.

"So, what have you got for me?" Logan asked.

Admittedly, Palmer was being less of a pain in the arse than usual, but the DCI was still keen to get the bugger out of his office as soon as humanly possible, ideally long before his real personality reared its ugly head again.

"Right. Yes." Palmer drew a breath in through his nose, straightened in the chair, and got down to business. "Hopefully this doesn't come as news to you, but it wasn't a suicide."

"Aye, we figured that out pretty sharpish."

"We've been at the place most of the evening, and think we've built up a decent picture. Ruby was killed first. We're assuming the stab wounds killed her, but pathology may say otherwise. Highly doubt it, though."

"How do you know she was first?" Logan asked.

"Blood. Her blood was on the stairs and in the living room. The mother's wasn't. The killer struck first upstairs, killed the child, came down, then killed the mother. Only way the blood trail makes sense," Palmer said. "Also..."

He pulled his briefcase onto his lap, fished inside, then produced a glossy photograph of a blood spot low down on the staircase wall.

"Note the teardrop shape? Suggests forward momentum when it hit, meaning whoever it dripped from was headed downstairs. There are no drips heading upwards."

Logan took the photograph, glanced at it to confirm, then sat it on his desk. "Right. Anything else?"

"We got a footprint. Size nine, which matches the husband."

Palmer handed over another photograph. This one showed an area of what appeared to be a kitchen floor. A bloody print was clearly visible in amongst the geometric pattern of the vinyl.

"Just the one?" Logan asked.

"One clean one. A few partials. Tread pattern matches on all of them."

"Fingerprints?"

Palmer nodded. "Three sets consistently throughout the house. Wife, daughter, and the husband's. None anywhere damning, though, so nothing that would stand up. There's a set we can't identify. Female, I'd reckon, judging by size and shape."

He took out another photograph, looked at it for a moment to check it was the right one, then passed it to Logan. The image showed the inside of a cupboard that was half-filled with junk.

"What's this?"

"Maybe nothing," Palmer said. "But three of us noted it. It was in the daughter's bedroom."

He said nothing more, leaving it hanging there like a challenge, defying the DCI to figure it out.

"It's a cupboard full of junk, Geoff," Logan said.

Palmer tutted patronisingly. "Come on, Jack. You should be able to see it. Man of your experience."

"I don't have time for games, Geoff. If there's something I should know, how about you just…"

A nagging little thought made its presence felt. Logan fell silent for a moment, considering the photograph. The cupboard wasn't much bigger than a phone box. The top half was lined with shelves that held towels and linen, but from about halfway down it was an open space that had clearly been used for storing toys.

All the boxes, board games, cars, and dolls were shoved into the corners and against the back and side walls of the cupboard, leaving an area in the middle almost completely clear.

"You think someone was hiding in there?" Logan asked.

Palmer was unable to hide his disappointment. Not that he made any real effort to. "Wow. OK. Truth be told, I'm surprised you figured it out. Still, took you long enough," he said, his true colours returning to the fore. "We're not sure. It's a possibility. We didn't find any prints in there beyond the usual three, but we did find some hair that we're getting tested. No saying it's recent, though."

"Likely to be from the family, surely?"

"Not a match for the mother or daughter. Wrong colour. It's darker."

Logan thought back to the wedding photo in the house. The husband's hair had been dark brown or black. Of course, finding a strand of a man's hair in a cupboard in his own house wasn't unusual. And there were plenty of explanations for the way the space had been cleared among the toys. Ruby could've used it as a den. Someone could've jumped in there while playing Hide and Seek.

He wasn't dismissing it completely, but Logan had his doubts that the cupboard would be a key factor in the case.

"That's pretty much your lot for now," Palmer said. "I've emailed the report over to DI Forde. Your email bounces back as 'unrecognisable address.'"

"Aye, well, I'll make sure they get that fixed."

Palmer sniffed. "Staying around then, are we?"

"I am."

Again, the SOC investigator made no attempt to hide his disappointment. "They not making you do the fitness test?"

Logan shifted his not-inconsiderable weight in his chair. "They are, aye."

"Right. I see," Palmer said, brightening considerably. "Well, in that case, given the state of you, this might not matter so much, but... can I say something to you? Man to man?"

Logan suspected Palmer's use of that phrase might see him in trouble under the Trade Descriptions Act, but gave his permission with a single nod. "Fire on."

"Right. It's Dr Maguire. Shona," Palmer began. His earlier uncertainty was gone, and he was puffing himself up before Logan's eyes.

"What about her?"

"I want you to stay away from her. Beyond... work-matters, I mean."

Logan's forward movement was slow and subtle, but calculated in its deliberateness. "I'm sorry?" he asked, half-smiling to suggest he'd *clearly* misheard the words that had come out of Palmer's mouth.

"She and I have a thing."

"A thing?" Logan echoed. "What do you mean?"

Palmer flinched, visibly irritated by the questions. "I mean there's a thing between us."

"Like what?" Logan snorted. "Two hundred feet and a

restraining order? Shona wouldn't touch you with a barge-pole, Geoff."

"Oh, wouldn't she? Wouldn't she?" Palmer spat, and Logan suddenly got the impression that there was more the man wanted to say. "Look, she's just... She's off-limits, OK? You had your chance, and you left. You made the decision to up and go, and leave her alone. Let someone else have a crack at her."

"Have a crack at her? Are you listening to the shite that's coming out of your mouth, Geoff?" Logan asked. "She's a grown woman. I think she can make her own decisions, don't you?"

"Oh, God, don't pretend to be all bloody feminist. You know what I mean," Palmer bit back. "You had your chance, and you blew it. Shona is moving on. With me."

He stood up, fiddling the buckle of his briefcase closed, his face a mask of righteous indignance.

"So, if you really care about her, then you'll do the decent thing," he concluded, finally getting the briefcase's metal clasp to snap shut. "You'll stay out of our way."

CHAPTER ELEVEN

SHONA MAGUIRE CHOKED, COUGHED, THEN EJECTED TWO
streams of *Barr's Red Kola* out through her nose, accompanied by a high-pitched wheeze and a gasped, "Fuck."

Logan politely looked away while she cleaned herself up
with a tissue, waited for her to finish coughing up the fizzy
red liquid, then turned back when she spoke.

"He said *what*?!"

"Just that, really. That you two had a thing."

"A thing? What did he mean, a thing? What kind of
thing?"

Logan shrugged. "He didn't specify. Just... a thing."

They were in Shona's office at Raigmore Hospital, the
site of their *Pot Noodle* lunch date that now felt like a life-
time ago. The pathologist placed a heel against the metal
base of a stool and kicked herself up into the seat.

"I bet it's that bloody lunch break," she said, scowling at
some memory Logan wasn't privy to.

"Lunch break?"

"We were on a course. One of your new boss's bloody

initiatives. Had to drive down to Falkirk for it, and then who's the first face I see when I walk into the room?"

"Sex Pest Palmer?"

"Sex Pest Palmer," Shona confirmed. "I couldn't shift the bastard all day. He was about me like a bad bloody smell. During the lunch break, he suggested we grab a bite to eat in the Costa next door from the venue. I didn't have the heart to say no."

Logan drew a breath in through his teeth. "Shite. Well, that's it, then. You've done it now."

"Done what?" Shona asked.

"That's pretty much you two married in Palmer's eyes. You let him buy you coffee. You belong to him now."

"I bought my own bloody coffee!" Shona protested. "Wasn't wanting him getting any ideas."

Logan wrinkled his nose. "How did that work out, do you think?"

Shona groaned. "Not perfect."

"There's a lesson to be learned here," Logan said.

"And what's that?" Shona asked, meeting his eye. "All men are arseholes? Way ahead of you."

She slid down from the high stool and washed her hands in the sink. "Anyway, enough with the chit-chat, get masked up," she instructed, her tone taking on a cooler edge.

With a tilt of her head, she indicated a selection of PPE over by the swing doors that led through to the mortuary.

"Because, Detective Chief Inspector, I am about to blow your tiny mind."

THERE WERE two mounds on two tables, covered by two sheets. Logan stood at one end of the larger mound, while Shona stood directly across from him.

He regarded the sheet, replaying what she'd just told him, confusion written all over his face. He'd seen the blood. He'd seen the injuries. What she was saying didn't make sense.

"Sorry," he said. "Say that again."

"The knife wounds didn't kill her," Shona repeated. "She drowned."

"Drowned?"

"Drowned."

"As in..."

"As in there was water in her lungs which would've quickly prevented her from breathing."

"She was in her living room," Logan reminded her. "How could she drown?"

He knew the answer to that almost before he'd finished asking the question. Shona had just started to shrug when he jumped in.

"There was a jug. I noticed it at the time. A water jug. It was on the arm of a chair."

"There you go, then," Shona said. "Doesn't take a lot of water to do the job."

She pulled the sheet down, unveiling the greying head and chest of the corpse of Lois Mann. She'd been cut open and put back together, and Logan could see the start of the incision between her breasts, now neatly sewn shut.

"Note the bruising here," she said, indicating the neck and both shoulders. Several dark blobs marked her skin all over these areas. "Pinned down, I'd say. Carpet burns on her back suggest she may have been dragged at some point, too."

"So, the killer held her down, poured the water down her throat, and she drowned?"

"Well, I doubt it was quite as straightforward as that. He'd have had to hold her for a while. Death isn't instant. When the body gets water in the lungs it reacts. Badly, as I'm sure you can imagine. Before long, the body starts to convulse. It has a fit."

"Aye. I've seen that happen. Not nice."

"Especially from her perspective, I'd have thought," Shona said, indicating the body stretched out between them. "The knife wounds to the wrists were done after she was dead using a kitchen knife found at the scene. Don't know what the purpose of those was. If it was to make it look like suicide, he did a terrible job."

"Aye, shoddy work, right enough," Logan agreed. "We got a time of death?"

"Mm. Yeah. Hang on." Shona unhooked a clipboard from the trolley and consulted the top couple of pages.

Logan watched her in silence. He should've kept in touch. Or at least told her he was going. What had he been thinking? She had every right to have moved on. If not with Geoff Palmer, then with someone else.

"Sunday night."

Logan blinked back to the here and now. "Hmm?"

"Body was found Wednesday afternoon at just after three. I'd put time of death as three days earlier, tail end of the day. The house was cool, which slowed decomposition. But, yeah. Later on Sunday evening, or the very early hours of Monday morning."

"So... seven through to one?"

"Ish, yeah. That sort of window."

She pulled the sheet up, allowing Lois Mann her final

scraps of dignity. Logan tensed when she walked over to the second bed with its smaller mound, and his feet were reluctant to follow.

"With the daughter, it was more straightforward," Shona said.

She stood a couple of feet from the head-end of the trolley, and crossed her hands in front of her like a show of respect. Logan plodded over to take up his spot at the opposite end, and mirrored her body language with his own.

"Nine, possibly ten stab wounds with a large, slightly curved blade. It doesn't match the knife that was found at the scene. The one used on Lois. This one was much thinner—narrower, I mean—and approximately nine to ten inches long. Carbon steel blade. Black."

Logan shot her a quizzical look.

"There were filings in the wounds that forensics tested. They think the blade had been sharpened very recently. Presumably in anticipation of..."

She gestured at the body beneath the sheet.

"And to think," Logan muttered. "I actually missed this."

"Here, no judgements from me," she told him. "I trained for years so I could poke about doing this."

Logan accepted the reassurance with a smile that she couldn't see behind his mask.

"From what I saw of the bed, looked like the blade went right through her," Logan said. "That right?"

Shona nodded grimly. "Yeah. All the way. She was sleeping on her back. He stabbed her through the covers, and the blade went through her into the mattress below. Not every time, but most. Pretty frenzied, too. No real pattern to it. Although, it would be hard to aim for anything specific with the quilt over her."

"She must've been scared out of her mind," Logan remarked.

"Would've been over quickly. But, aye, just bloody horrible while it lasted." Shona motioned to the sheet. "Want a look?"

Logan tried very hard not to flinch at the thought of it. "Would it help?"

Shona hesitated for just a moment, then stepped back, crossing her hands in front of her again. "No," she said, and for just a moment there was something behind her eyes. Something haunted. "It would not."

THE GLOVES CAME off with a series of elastic *snaps*. Shona pressed down the pedal of the contaminated waste bin until Logan had deposited his PPE, then dumped her own and let the lid fall closed.

The pathologist hadn't been able to determine which of the victims had died first, just that it must've been roughly around the same time. Lois Mann had been drinking quite heavily. Not *three sheets to the wind* levels of drunkenness, but not a kick in the arse off it.

"She'd likely still be in control, depending on her levels of tolerance," Shona had explained. "But reactions and reasoning would've been reasonably impaired."

Both victims had been in good health, although there was some bruising on Lois's hands that were consistent with someone who'd recently been hitting something.

"The attacker?" Logan had asked, but Shona had dismissed it.

The bruises were older—days before the death. From

their position on the outside of each hand, she could've been raining hammer-strikes on something. If Shona had to guess what, she'd say the floor, as there was a suggestion of a carpet burn among the bruises on one of the hands, although the two things, she'd stressed, could well be completely unrelated.

"Thank you," Logan said, once he'd ridded himself of the gloves and mask. "A roller-coaster, as always."

"Best ride in Inverness," Shona said, then her eyes widened with horror and what felt like all the blood in her body rushed to fill her cheeks. "I mean... I don't... That's not... Jesus. Scrub that from the record."

"Consider it scrubbed," said Logan, trying very hard to save her further embarrassment by not smiling, although with only moderate success.

"You've shaved, then," Shona said, hurriedly changing the subject.

"Aye, no' much gets past you," Logan replied. It was supposed to be a joke, but it came out sounding a little too direct. "Boss's orders," he continued, trying to soften the previous sentence. "Shame. It hid the additional chins."

"Didn't hide the grey, though," Shona said. Her mouth formed various shapes, like she was testing out sentences before abandoning them. Eventually, she settled on: "You're hanging around, then?"

"Aye. That's the plan. Assuming I pass the fitness test on Monday, I'm here for the duration."

"You're not going to go swanning off to some far flung island again next month?"

"I'd hardly call Orkney 'far flung.'"

"I've driven that Thurso road," Shona said, shuddering. "It's far flung enough."

"You should try it with DC Neish spewing his ring up front sometime. Adds a whole new dimension to it."

"What are you doing at half-five tomorrow morning?" Shona asked, blurting the sentence out in one big breath, like she was worried she might otherwise cut it short.

"Eh, sleeping, I hope. Why?"

"Come to mine," Shona told him.

"Yours?" Logan frowned. "At half-five in the morning? You needing a hand with a paper round, or something?"

"No. I'm going to help get you ready for your fitness test." Shona reached up and tapped the DCI's double chin with a curved index finger. "Boop! You and me are going jogging."

CHAPTER TWELVE

"Right. Any word on our vanishing minister yet?" Logan demanded, throwing open the doors to the Incident Room and barrelling in. "Because I want the bastard in here, pronto."

Logan stopped, his coat half-off, when he realised he was talking to an almost completely empty room. None of the faces he'd expected to see were in the places he'd expected to see them. Instead, a solitary uniformed constable sat at a desk in the corner, an assortment of evidence spread out before him, all bagged and tagged.

It was hard to judge his height sitting down, but he was broad. Not fat, more like he could bench-press a Vauxhall Corsa without breaking a sweat. His neck was probably normal length, but the way his shoulder muscles almost came up to meet his chin made it look much shorter.

"Who are you?" Logan asked.

The constable looked up from the desk, tapped the side of his head in a relaxed salute, and smiled. "Morning, sir. Constable Davidson. David. Dave to my mates."

"David Davidson?"

The smile broadened, like the officer had just been reminded of his all-time favourite joke. "That's me! The only explanation I can offer is that my parents were a pair of arseholes."

This made Logan warm to him immensely. The DCI chuckled and finished taking off his coat. "Aye, sounds like it, right enough," he agreed. He gestured to the evidence bags. "You on Exhibits?"

"That I am, sir. Hence all the bags and that," Dave said. His accent was local, but there was a brightness running through it like he was only ever a few seconds away from a spontaneous outburst of laughter. "Detective Superintendent Mitchell assigned me personally. She also asked me to keep an eye on you. But secretly, like. You're not to know, obviously."

Yes, Logan was definitely going to like this one.

"Obviously. And that sounds sensible," he said. "Never know what I'm going to get up to."

"So they tell me, aye."

"Who's 'they'?"

"Oh, you know, just the general 'They.' The wee birdies. The dwellers on the grapevine," Dave said. "And, in answer to the question you asked when you came in, no, no definite word on the minister yet. Sinead and... the young fella." Dave pouted like an Instagram influencer taking a selfie. "Can't mind his name."

"Tyler."

"Him. Aye. They've got addresses for a couple of the minister's family members. One in Elgin, one in Nairn. They're off to check there. Detective Sergeant..." He left a space that Logan stepped in to fill.

"Khaled."

"That's the boy. He's off with DI Forde. Something about a church key. He said it'd make sense."

"Aye. It does," Logan confirmed.

He picked an empty desk near the middle of the room and headed for it. The furniture had been jigged about a bit since his last stint here, and so it wasn't the same desk that he'd used in the past, and wasn't in *quite* the same spot, but it would do the job.

Logan had just hung his coat over the back of his seat when he noticed Dave's chair. Specifically, he noticed its wheels.

"Car accident eighteen months ago," Dave said, and Logan realised he must've been staring. He blinked and snapped his head up until he met the other man's eye. "Chase on the A9. Another vehicle pulled out in front. Tried to avoid, but—"

He punched a fist into the opposite palm, and the *thack* it made suggested a heavy impact.

"Shite. I'm sorry."

Dave ratcheted his smile up a little higher. "You think this is bad? You should see the other guy!" he said, then he shook his head. "Actually, he's fine. He was in a fuck-off big truck. Got a fine and points on his license, though, so I had the last laugh."

"I'm sorry," Logan said again. It didn't feel enough, but nor could he think of anything else to say that would be.

"Shit happens, sir. We get up, dust ourselves down, and we move on." Dave looked down at the floor for a moment, as if to compose himself. When he spoke, his voice was hushed. Sombre. "You know what I said, sir? Right after the accident? Do you know what I said?"

Logan shook his head. "No. What?"

Dave raised his voice to a shrill, panicked shout and slammed the flat of one hand on the desktop with enough force to make Logan jump. "*My legs! I can't feel my legs!*"

Logan stared at the grinning man in the wheelchair, temporarily struck dumb. And then, he cracked. The laughter came as a snort, then rose quickly until the DCI's shoulders heaved, and tears rolled down his face.

"You're a sick man, David Davidson," he wheezed, when he eventually managed to pull himself back together. "I think you're going to fit in here just fine."

A ringing phone brought the conversation to an end. It took Logan a couple of seconds to pinpoint which of the many telephones on the many desks was ringing, but he eventually traced it to Ben's.

Dave went back to cataloguing the evidence bags while Logan grabbed the handset and brought it to his ear. "DCI Logan."

He listened to the voice on the other end for a few seconds, checked his watch, then nodded. "Interview Room Three. Right. Make him comfortable, get him a cup of tea and some biscuits, and give me five minutes."

He hung up, then turned and looked along the walls until he spotted where the stationery cupboard had been moved to in the shift-around.

"They found your man, sir?" Dave asked.

"No, sadly not. It's the postie," Logan replied, heading for the wardrobe-sized cabinet he knew housed the note-books and pens.

"Does he no' just usually pop the letters in at the front desk?" Dave asked.

"Not our postie. From the case. He found the bodies and raised the alarm."

"Ah. That makes more sense, right enough," Dave said. "I thought, Christ, have I been doing it wrong all these years? Am I meant to be making the bastard lunch?"

Logan opened the doors to the stationery cupboard. Last time he'd looked, it had been crammed with more pens, folders, and notepads than a branch of *Rymans*. Now, there were three A4 pads, two ring binders, half a box of cheap ballpoint pens, and several matchbox-sized plastic containers, each containing twenty or so paperclips.

"Where is everything?" he wondered aloud.

"Detective Superintendent Mitchell reckoned we were all wasting resources, sir," Dave explained. "She cut everything right back to basics, and even then you're meant to note what you use. I mostly buy my own stuff now."

He held up the pen he was using to record the exhibits. It had a furry blue creature on the top with a shock of pink hair.

"From *Smiggle* in the Eastgate," Dave said. He brought it to his nose and inhaled. "Smells of strawberries, too. I mean, I don't quite get what the connection is between this wee hairy gonk fella and strawberries, but I'm no' complaining." He held the pen out. "Want a sniff?"

Logan took a notepad and pen from the cabinet, shot the bare shelves a disparaging look, then closed the doors.

"Another time, maybe," he said. He checked his watch, nodded once, then headed for the door. "If anyone calls or comes looking for me, tell them I won't be long."

"Right you are, sir," Dave replied. He winked and gave a double thumbs-up. "And I'll pass on to the Detective Super that so far, so good."

"Sᴏʀʀʏ ᴛᴏ ᴋᴇᴇᴘ ʏᴏᴜ, Mʀ..."

The man on the other side of the interview desk rose to his feet and practically curtsied when Logan entered.

"Dugdale. Gwynn Dugdale," he said, the accent giving away his Welsh origins, and the name just helping to confirm it.

Logan extended a hand and Gwynn hurriedly shook it. The palm was sweaty against Logan's own, the fingers rough and calloused.

"You alright for tea there?" Logan asked, releasing his grip and subtly wiping his hand on the back of his trouser leg. "More biscuits?"

"No, no, I'm fine. Fine. This is great. Lovely. Thanks," Gwynn gushed. "Very generous. I've never been in trouble with the police before, so I didn't know what to expect."

"You're not in trouble now, Mr Dugdale," Logan assured him. "And if you were, you'd be on the Tesco Savers Rich Teas, no' the chocolate Hobnobs."

He pulled out his chair, and motioned for Gwynn to return to his own seat. The postman wasn't wearing his uniform, and instead was dressed in a short-sleeved blue shirt and a pair of tan cords. Probably not the smartest clobber in his wardrobe—he wasn't having lunch at Balmoral—but he'd made an effort.

"Day off today?" Logan asked.

"Yeah. They've given me a few days," Gwynn confirmed. His eyes darted around, like he was trying to resist focusing on some mental image. "After... what I saw, and everything. They thought I could do with some time away."

"Good of them," Logan said.

Gwynn nodded. "Yeah. They seem like a good bunch. I've not actually been in the job all that long." His eyes went wandering again. "Nobody told me about anything like... Like..."

He cleared his throat and seemed to centre himself.

"I hear the wee girl was found upstairs, too. I didn't see her, thank God. Just the woman. Mrs Mann."

"You knew her?" Logan asked.

"Just the name. From her mail. Lois, wasn't it? Like in Superman."

"That's right," Logan confirmed. He gave a smile of encouragement, and pitched his voice at a well-rehearsed level of comforting. "I know it's not particularly pleasant, but do you mind taking me through what happened yesterday?"

Gwynn clasped his hands on the table in front of him, as if in prayer. "Of course," he said resolutely, despite his shaking legs that Logan could feel vibrating through the table and across the floor between them. "I was... It was afternoon. We were running a bit late."

"We?"

"Me. I just mean all of us have been running late lately. There's a few folk off sick, and one of the posts that was advertised at same time as mine still hasn't been filled, so we're chasing our tails at lot."

"But you were on your own?"

Gwynn nodded. "Yeah. On my own. I turned up at the house—"

"What time, roughly?" Logan interjected. He'd long ago found that turning it into a conversation could help the nerves of an anxious witness. Fire in a few questions, and they became so focused on giving the answers that they forgot to be nervous.

"Three fifteen, three twenty or so. Steve Wright was on the radio. The Big Show. They had Paul McKenna on. You know, the hypnotist? Talking about stopping smoking."

Logan instinctively stole a look at the other man's clasped fingers, and saw the yellow staining around the tips.

"Sorry, I'm waffling," Gwynn said.

"Just take your time, Mr Dugdale. You're fine."

Gwynn sipped in a few breaths, then exhaled them all at once and nodded. "Right. Yes. Sorry. So... I went to the house, as I normally would. Knocked. No answer. Knocked again, listened, and I was sure I could hear someone inside."

"Someone moving around?"

"Talking. It was the TV, I later found out," Gwynn said. "Didn't know it at the time, though. Thought it was people having a conversation. Thought maybe they just hadn't heard. I'd have just tried the door and chucked... I mean, *put* the package in, but it needed a signature. First Class Tracked."

He reached for his cup with a trembling hand. Concentrating so as not to spill it, he took a sip of his milky white tea.

"So... So, I went to the living room window. And I looked." His voice wobbled, but didn't break all the way. Not quite. "And there she was. Just lying there. Mrs Mann. On the floor."

He zoned out for a few seconds, replaying it in his mind's eye.

"Did you go inside?" Logan asked. "Try to help her?"

"I didn't want to," Gwynn said. "But the woman on the phone—nine-nine-nine—she told me to check on her. I said she was dead. I could tell from the window she was dead. But, she made me go in, anyway. She told me to check for a pulse, but... God. I told her there was no point, but she kept saying it. 'Check for a pulse. Is she conscious? Is she breathing?'"

He swallowed down another breath, then looked across at Logan, worry blazing behind his eyes. "I lied to her. I said I'd checked, but I didn't. I didn't want to touch her. I knew. That she was dead, I mean. It was obvious. I knew."

"I understand. What did you do after that, Mr Dugdale?"

"After I'd got the operator to understand that there was no point doing CPR, she told me to get out. Told me not to touch anything. Said police and ambulance were on the way. So, I did. I went outside. I waited. And then, five minutes later, police car shows up and... yeah. Everything kicks off. Sirens, lights, paramedics, more police. I got asked who I was, like, twenty times. I wasn't sure what I was meant to be doing, but someone eventually came and took a statement, and said I could go home, but that I should report in here today." He pulled together some faint vestige of a smile. "And so, here I am."

Logan had been jotting down a few notes while the postman had recited the events of the day before. He tapped his pen against one of the words he'd circled. "You said you were delivering a package."

"That's right. Needed to be signed for."

"And presumably nobody was in any fit state to sign for it? So, what happened to it?"

A couple of creases formed above the bridge of Gwynn's nose. "Um... I'm not sure," he admitted. "I had it in my hand when I went to the window, then... Did I take it in the house? Was it in the house?"

"Not that I'm aware of," Logan said. "I'd have to check to

be sure, but I don't remember seeing it or hearing it mentioned."

"I... I think it's probably in the house," Gwynn said. "Or outside, maybe? I might have dropped it when I saw... everything. It was soft. Clothes, I think. A blue bag. Greyish-blue. Didn't say where it was from, or not that I noticed, anyway. It must be at the house, or..."

He leaned back, rubbing his chin, his frown deepening. "Did I take it back to the van? I had to go back for my phone." His expression became an apology. "Shit. I might've left it in the van."

"It's fine, nothing to worry about, Mr Dugdale. Probably completely irrelevant. I'll look into it from this end, but if you could have someone check the van for us, that would be useful."

"Of course. I can phone now, if you like?"

Logan looked at his watch, groaned quietly, then folded his notepad closed. "Aye, that would be good. I'll have someone from Uniform come check with you and see you out." He reached across the table, shook Gwynn's hand again, then stood up. "Unfortunately, I have another appointment. Whether I like it or not."

CHAPTER THIRTEEN

THE INSIDE OF THE CHURCH WAS GLOOMY AND unwelcoming. On a bright day, the narrow windows might've let in enough sunlight to burn away the shadows, but on a dreich afternoon in the Highlands, it barely nudged them aside.

The electric lights had been retrofitted at some point in the church's history, and had been poorly maintained ever since. They were high up near the ceiling, and several of the bulbs needed replacing. Even with all the switches flipped, the lights more coloured the darkness than eliminated it.

"Welcoming place," Hamza remarked. He indicated a carving at the far end with a tilt of his head. "Old Jesus there."

"Aye, the Big Man Himself," Ben said. He tipped an imaginary hat in the Son of God's direction. "Don't mind us. Just having a poke around."

He clicked on his torch and swept the beam across the rows of polished wooden pews. Blurred shadows raced up the walls away from the torchlight, before dropping into place again the moment it had passed.

"Hello? Mr Mann?" Hamza called, then the name clicked and he turned to DI Forde and spoke in a whisper. "Mr Mann! I hadn't thought of that. Poor bastard."

Ben gave him a gentle dunt on the arm. "You're no' supposed to swear in front of Jesus," he said. He pulled a face that agreed on the 'poor bastard,' sentiment without him having to say the words. "But aye, that's unfortunate, right enough. It's probably why he became a Minister, so he could change it."

"Oh. Aye. Forgot. You there, Reverend Mann? We need to talk to you," Hamza said, raising the volume of his voice again. The words bounced off the white-painted stone walls, and up to the rafters, and the only reply that came was the returning echo.

Ben and Hamza continued down the aisle, side by side, both now shining their torches along the gaps between the pews.

When they reached the front, Hamza got down onto his knees, did a quick check below the benches, then stood up and dusted the front of his trousers down.

"No sign, sir."

Ben flicked the beam of his torch towards a curtain hanging on the far corner of the wall behind the pulpit. It was—not accidentally—slightly larger than a door.

They approached it in silence, Hamza taking point, Ben following with his torch fixed on the thick red fabric drape. Cautiously, DS Khaled caught one edge of the curtain and pulled it aside just enough to peek behind it.

There was, unsurprisingly, a door there. The handle was an iron ring that turned with a scraping sound. Something on the other side *clunked* and the door sprung open almost a foot, like it had been jammed into the frame against its will.

For a moment, Hamza thought it had been yanked open from the other side, and he stepped back quickly, letting the curtain fall back into place as he raised his hands to protect himself.

When it became apparent what had happened, and that nobody was about to come leaping out at them, he reached for the drape again, studiously avoiding the twinkly-eyed look of amusement he knew fine well DI Forde would currently be giving him.

"Mr Mann? This is the police. If you're in there, we're coming in now," Hamza announced.

They waited for a response.

None came.

"We're coming in now," Hamza said, then he slid the curtain fully aside, pushed open the door, and stepped into what appeared to be a small store room.

Boxes of hymn books and Bibles gathered dust on racks of plastic shelving. Half a dozen bulging black bags were piled up in one corner below a hand-written sign marked, "Donations," that was stuck to the wall with a push-pin.

There were two folding wooden chairs and a small round table that held a kettle, an open box of tea bags—*Scottish Blend*, Ben noted, none of your own brand shite—and four mugs that were ringed inside with brown lines to varying degrees of severity, as if the closest they ever got to being cleaned was a quick skoosh under the cold tap of the big square white porcelain sink in the corner.

The inside of the fire door that Logan had described seeing from outside was at the back of this room, providing the only other way in or out of the building.

With this room being smaller, the weak sunlight seeping in through the one and only window was enough to light it up. Motes of dust danced in the air as Hamza went creaking across the scuffed wooden floor and pressed a hand against the side of the kettle.

"Cold," he said.

"Pity," Ben said, although he wasn't particularly surprised. If Reverend Mann had killed his family, he'd be an idiot to try hiding here. He'd have known it would be the first place they'd come looking for him.

After a quick poke around in the boxes—the hymn books were tatty, dog-eared things—and in a couple of the black bags—men's clothes, bundled up in knots—they'd returned to the main part of the church, pulled the store room door closed, and swished the curtain back into place.

By the time they made it outside and locked the church entrance again, the woman from yesterday was back sitting on the same spot on the bench.

"Still no sign?" she asked, her nostrils flared in irritation.

"Uh, sir, this is..." Hamza searched for the name. "Elizabeth Strand?"

"Are you asking him or telling him?" Elizabeth snapped.

"Sorry. Elizabeth Strand," Hamza said. "She's a parishioner here."

"For fifty-two years. Woman and girl." She gestured at the church with her Kindle. "No sign of the Reverend?"

"I'm afraid not," Ben told her. "I'm Detective Inspector Forde, by the way, it's nice to—"

"Did he do it?"

Ben's face remained impassive, years of experience allowing him to successfully mask his surprise. Not that he should've been surprised, of course. Fort Augustus wasn't a big place, and news—particularly of this nature—travelled fast.

"Do what?" Ben asked.

"Come off it," Elizabeth said, rolling her eyes. "I know what happened. You know what happened. Lois and Ruby, the poor creatures. It's all over town. Murdered. Everyone's talking about it. Horrible."

"Aye, well. There'll be an official statement released soon," Ben said. "But, between you and me, we're pursuing various lines of inquiry. We'd like to speak to Reverend Mann, of course, but there's no saying he's responsible."

"What's he like? Hamza asked. "Reverend Mann?"

"Do you mean, do I think he's capable of murdering his wife and daughter?" Elizabeth asked, seeing through the question immediately. "No, of course not. He's always been lovely. He plays guitar, you know. One of the nice ones, not the pluggy-in ones that make that horrible racket. A proper guitar. Voice of an angel, so he has. Voice of an angel."

She looked up at the church, then aimed her eyes at the Heavens on high, as if searching for guidance.

"I've never so much as heard him raise his voice, except to rejoice," Elizabeth continued. "So, do I think he's capable of murder? No. But then, I'd like to think that nobody else was, either." The thought seemed to sadden her, and her gaze returned to ground level. "So what do I know?"

"What was their relationship like? Do you know?" Hamza asked. "Reverend Mann and his wife."

Elizabeth's expression barely changed, but she somehow gave the impression she'd taken personal offence at the question, like the Detective Sergeant was accusing her of something.

"And why would I know something like that? I'm not

some busybody, I'll have you know. It's none of my business," she said, rounding the response off with an indignant sniff.

"No. Sorry," Hamza said.

Elizabeth's eyes darted left and right. She leaned forwards a fraction and dropped her voice by a handful of decibels. "If anyone would know, it would be that Kerry Philip. You know? From up in Drum?"

Hamza produced his notebook and began to write. "I don't believe we've come across the name, no."

"Kerry *Philip*. Just the one L," Elizabeth said. "Young thing. Too pretty for her own good, if you know what I mean. Married. Well, if you can call it that. But it's not my place to say. Couple of young children. It's really none of my business." She pointed with the Kindle at Hamza, then Ben. "But, if you want my advice, have a word. She'll know a thing or two about a thing or two, I'm sure. I'll say no more on the matter than that."

"Don't suppose you know an address?" Hamza asked.

Elizabeth gazed pointedly at Ben. "Did he not hear what I just said? I'll say no more on the matter than that. Of course, I don't have her address. But she works at the Monster Exhibition Centre." The old woman folded her arms in front of her, tucking her Kindle in against the front of her coat. "And that's the last I intend to say on the matter."

"Thank you. You've been very helpful," Ben said. "Mind if we take your contact details, just in case we need to ask you any more questions?"

Elizabeth didn't appear particularly happy about that, but recited her address and phone number with some gentle encouragement and a promise she wouldn't be added to any junk mail lists now, or at any point in the future.

"You can phone me to let me know when the church is

going to open again," she instructed, once they'd said their goodbyes and were starting to move away. "And what about Tomdoun?"

Ben and Hamza stopped and turned. "Tomdoun?" Ben asked.

"The wee church there. Reverend Mann runs a monthly service for those who can't make it into town. Out in the sticks. Will that one be up and running this month?"

The detectives swapped looks, the same thought occurring to them both at the same time.

Hamza flipped open his notepad again. "Tomdoun," he began. "Can you maybe spell that for us?"

CHAPTER FOURTEEN

It was not Logan's first experience of Professional Standards. And, despite the assurances he'd given Detective Superintendent Mitchell, he was quietly confident that nor would it be his last.

There was a greyness to the man and woman sitting across the table from him. Not to their appearance, exactly—both were in their forties, and neither one was showing any signs of premature ageing—but to their very presence.

Logan didn't believe in auras, in much the same way he didn't believe in such things as ghosts, or fairies, or a peaceful Saturday night on Sauchiehall Street. If he had believed in auras, though, he was confident that the colours radiating off this pair of bastards would've been steadfastly monotone.

They'd already run through what they described as 'the most troublesome points,' and he hadn't really been able to argue with any of them. He'd removed evidence from a crime scene (once, that they knew of). He'd neglected to follow the proper chain of command (multiple times). He'd broken into private premises without a warrant, had orchestrated the abduction of a minor, and caused extensive criminal damage.

And, what seemed to bother them most, was that he hadn't filled out the paperwork for any of it.

Of the two Conduct Unit officers holding the interview, the man seemed the least impressed—close run thing as it was. He'd given Logan his name when the DCI had entered the office, but he was so tedious the name had almost immediately fallen straight out of Logan's other ear.

Randall, he thought. Or *Henley*. Something with an L in it.

Williams? Aye, that might be it.

Whatever his name was, he tutted and shook his head reproachfully, while his partner had read through her list of points.

When she was finished, he removed the wire-framed glasses he'd had perched on the end of his nose, folded the legs closed, then tucked them into his shirt pocket.

"Frankly, Detective Chief Inspector, we can't comprehend why you've been allowed back," he said. "Granted, your methods have been effective, but that's only half the battle, as we know."

Logan disagreed, but opted to keep his mouth shut.

"We must be beyond reproach. We are the police, after all. And this is Inverness, not the Wild West, or... or... the Gaza Strip," Williams said. Or *Hillary*, maybe? "We don't get to rain rockets on the general populace here, or go kicking in the saloon door."

Logan thought about pointing out that kicking in a saloon door was likely to be pretty ineffectual, but didn't want to prolong this whole experience any longer than was absolutely necessary.

"I think what my colleague is saying is that, fundamentally, you've proven yourself to be a rogue element," the woman said. Her name was Livingstone. He'd caught that much.

"Thanks very much," Logan said.

"It isn't a compliment."

"Aye, well, I'm going to go ahead and take it as one," the DCI told her.

She looked very deliberately down at her notes, ringed something with her pen, then raised her head again. "I get the feeling you're not taking this very seriously, Detective Chief Inspector. I assure you, it's a very serious matter."

"A very serious matter indeed," confirmed her partner.

Logan checked his watch, and made damn sure that they both noticed. He'd been in this room for almost an hour now. Didn't they realise there was a bloody murder investigation on?

"Look, on the one hand, I completely agree," Logan told them. "I was out of order, and I apologise. You can write that down, if you like. I'll even sign it for you, if that helps."

It was the turn of Williams, or Hillary, or whatever his bloody name was, to chime in. "And, on the other hand?"

"On the other hand, here I am. Sat here, back in the job." He leaned forward and jabbed a meaty index finger down on the bundle of notes stacked equidistant between the two Conduct Unit officers. "And this? You knew this beforehand. You've known it for months. You've held your investigation, you've considered all the evidence, and *you*—the polis, I mean, not you two personally—came looking for *me*. Not the other way around. I'm back here because I was asked. Because I was invited."

Both officers were staring back at him in silence now,

their hands clasped in front of them, each of them mirroring the body language of the other and sharing the same unimpressed expression.

"So, we can either go around in circles, with you telling me all the many things you say I've done wrong and me promising not to do any of it again," Logan said. "Or, we can knock this whole charade on the head, you two can fuck off back to wherever it is you came from, and I'll go find the bastard who murdered a mother and her young daughter."

He sat back, crossed his arms, and flashed a Cheshire Cat grin in their general direction.

"So?" he asked. "How does that sound?"

DAVE DAVIDSON WAS STILL the only one in the office when Logan returned. He had a small pile of clear plastic evidence bags on the desk in front of him, a single crumpled receipt in each one.

"You sacked, then?" he asked, looking up just long enough to be polite.

"No. Though, not for want of trying," Logan replied. "Any word from..." He gestured around the room. "...anyone?"

"No one called in, no," said Dave.

"What's that?" Logan asked, eyes going to the mound of bags. "Receipts?"

"Bloody dozens of them, aye. Debenhams. Petrol station. Some boat trip. Loads of the bloody things. They were in the glove box of her car, apparently."

"Might help us build up a picture of her movements before she died."

Dave screwed up his face. "Doubt it. Some of them are months old. Most recent is from about three weeks ago." He slid the top few bags aside, searching for one in particular. "Here it is. Bottle of milk and a prawn sandwich. Suspect we won't get a conviction out of that."

"Wait. Hang on," said Logan, realising he'd skipped over a key detail. "Her car? Or a family car?"

Dave shrugged his rounded shoulders. "Not a clue. Want me to find out?"

Before Logan could answer, the Incident Room door swung open, and DC Neish came strolling in, whistling quietly.

"Alright, boss?" he asked. His gaze shifted to the man in the wheelchair. "Alright, eh...?"

"Dave. And not bad, thanks."

"Exhibits?" Tyler asked.

Dave indicated the bags in front of him in the style of a magician's assistant showing off the cabinet in which she was about to be cut in half.

"Where the bloody hell have you been?" Logan demanded, signalling the introductions were over. "And where's Sinead?"

"Sorry, boss. Reverend Mann has a brother-in-law in Nairn and an aunt in Elgin. I took the brother-in-law, Sinead took the auntie."

"How does the brother-in-law connect in?" Logan asked.

"He was married to the Reverend's sister. Was. Past tense."

"Divorced?"

"Dead, boss," Tyler said. He quickly interpreted the questioning look on the DCI's face. "Cancer a few years back. Nothing suspect. He hasn't heard from Mann in about a year, other than a Christmas card and a couple of texts on the anniversary of the sister's death."

"Sinead have any more luck?"

Tyler shook his head. "Not really. Spoke to her on the drive back. She's headed down the road from Elgin now. Aunt's in her eighties. Care home. By the sounds of it she doesn't remember who she is, much less her nephew."

Logan tutted. "Damn. Right, well, it is what it is," he said, then he pointed to Tyler's computer. "Hamza's no' here, so I'll need you to use your brains for once. Find out how many cars were in the household. We've got the victim's, but I want to know if the husband has one, too."

"Right, boss," Tyler said, moving to pass him.

"I'm not done," Logan said, blocking the way. "There should be a location request in to whichever phone network Mann is with. Find out if we've got anything back yet, and if not shout at them."

"Shout?"

"Aye. Shout. I don't care what you shout, just shout. Put a firework up them. I want to know where his phone's been, and—more importantly—where it is now."

"On it, boss."

"At-at-at!" Logan ejected, stepping into Tyler's path again. Dave chuckled quietly at this, but kept his head down and said nothing. "Get onto the computer forensics bods," continued Logan. "What was on her laptop? Have they got location data from her phone? If not, take that up with her network, too. I want to know all her movements in the run-up to the murder."

Tyler waited, going nowhere and saying nothing.

"Well?" Logan barked. "Why are you standing there with your finger up your arse? Get a move on."

"Right, boss. Consider it done," Tyler said, springing into action. He stopped again almost immediately. "Just checking, though, what order do you want me to—"

"Mind that part I mentioned about using your brain? That's where that would come in," Logan said. "Figure it out, son."

Tyler smiled grimly, like he wasn't overjoyed at the prospect, but nodded and then scuttled over to his desk to get started.

"When Sinead gets in, ask her to start putting together the Big Board for us," Logan said. He groaned inwardly, sighed outwardly, then took a long, solemn look at his office door. "I've got a date with a big pile of paperwork."

CHAPTER FIFTEEN

Tomdoun was further away than they'd expected. Getting to it involved a drive south until they reached Loch Oich, then a right turn at the Invergarry junction, followed by another twenty-odd minutes of winding roads that didn't feel a whole lot wider than the car they were travelling in.

There were only a handful of passing places on the road, and the whole journey was spent dreading seeing another vehicle rounding one of the many bends up ahead. As luck would have it, they saw nothing but a couple of Lycra-clad cyclists and the occasional lonely-looking sheep.

It wasn't an area either of them was familiar with, and they spent a good ten minutes second-guessing turn-offs, slowing at every one of the old stone buildings they passed, and cursing Google Maps for pretty much drawing a blank on the church's whereabouts.

Finally, they'd found a small hotel and Hamza had gone inside to ask for directions. The owner had been gazing out through the front window, and at first looked shocked, then visibly delighted when the Detective Sergeant had come clopping up the narrow steps to the front door.

His joy had quickly faded, though, when he realised Hamza wasn't looking to check in, and he drew a map to the church without another word.

In hindsight, the map was really overkill, Ben thought. Four words—"Straight on, next right,"—would've served the purpose equally as well. Although, he supposed you couldn't do that on hotel headed notepaper with the website address and phone number on it.

There was an old-style red phone box standing across from the next junction. The lack of mobile network coverage in the area was probably the reason for it, but Ben had counted four houses in the last three miles, and he imagined most of them had landlines of their own.

Tomdoun Church was up a side road that made the previous single-track route feel like a US interstate. DI Forde's car creaked and *thunked* over the potholes and bumps, the branches of bushes on either side of the road dragging along the windows and paintwork.

"Is this even a road, sir?" Hamza wondered aloud.

"It's on the map," Ben said, pointing to his phone screen. "It's about the only bloody thing that *is* on the map."

Hamza wasn't convinced. He was quietly confident they were driving up a footpath, regardless of what the map was telling them. Surely nobody would build a road a full 5% narrower than the vehicles driving along it? Not unless they were particularly evil and twisted.

The Detective Sergeant spent a few moments thinking about the Highland Council Road Planning department, then turned to the man in the driver's seat.

"Aye, this probably is the way, right enough, sir," he said.

A sharp left-hand bend led into a wide driveway of packed dirt and rough aggregate. One side of the drive led to an L-shaped stone bungalow. Sticking to the outside lane, Ben followed the drive around the back of the house, and slowed as he approached the church building.

It was of a similar shape to the house—two rectangles set at a ninety degree junction, and no upstairs. Both buildings were made of the same grey stone and mortar, but the church boasted an extra-large window that looked out across the rolling green landscape in the direction of Loch Garry.

Or it would've done, at least, had a copse of trees not seen fit to spring up in the wrong place, almost completely obscuring the view.

"Looks like the place," Hamza said, as Ben pulled the car onto a verge that he was going to go ahead and assume was used for parking. "Reckon he's inside?"

Ben regarded the darkened church. It looked cold and inhospitable, and nothing like a church should be. "Fingers crossed," he said, unclipping his seat belt and opening the door. "But I'm no' going to get my hopes up."

He knelt by the window, concealed by the half-shut curtains and the reflected sunlight playing across the glass. He hid there, humming to himself as he watched them approach. Both of them. Together. Strolling up the path, side-by-side, chatting away like they didn't have a care in the world.

Of course they didn't. No cares. No clue about what was to come.

Not them. Not yet.

But soon.

This was their fault. All of it. Everything. The failing of his marriage. The end of his livelihood. The collapse of his whole fucking life.

He had been someone once. Someone better. Someone loved. And then, these two had taken that away. These two, and all the others. They had done this. Caused this. Brought this upon themselves.

He wasn't a killer. Not as far as he was concerned, anyway. Not really. Not any more than a gun, or a knife, or a lungful of water could be classed as such. He was merely the weapon. The righteous instrument of their long-overdue downfall.

And he would enjoy watching their plunge.

His tuneless humming evolved into murmured words as he watched them approaching along the path.

"The animals went in two by two, hurrah! Hurrah!" he sang to himself.

His voice was stone scraping on metal. The sharpening of a blade.

As an instrument, he was a blunt one—he'd shown that with his last attempt—but he was finding his edge. Refining it. Honing himself.

Preparing for everything that was to come.

The front door opened. He retreated from the window.

And the shadows welcomed him into their embrace.

DETECTIVE SUPERINTENDENT MITCHELL gave the bundle of paperwork on her desk a brief, disinterested glance, then tapped the top sheet with a pen.

"It's all signed?"

"Three places. You already had the National Insurance details, and all that stuff, but I filled it in, anyway," Logan told her. "For address, I've put Ben's new place down. I'll update it when I've found somewhere of my own."

"I'm impressed. I was led to believe that getting you to complete paperwork was akin to one of the Twelve Tasks of Hercules. Perhaps we're going to get along better than I thought," Mitchell said. "How is he?"

"Who, Hercules?"

"DI Forde."

"Oh. Ben? He's..." Logan gave this some consideration before replying. "Dealing, I suppose."

"It'll require some adjustment," Mitchell said. Had Logan not known from context, he might've assumed from her tone that she was talking about a spreadsheet, or a leaky tap, not a human being.

"Aye. It won't be easy," he agreed.

"And how was your meeting with Professional Standards?" Mitchell pressed. "Some lessons learned, I hope?"

Logan rocked his weight back onto his heels and put his hands in the pockets of his overcoat. "I'd say both parties came away with a better sense of their role," he said.

The Detective Superintendent held his gaze for a long time, neither one flinching.

"Yes. Well," she said, at last. "As I was the one who requested the meeting, they'll be sending me their report. Do I want to read it?"

"You'll find my full and frank apology in there," Logan told her, then he shrugged. "Might want to skip out the last couple of pages, though."

Mitchell appeared wholly unimpressed, but chose not to

enquire further. Instead, she sidestepped onto an entirely different subject.

"You've met Constable Davidson?"

"I have."

"Thoughts?"

"Seems alright. First impression was that he could probably bench press a small caravan. He was in an accident, he tells me."

"Yes. Horrible incident during a high-speed pursuit," Mitchell confirmed. "Got quite a lot of compensation for it."

Something that had been buried at the back of Logan's subconscious suddenly flicked on like a lightbulb. "God, aye. I remember now. Half a million or something, wasn't it?"

"Closer to three quarters," said the DSup.

"And he came back?"

"He did. As soon as he was able," Mitchell confirmed. "Money or not, he wants to make a difference. I felt he'd be a good fit. And, I wanted him to keep an eye on you." She raised an eyebrow. "But I'm sure he's already told you that."

"I couldn't possibly comment, ma'am."

"Hmm. Well," Mitchell poked the stack of paperwork with her pen, like she wanted to double-check it was really there. "Was there anything else?"

"Aye, just one thing," Logan said. "I'm going to need a car. The Volvo I had before was fine. I don't need anything too flash or—"

"Ah, yes!" said Mitchell, and the way her face came alive made Logan feel suddenly apprehensive.

She opened her desk drawer and immediately produced a silver key topped with a disk of black plastic. The vehicle's registration was written on the plastic keyring, and Logan clocked right away that whatever he was about to be saddled with was three years older than his Volvo had been.

Mitchell tossed the key onto the desk between them, then gestured to it, inviting Logan to pick it up.

"I hope you approve," she said. "I hand-picked it for you personally."

———

"ALRIGHT, SIR?"

Logan turned his head just enough to catch sight of Sinead's reflection in the windscreen, nodded mutely, then went back to staring at his new car.

At least, it was new to him. Not new in general. Not even all that close to new. It was pushing six years old, and had all the paint chips, scratches, and little dents to show it.

The '65 number plate was partially obscured by a congealed mass of tiny dead insects. They coated the front bumper and dotted the headlights, too.

Where was the thing last driven? he wondered. *The Amazon bloody Rainforest?*

"Everything alright, sir?" Sinead pressed, joining him in front of the car. She gave the vehicle a quick look over, then glanced out past the car park entrance to the road beyond. "Not abandoned, is it? Be a bold place to ditch it, you've got to give them that."

"No, it's not abandoned," Logan said. He sighed through his nose, then leaned forward and rapped his knuckles on the faded forest green bonnet of the Ford Fiesta. "It's mine."

"Yours?!" Sinead gasped.

"Aye. Detective Superintendent Mitchell chose it herself, she tells me."

"God." Sinead looked the car over. "She proper hates you, eh?"

"Apparently."

"What are you going to do with it, sir?" Sinead asked. "Wear it as a hat? I mean, it's not exactly spacious, is it? And you're..."

"Yes, thank you, Detective Constable. You can drop the rest of that sentence."

Sinead was right. While he'd never had any issues or complaints with Ford's Fiesta range, this was largely because he'd never driven one in his life. It was a small car. He was a big man. It was not a vehicular match he'd ever even contemplated before.

He opened the driver's door, ducked his head inside, and spent a few seconds checking the inside of the vehicle over. "There's a scene in one of the *Police Academy* movies where the big tall fella rips out the front seat and just sits in the back. I might try that."

"Police Academy, sir?"

"Aye. Steve Guttenberg. There were about twelve of the bloody things."

"Never seen them, sir," Sinead said. "Bit before my time."

"Some people have all the bloody luck," Logan told her.

He closed the door with enough of a slam to rock the car on its wheels, then spent the next thirty seconds pressing the same two buttons on the remote in the hope that one of them would lock the bloody thing.

Or, preferably, blow it to bits.

"Bugger it. Maybe if I leave the bastard unlocked, someone will come along and nick it," he said, shoving the keys in his coat pocket. He indicated the restaurant and takeaway across on the other side of the dual carriageway with a jab of a thumb. "I'm going to get coffee. Do me a favour and check with Tyler and Dave, will you? Text me your order and I'll pick it up."

"Dave?"

"David. David Davidson."

Sinead's face lit up. "Oh, *Dave*! Is he with us? What's he doing?"

"Exhibits. The Detective Superintendent thought he'd be a good fit."

"Oh, he will. Dave's great," Sinead said. "I shadowed him for a while when I was training up here. Horrible what happened."

Logan agreed that it was, then his desire for caffeine overrode his interest in continuing the conversation, and he set off towards the car park exit. "Let me know what everyone wants. Won't be long."

"Right you are, sir," Sinead said.

Logan stopped halfway across the car park, then turned, a thought occurring to him. "Oh, and Sinead? Where's the best place round here to get a pair of trainers?" He looked down at his feet, then back up again. "Big ones."

CHAPTER SIXTEEN

IF THE CHURCH IN FORT AUGUSTUS HAD BEEN SMALL, then Tomdoun barely qualified as fun-sized. A dozen parishioners could probably squeeze in at a push, provided they'd all kept themselves in shape, maintained excellent personal hygiene, and none of them had recently eaten garlic.

It had taken just a few seconds to find the right key in the bundle taken from the Mann family's cottage. It was a thick old cast iron thing, pitted across its surface with flecks of brown rust. It was the kind of key that would be completely inappropriate for anything other than a church or a dungeon, and it rattled in the slot when Hamza jiggled it inside.

It was only when he had spent twenty seconds trying to get the bloody thing to turn in the lock that he realised the door hadn't been locked in the first place.

The church exhaled as they entered, a breath of stale, moth-eaten air rolling out over them in its rush to escape into the world beyond.

The floorboards creaked. The doors, too. There was no space in the church for an organ or piano, so it was possible the creaks were deliberate, designed to be used as a musical accompaniment during the hymns.

"Unlikely, I'd have thought," Ben said, after Hamza floated the theory, and the DS was surprised by the sharply impatient tone of the response.

During their drive up to the church building, they'd been able to see that a search—even an extremely thorough one— wasn't going to take them long. They were still surprised, though, by just how brief an exercise it turned out to be.

They found him sitting on the frontmost pew, hands clasped between his knees, head lowered in grief or in prayer, and very probably both.

He didn't look up as they entered. It wasn't until they said his name, and its echo had been absorbed by the cold stone walls, that he straightened his back and held his head high.

"Yes," he said, slowly getting to his feet. His voice was hoarse, his words scraping in his throat like broken glass. "Yes. That's me. I suppose you've come to—"

He stopped when he saw them, his expression a blend of surprise and confusion. Clearly, he'd been expecting someone else.

Reverend Mann was in his late thirties, with a short, fashionable haircut, and a face that would've been positively cherubic had it not been for the scrappy beard growth that was shadowing his jaw, and the purple shiner beaming from one eye socket.

"Who are you?" he asked, his gaze flitting between them.

"Detective Inspector Ben Forde. Police Scotland Major Investigations," Ben said. He flashed his ID, despite the other man being too far away to read it. "This is Detective Sergeant Hamza Khaled, also of the MIT."

"Police? No." The Reverend shook his head. "Who called you? You're not supposed to be here. I don't want to press charges. It's a private matter."

Ben felt Hamza's sideways look, even if he didn't see it.

"I'm afraid you misunderstand, we're not—"

"No, I'm sorry. I'm not... I'm not interested," Mann told them, emphasising this with a series of adamant *shooing* hand gestures. "If I don't report it, if... if... I refuse to be a witness and give evidence, there's nothing you can do. That's right, isn't it?"

"A witness? I'm afraid we're talking at cross-purposes here, son," Ben said. He cleared his throat and projected, making sure there could be no misunderstanding. "Gareth Mann, we're arresting you on the suspicion of the murder of Lois and Ruby Mann."

He smiled. A strange mixture of curiosity and relief.

"Ha!" he ejected, and the sound reverberated its way around the church half a dozen times before eventually fading into silence.

He looked from Hamza to Ben and back again, eyes flicking faster and faster, like he was becoming increasingly desperate for them to hurry up and deliver the punchline.

"What?" he finally said, the smile falling away as he concluded that there was no punchline coming. "This is... What?"

The Reverend jerked a few steps closer, moving as if on strings he wasn't in control of. His eyes became wider, his body language growing erratic and more agitated, like there were bugs crawling over him that he was trying desperately to ignore.

"You're not... What? *Murder?* What are you talking

about? Lois and Ruby? What are you talking about? What are you saying?" he demanded. "What are you...?"

The smile returned. Wider. Even more desperate. Pleading with them to say they were lying. To say it wasn't true. For them to stop this sick game.

"We'll talk about it at the station, son," Ben told him. "Come away with us."

"The station? No. I... This isn't... You're not..."

Words failed him, and he just stood there, motionless. The colour had drained from his face, making the purple-black bruise appear even more prominent.

He remained like that for several long seconds, frozen and immobile like a ruined, broken thing.

Then, he turned and shot a look back at a painting of Jesus on the wall above the pulpit, like he might get some guidance from Him. Some sign. Some reassurance that this was a mistake, and that everything was going to be OK.

But, there was no comfort to be found there. Shaking, Reverend Mann dropped to his knees in the centre of the narrow aisle.

And his cries rose as high as the heavens.

———

LOGAN DUMPED the cardboard tray containing the teas and coffees on his desk, and began the process of dishing them out.

"Tea," he said, placing one of the paper cups on Dave's desk.

"Nice one, ta. What do I owe you?"

Logan shot that idea down with a look, then handed Sinead her cup. "Latte."

"Cheers, sir."

He set a third cup down on Tyler's desk. "Latte."

Tyler's brow furrowed. "What? I asked for a Caramel Macchiato, boss."

"Latte's where I draw the line, son. Anything more than that isn't coffee, it's a bloody dessert." He fished inside the paper bag he'd brought in with the drinks. "Although, speaking of which..."

With a flourish, he produced a four-pack of strawberry tarts from the bag, presenting them like they were a gift from the gods themselves.

"Don't say I'm not good to you."

"Get in," cheered Dave, gladly accepting the offered pastry.

"Beauty, boss, cheers," Tyler said, helping himself as the tray was wafted under his nose.

Sinead shook her head. "I'm fine, sir, cheers," she said. "Watching my weight."

"Why? There's nothing bloody of you," Logan told her. "Have a strawberry tart."

"I'll have hers, if it's going," Tyler said. He was halfway through his own, and sprayed crumbs down his front when he spoke, but felt it important to call dibs before the new guy got any ideas.

"They're about four hundred calories each," Sinead pointed out. She looked up at Logan and smiled encouragingly. "But you go on, sir. Don't let me stop you. Or, you know, your fitness test. When is that again? Monday, was it?"

Logan's eyes crept to the two remaining strawberry tarts. They nestled there in their plastic and foil, all creamy and jammy and crumbly. And fruity, obviously, although that wasn't as tempting as all those other qualities.

His gaze diverted from the tarts to his stomach. It strained at the buttons of his shirt, like it was fighting to get free.

"Bugger it," he muttered, then he closed over the lid, set the pack down on the desk, and shot Sinead a far-from-grateful look. "Thanks a bloody lot."

"Anytime, sir," Sinead replied, choosing to ignore the sarcasm and take the comment entirely at face value.

"So... there's two going spare?" Tyler asked, squashing the now empty foil container into a half-circle as he hungrily eyed the pack on the DCI's desk.

Right then, the door to the Incident Room swung open, and all eyes went to Ben and Hamza as they strode triumphantly in.

"Well?" Logan asked.

"We got him," DI Forde announced. "He's being checked in and stuck in an interview room now. Should be ready to talk to in— Ooh. Are those strawberry tarts?"

Hamza's head whipped around, his gaze sweeping the area until it locked onto the pastries.

"They going spare?" Ben asked.

Logan could feel Sinead watching him. He sighed, picked up the plastic packaging and, to his own and Tyler's disappointment, handed it to Ben. "Knock yourselves out," he told them, then he clicked his fingers and pointed to DC Neish. "Tyler, go make sure the Reverend Mann gets checked in pronto." He rolled his head around, limbering up his neck muscles, then cracked his knuckles. "I've got some frustration I need to take out."

CHAPTER SEVENTEEN

REVEREND MANN DECLINED THE CHANCE TO HAVE A solicitor present. He'd never had one, he said. Never had the need. And, although Logan offered for one to be provided, he held firm. He had God on his side, he insisted. Guiding him, steering him. What lawyer could compete with that?

Logan chose to bring Ben in on the interview, for better or worse. He'd been the arresting officer, and he had more experience of these things than anyone else on the team, with the possible exception of Logan himself. Even then, it was a close run thing.

And yet, the religious element had almost changed his mind. He didn't know enough yet about Ben's new church, or how his newly-discovered love of the Lord might influence him. He trusted the DI completely, of course, but Ben was still dealing with the death of his own wife. There was no saying what coming face-to-face with someone accused of killing theirs—a supposed man of God, no less—might do to him.

It was only Ben's keenness that convinced Logan to bring him in. He wanted to nail the bastard for what he'd done, and he assured the DCI that he was more than up to the job.

Mann sat with his hands clasped in prayer when the detectives entered, his lips moving. They both waited just inside the doorway until he'd finished, then took their seats across from him and Logan introduced himself.

He looked younger than his age, despite the red rings of grief around his eyes. He could've passed for thirty. Perhaps even younger, in the right lighting conditions, although the bruising on the left side of his face aged him up a little.

Ben had filled Logan in on the Reverend's reaction to the news of his wife and daughter's death as they'd walked down the stairs to the interview room. The DI had described it as, "Quite the performance," although by the time they were back at Invergarry, the minister had mostly calmed down. And, aside from a minute or two of terse silence when they'd denied his request to stop for a few minutes at the church in Fort Augustus, he'd been borderline chatty.

Ben and Hamza had made it clear that they weren't going to discuss the details of the case until he was checked in at the station, so he'd started talking about the weather, how warm it still was for the time of year, and how the nights would soon be starting to draw in.

He'd burst into tears completely out of the blue when they'd pulled in at the station. They'd given him a few minutes to pull himself together, then brought him inside and left him for processing.

And now, here they all were, together in the interview room. Them, three-and-a-half featureless walls, and one big mirror.

Having done all the necessary commentary for the recording, Logan clasped his hands together in a reflection of Reverend Mann's, and offered a thin, supportive sort of smile.

"You mind if I call you Gareth?" he asked.

Mann shook his head. "It's fine."

"Right. Well, do you know why you're here, Gareth?"

"Someone killed my wife and daughter," the Reverend replied. He pointed to Ben. "That's what he said. Is it... is it true?"

"It is," Logan confirmed. "But, I don't think you needed to be told. Did you, son? I think you already knew. I think you knew since Sunday."

"Sunday? Why Sunday?"

"Oh, I don't know, Gareth. You tell me. What happened on Sunday evening?"

"I don't... I'm not sure what you mean."

"Come off it, Gareth," Logan said, his tone clipped and irritable. He leaned forward and lowered his voice like he was sharing a secret. "What if I told you that a neighbour heard you arguing? Heard raised voices? Your raised voice?"

They hadn't, of course. As far as Logan was aware, no neighbour had heard any such thing. But then, he wasn't claiming they had. Implying it? God, aye. But what the Reverend chose to infer from the question was entirely up to him.

"I don't... When? What neighbour?"

"So, you don't deny that you had a row?" Logan asked, seizing on the response. He pressed on quickly, keeping the other man off-balance. "What was it about?"

Judging by his body-language, Mann was already on the ropes. He glanced upwards, either seeking guidance or hoping for the Rapture to whisk him off to Heaven right there and then.

The latter failed to happen and, judging by his stammered answer, so did the former.

"It was... There was... Nothing. It just..."

"Look, couples argue, Gareth. No one is saying otherwise, and especially no' me. I've got an ex-wife. You're preaching to the converted here." Logan re-established the smile on his face and opened his hands in a welcoming gesture. "We just need to know what it was about, so we can get all this cleared up and squared away."

Gareth looked upwards again. There was something slightly accusatory in the way he did it, like he was rapidly coming to the conclusion that the Lord had forsaken him.

"I was moving out," he said. The words were whispered, and spoken towards the ceiling.

"Can you say that again for the tape?" Logan asked.

Mann tore his eyes from the ceiling and spoke more loudly. "I was moving out. We were... taking a break."

"And whose idea was that?" asked Ben.

"Hers. Mine, I mean." The Reverend shook his head and sighed. "It was a mutual decision."

"And what prompted that decision?" Logan asked.

Mann's shoulders rose then fell in a dejected sort of slump. "I don't know. We'd grown apart, I suppose. She... she wanted a divorce."

"So, if you couldn't have her, no one could?" Logan said.

The Reverend's eyes widened, shocked. "What? No! Of course not! I'd never do... I couldn't..."

"How'd you get the black eye?" Ben asked. "Quite a shiner, that."

Mann's fingers came up and traced the outline of the bruise.

"You said you didn't want to press charges," Ben reminded him. "Why? Who did it?"

"Was it Lois?" Logan asked. "Did she do that to you?"

Mann nodded. It was brief, and subtle, and possibly not even intentional, but both detectives spotted it.

"You need to say it for the tape, son," Logan told him.

"Yes. Yes, Lois did it," the Reverend confirmed. "But it wasn't... She didn't mean to..." He groaned, fully aware of what a mess he was making of this whole thing, then tried again. "She was angry. It was my fault."

"What happened? Talk us through it," Logan urged.

"She threw a shoe," Mann explained. "One of mine. It caught me off-guard and..." He indicated the black eye. "Well, you see the result."

Ben asked the obvious question. "Why did she throw a shoe at you?"

The Reverend shrugged. "Because I was leaving, I suppose. She'd gathered up my stuff. Gave me most of it in black bags. Chucked some of it at me. She was upset."

"Aye, sounds like it," Logan agreed. "Although, I have to say, this break up doesn't sound like it was by 'mutual agreement.' Not if one party's lobbing shoes at the other."

"What really happened, Gareth?" Ben added. "Why did you really split up?"

He hesitated. For a moment, it looked like he was going to change his story, but then he gave a single shake of his head and recited his next words like he was reading them from a script. "I told you. We'd grown apart. It was a mutual decision. Things just got a little heated, that's all."

Logan shifted lanes. He opened one of the cardboard folders he'd brought in with him and glanced down at the top printout contained inside. "A colleague has been going through your phone records, Gareth. They make for interesting reading. What can you tell me about the calls you made on Sunday evening?"

"Calls?"

"One around four, and one around half-six," Logan prompted. "Were those before or after you murdered your family?"

Mann looked from Logan to Ben, hoping desperately for some support that didn't come.

"I didn't murder them. God. I wouldn't... I couldn't... I don't know what happened. I don't know when," he babbled, his voice little more than a throaty squeak. "Nobody's told me. Nobody's told me anything."

"Because we're waiting on you telling us, Gareth. You're the man with all the info. You're the only one who can put all this to bed," Logan said. "It's very Biblical, isn't it? Drowning?"

"Drowning? What?"

"Big flood, and all that. Purifying the Earth. That's what that was all about, wasn't it? Noah and the Ark. Big flood to drown the non-believers and the unworthy." Logan raised his eyes and pointed upwards. "He tell you to do it, did He? The Big Man Upstairs?"

"What? No!"

"Then why did you?"

"I didn't! I didn't kill anyone! You have to believe me. Please. How could I? I *loved* them! I loved them both. More than anything."

"But she kicked you out. She tore the family apart," Logan said, his tone becoming harsher. "Did she say you weren't going to get to see Ruby? Was that? Was she trying to stop you seeing your child? That must've been hard, son."

"Is that what set you off?" Ben asked.

"Thou Shalt Not Kill!" Mann said, his breathing coming as a throaty sob as he thumped a fist down on the table. "Thou Shalt Not Kill. It's there, in black and white. I believe that! I live my life by the Book! I didn't kill them. I couldn't. I don't have it in me. Not in here." He slapped himself in the centre of the chest, pleading with his eyes for them to believe him. "I don't have it in here!"

He broke then, tears bubbling to the surface, words failing him until all that was left was a raw, inhuman wail.

When he finally found the ability to speak again, it was just one word, repeated over and over. He flinched at each one, like the very utterance of it was slicing him open and pouring his insides onto the interview room table for all to see.

"Ruby," he whimpered. "*Ruby*."

He grabbed at his hair, twisting it around his fingers, his face contorting in pain and grief. Or a very good approximation of it.

"Oh God," he spat. "Not her. Not my little girl!"

"You think he did it?"

Logan sat in Ben's front room, looking out onto the identical house across the road. There was only room for one car in the drive, so he'd parked the Fiesta on the street, and had considered leaving the keys in the ignition with a

'Free to a Good Home' sign taped to the driver's side window.

The interview had continued for several hours, with a couple of breaks for the Reverend to pull himself together. By the end of it, Mann had gone over his story from every angle. Annoyingly, it had remained mostly consistent, although there were enough gaps in it to warrant keeping him in for the night.

He'd come home from talking with a parishioner around half-four in the afternoon, he claimed. He wouldn't say who, citing their request for anonymity, just that they'd been having suicidal thoughts, and that he'd done his best to comfort and console them.

After getting home, he, Lois, and Ruby had eaten dinner together, then he'd taken Lois aside and broken the news that he was moving out. It had been on the cards for months, he claimed, but it was the conversation with the parishioner that had helped him make the decision—helped him realise that life was short, and that we all had a duty to God to make the most of however many years He saw fit to give us.

She hadn't taken it well. They'd fought. She'd bagged up his clothes and thrown them at him, then clocked him in the coupon with a well-aimed shoe. He'd left around six, carrying his belongings with him in half a dozen black bags.

He'd dropped them at the church in Fort Augustus, in the space usually left for the charity shop drop-off point, and then taken a taxi out to the smaller church at Tomdoun.

"To get my head together," he'd explained. "I couldn't face people. I didn't want people knowing what had happened."

"That you'd killed your wife and child, you mean?"

"No! That my marriage had failed. I'm supposed to have

it all together. They come to me for guidance. I'm meant to help them with their problems. What right do I have to do that when I couldn't even keep my family together?"

The detectives had taken it in turns to try to steer him onto other narratives. They'd talked through a few variations on how he'd killed Lois and Ruby, feeding him just enough rope with which to hang himself.

But, he'd stuck to his story. There were several big gaps in what he told them, but everything he did say remained annoyingly consistent.

"Honestly? I don't know if he did," Logan admitted. "Before we brought him in, I'd have put money on it being him. Now, though?" He massaged the back of his scalp and ran his fingers down his neck, trying to ease the tension building there. "I don't know. There's a lot he's not telling us."

"There's a lot we haven't even asked," Ben pointed out. "I was waiting for you to say something about Kerry Philip."

A line appeared on Logan's forehead. Ben knew from experience what that particular crease meant.

"The tip-off we got from the woman at the church. The one she said we should talk to about the state of the minister's marriage."

"Oh. Aye. Her. Did Hamza track her down?"

"He did, aye. Going round to talk to her in the morning."

Logan scratched at his stomach like he was scratching a loyal dog behind the ears. "Get him to bring her in. We'll time it so Mann sees her. That should shake the bastard up a bit."

Ben took out his phone, pulled on his reading glasses, and began the painstaking process of typing out a text.

"We'll need to be on him from early tomorrow. Mann, I

mean," Ben said. "We'll have to make a decision by dinner time."

"Might be able to get an extension, given the circumstances."

"Maybe, aye," Ben agreed.

Logan squirmed in his chair like the cushions were full of nails. "Are you, eh, are you alright being in on the questioning?"

Ben glanced up from his phone and peered at Logan over the top of his glasses. "Am I what?"

"Given the, eh, nature of the case," Logan said, having a rare stab at diplomacy. "The man potentially murdered his wife. It's not too... difficult, is it?"

"Why would it be too difficult?" Ben asked, clearly annoyed by the suggestion. "Because of what happened to herself? I'm a police officer, Jack. I'm more than capable of setting that stuff aside."

"Because of what happened to *Alice*," Logan said.

Something raw flashed across Ben's face, like the mention of the name had wounded him.

"It wasn't your fault, Ben," Logan insisted. "What happened. None of it was your fault."

"Aye. I know that."

"Do you? Because I'm not convinced you do."

"I'm fine. I'm a big boy," Ben said, the words short and clipped. He finished sending the text, checked the time, then slapped his hands on his thighs and stood up. "Right, it's past midnight. That's me."

Logan thought about pursuing the Alice conversation further, but could tell there would be little point. Not now. Not yet.

He checked his own watch, then groaned and shot a look

of contempt at the *Sports Direct* carrier bag that sat in the corner of the room, an oversized shoe box and some mismatched running gear lurking inside like a bad smell.

"Aye, best get some rest," he said, standing. "I've a feeling we're going to need it with this case. Never mind the fact that Shona's dragging me out jogging tomorrow."

Ben did a double-take, his eyes widening in surprise. "She's what?! At your age?"

"What do you mean at my bloody age?" Logan asked. "There's life in the old dog yet, Benjamin."

"Evidently," Ben said. He looked the DCI up and down, then shook his head. "I don't see the appeal in that sort of thing myself. But, each to their own, I suppose. Although, I never had you pegged as... that sort."

"Believe me, I'm not. Every time I've tried it before, I've hated every bloody minute."

"You've tried it before?!" gasped Ben.

"Aye. A few times. Never took to it. Shona can be pretty persuasive when she wants to be, though."

"So it seems. Well, I bloody never," Ben muttered. He gave another shake of his head. "But you'd better watch you don't get yourself caught, for Christ's sake. If you do, keep my name out of it."

Logan frowned. "Caught?"

"I mean, I'm as open-minded as the next man, Jack, but... You do know it's illegal, yes? What am I saying? Of course you do. Well, on your own bloody head be it, that's all I'm saying."

"*Jogging*," Logan said, stressing the J. "I'm going *jogging*, Benjamin. No' bloody dogging."

Ben exhaled sharply. "Oh!" he said, breaking into a chuckle. "Oh, thank God for that! You had me worried for a moment there," Ben told him. "May be time to get the old ears tested."

"May be time to get your mind out of the bloody gutter, more like."

"Aye, maybe that, too," Ben agreed, still chortling away to himself. "Anyway, that's me. Night, Jack."

"Goodnight," Logan replied. "Ye dirty old bastard."

CHAPTER EIGHTEEN

THIS WAS PAYBACK. IT HAD TO BE. THIS WAS HER revenge for him leaving without saying goodbye.

Everything hurt. It had been doing so for some time now, and he suspected there was little chance of it stopping anytime soon.

He had spent the last quarter of a mile trying to work out which of the many individual pains and discomforts was the worst. His cramping lungs definitely ranked as a contender. His burning thighs and calves were both surely in with a good shout.

Or his knees. Christ, his knees. Each jarring step sent little stabs of agony through his feet and up his shins, before exploding just behind the kneecap.

Perhaps worse, though, were the smaller indignities. The involuntary groans. The sweat that was slicking his t-shirt to his back, and plastering his hair to his forehead. The way the exertion was making his nose run, so he had to sniff every four steps, or risk leaving a slug-trail of snot on the path behind him.

Or the way that, despite his slow speed, no two parts of him were jiggling the same way.

They were running up what Shona had described as, "A gentle incline," out behind her house, but which all available evidence said was Mount bloody Everest. It hadn't looked all that bad from the bottom, although that was before they'd started the warm-up walk. Ten seconds into that, and Logan had realised he may have made a mistake.

The top of the hill was in sight now. He was taking comfort from that, but trying not to get his hopes up. He'd thought the top had been in sight twice before, only to reach a false summit and have Shona urge him on with promises of, "Not far now!"

They'd chatted to start with, Shona talking about everything and nothing, and Logan emitting the occasional grunt of acknowledgement as he focused all his efforts on continuing to breathe.

As the climb had become steeper, the one-sided conversation had become no-sided, and they'd both puffed and wheezed their way onwards and upwards, conserving their breath and—in Logan's case—trying not to vomit up his breakfast.

This would've been particularly impressive, given that he hadn't actually eaten breakfast yet.

He should've stopped long before reaching that point. His body had made that extremely clear. But stopping was giving up, and he'd never been one for giving up. Doubly so with Shona there to witness it.

Which was why, half an hour after taking the balls of paper out of his new trainers and wrestling his size thirteens into them, Logan gasped his way to the top of the hill, and almost collapsed onto the damp early-morning grass.

"Jesus Christ," he coughed, sniffing for the four-hundredth time. Every one of his muscles screamed at him, demanding to know what the hell he thought he was playing at. "I thought you said it was a gentle incline?"

"It was," Shona said. Her breathing was heavy, but controlled.

"Compared to what? The north face of the Eiger? At one point, I thought I was going to have to run back for crampons and a bloody ice axe."

Shona laughed. Logan was impressed that there was enough air in her lungs to facilitate this. The way he felt right now, anything above a wry chuckle was likely to spell certain death.

"Worth it, though, eh?" Shona said.

Logan looked down at his gut. It was still the same size as when they'd set out, which felt like a right slap in the face, given what he'd just gone through.

Shona laughed again. Now she was just showing off.

"Not that. That."

Logan followed the direction she was pointing, and temporarily forgot the way his body hummed with pain.

From the top of the hill, they could see all the way to where the Kessock Bridge split the Moray and Beauly Firths, and beyond that to where Inverness sat glinting in the orange-pink glow of the rising sun.

The whole of Scotland's newest city sat nestled there, its long shadows shrinking as the morning came upon it.

"If you squint, you can see Nairn," Shona said. "That way."

She put a hand on his back to guide him, and he let out an embarrassingly high-pitched yelp of shock when the now freezing cold sweat on his t-shirt touched his warm back.

"Sorry!" Shona said, biting her lip to hold back more laughter. She pointed to a distant gathering of buildings out by the horizon. "There. That's Nairn. Have you been?"

"To Nairn?" Logan asked. He tried to raise a sardonic eyebrow, but his face was as knackered as the rest of him, and it barely budged. "Aye. I've been to Nairn."

"But have you stopped, I mean? Properly? There's a beach. It's nice. Bloody Baltic, obviously, and you'd have to be a masochist to go swimming." She shrugged. "But it's nice. You should go sometime."

Logan ran his fingers through his hair, unpeeling it from his forehead. "Aye. Maybe," he said. He cleared his throat. This also hurt more than he'd ideally have liked it to, but he battled through. "We both could. Go, I mean. If you wanted."

"I don't... I'm not sure..." Shona said.

Logan sniffed, for about the four-hundred-*and-first* time that morning. "Oh. Aye. No, I shouldn't have... That's—"

"I mean, I'd have to ask Geoff..."

It took Logan a moment to realise she was on the wind-up. He blamed the lack of oxygen. "Aye, obviously. We'd need permission from him first. Goes without saying."

"Sunday?" Shona suggested.

"I haven't seen the weather, but—"

"Pishing down," Shona told him. She shrugged. "Just means we'll have the place to ourselves."

Her face shone with the colours of the rising sun. And sweat. Mostly sweat, in fact, but Logan found it mesmerising, all the same.

"Aye," he said. "OK. Sunday it is."

"Good. Right, then." She jogged on the spot for a few

seconds, warming up, then set off down the hill. "Race you to the bottom."

LOGAN GRIMACED OUT A LOW, pained whimper as he heaved himself out of Ben's car and gingerly stretched a foot out until it eventually found the surface of the car park.

His plan had been to drive to the station himself, but all those parts of his body that were designed to bend, flex, or in any way move had come to the decision that they really didn't want to even contemplate anything of the sort right now, and so the idea of wrestling himself into the Fiesta had felt like an accident waiting to happen

Once out Ben's car, it took him a second or two to fully straighten up, then a couple more to convince his legs to carry him in the direction of the front door.

"You alright there, Jack?" Ben asked, watching the DCI's laboured movements.

"Oh, aye. Just dandy. But, I'm telling you now, there better not be a problem with the lift," Logan replied. He winced. "Or we'll be doing this interview across the bloody reception desk."

"You OK, SIR? WHAT HAPPENED?" asked Sinead, hurrying to meet Logan as he came hobbling into the Incident Room.

"Jesus. You been in an accident, boss?" Tyler added.

"No, I haven't been in an accident," Logan replied through gritted teeth.

"Did someone give you a doing?" asked Dave from his spot at the Exhibits desk.

"No! I went running, alright?" Logan explained.

"Running?" Tyler looked the DCI up and down. "What was it, boss? One of them ultra-marathons?"

"Funny. No. It was up some big bastard of a hill."

"At half-five this morning, no less," Ben said. He put the back of his hand to the side of his mouth, as if sharing some big secret. "With a certain pathologist, who shall remain nameless."

Given there were only two pathologists in the area, and one of them was a man in his early seventies, Ben's subtle clue didn't take a lot of figuring out, and there came a chorus of "*oohs*" from Tyler and Sinead, which Logan promptly knocked on the head with a single glare.

"You can cut that out for a start," he told them. "She's helping me train for the bleep test on Monday."

"Ugh. I hated that bloody bleep test," Dave chipped in. "You have my sympathies."

Tyler turned to the uniformed constable. "What? They didn't make you do it, did they?"

Dave frowned. "Aye. Of course. Everyone does it."

Tyler raised his eyebrows and whistled through his teeth, clearly impressed. "How the hell did you manage that?"

"I mean... I could walk then, like," Dave pointed out. "Doubt they'd make me do it now."

"Ah. Right. Yeah. That makes more sense," said Tyler, blushing slightly. He caught Sinead shaking her head and smirking at him, then turned his attention back to Logan and Ben and hurriedly changed the subject. "Ham's on his way back with Kerry Philip. Says he'll be about twenty minutes, but he can hold-off if you need him to."

Logan checked his watch. There was either a set of stairs between here and the interview rooms, or a long walk to the elevator in both directions.

Christ.

"Maybe get him to circle the block a couple of times," Logan suggested.

"On it, boss," Tyler said, taking out his phone.

Logan turned to Sinead. "Anything we need to get caught up on before we go in?"

"One or two updates, sir, yeah," she confirmed.

"Right, then. We'll hear it in a minute," Logan said. He looked between her and Ben. Even that small neck movement made his muscles grumble in complaint. "But first, someone help me get this bloody coat off."

THE UPDATES WERE RELATIVELY SIGNIFICANT, although they did nothing to implicate or exonerate Reverend Mann in any way.

The murder weapon had been found. Ruby Mann's murder weapon, at least. The cuts in Lois Mann's wrists had been done with the kitchen knife found at the scene, but she'd almost certainly been dead by that point.

"Looks like it was ditched in a drain a couple of streets away, sir," Sinead told him. "As luck would have it, it caused a blockage. A boy from Scottish Water found it and called it in. Forensics are looking at it now, and Geoff Palmer's team are out checking the area."

She pointed to a printout of a map she'd pinned to the Big Board, and drew Logan's attention to the three different routes she'd plotted in different coloured pens. "To pass that drain, he'd have had to head in one of these directions from the house."

"Any of them head in the direction of the church?" Ben asked.

"No, sir."

"It was a wild night. Could he have dumped it in a drain closer to the house and the rainwater carried it to that one?"

Sinead shook her head, and a suggestion of self-satisfaction flitted across her face. "No, sir. I asked that same question. Apparently, it doesn't work like that. You can't drop something in one drain, then run along the street and see it passing. They all run to the central pipe. And, the pipe running from most of them have debris filters on the end. Including this one." She tapped the spot she'd circled on the map. "He was there. He physically dropped it into that drain. No question."

"We're checking for CCTV, boss," Tyler added. "It's mostly residential, so not holding out a lot of hope, but worth a bash."

"Aye. Good," Logan said. "What else have we got?"

"Tech stuff mostly, boss," Tyler said, picking up a sheet of A4 paper he'd scrawled notes on. "Bit of interest on the laptop. Lois was on Mumsnet the night she died. She didn't make any posts herself, but replied to a lot of different posts from women saying their husbands had been cheating on them."

"Saying what?"

"Nothing major. Little heart emojis, mostly. Offering hugs. That sort of thing. There was one that was interesting, though. I'll get Sinead to read it, for full effect."

Taking her cue, Sinead cleared her throat and began reading from a print-out. "I—"

Tyler interrupted before she could get any further. "This was in response to a post from a woman who found out her husband was shagging someone at work." He caught the look from Sinead and smiled apologetically. "Sorry. On you go."

"'I completely understand what you're going through,'" she read. "'You think you've found the right one, you give them everything—your body, your trust, your heart and soul —and they betray it all for the sake of some slut half their age. All men are shits. We're better off without them.'" Sinead lowered the page. "And then she signs off with an angry face emoji and a couple of hearts."

"And what time was that posted?" Logan asked.

"Just after three," Sinead said, checking the header. "The original post was from a couple of weeks before. There hadn't been any comments on it in days."

Ben stared blankly back at her. "Meaning?"

"Meaning she probably went searching for posts about cheating and infidelity," Tyler said. "Those forums are mental, there's thousands of new posts a day. No way she'd just stumble upon it without looking for it."

"So, cheating husbands were on her mind, then," Logan mused. "This woman we're bringing in."

"Kerry Philip," Sinead said.

"What age is she?"

"Twenty-one."

Logan reached to smooth down his beard, found it missing, and scratched his chin instead. "Not half his age, then, but a good bit younger."

"You think they were at it, boss?"

"I guess we'll soon find out," Logan replied. "You said there was more tech stuff?"

THE BIG MAN UPSTAIRS 151

Tyler consulted his scrawled notes again. "Aye. We were able to get the Reverend's whereabouts from his phone. The timings at the house seem to tie in with what he said. But he wasn't visiting a parishioner before he came home. He was at the church in Fort Augustus all afternoon, then headed home."

"And afterwards?" Ben asked.

"Back to the church. Nowhere near the drain where the knife was found."

"So... that's that, then?" said Ben. "It wasn't him?"

"He could've gone back to the church, dumped his bags and the phone, and then disposed of the knife afterwards," Logan suggested. With some difficulty and a few pained grunts, he stood up and approached the Big Board. "That drain's almost exactly the opposite direction from the church. Could be his way of throwing us off the scent."

"That's what I said, boss," Tyler crowed, looking pleased with himself. He shot Sinead a patronising look. "You disagreed though, didn't you?"

"Why?" Logan asked, ignoring Tyler and rounding on the newest DC.

Sinead shifted uncomfortably, aware of all the eyes now on her. "Well, I just thought... At the house. He tried to make it look like a murder suicide, but he made a mess of it. The attack on the wee girl was pretty frenzied. Aye, drowning Lois was more calculated, but slitting her wrists as a cover story? Clearly, we're not exactly dealing with a criminal mastermind here."

She indicated the map, and the routes marked out on it. "It's a six minute walk from the house to the drain. Quickest route from the church to that spot is eighteen minutes, and that's if you go right past the house. Otherwise, you have to take the long way, and you're looking at half an hour there and the same again back."

Sinead shrugged. Her cheeks had reddened as she'd explained her thinking to her completely silent and unresponsive audience.

"If he'd murdered his wife and daughter, it seems a bit risky to walk for that long carrying the knife he used to kill one of them. Especially when he's well-known locally, and people were likely to approach him."

The smug look on Tyler's face had all-but faded away. He tried to revive it by pointing at the map and saying, "Aye, but..." then concluded that it probably wasn't worth the effort. "I mean, I suppose that does sort of make sense," he admitted. Begrudgingly.

His phone buzzed and he checked the screen.

"That Hamza?" Logan asked.

"That's them arriving now, boss," the DC confirmed.

"Shite. Right, go get Mann in interview room one. Leave the door open. Get Hamza to bring Kerry Philip past there and into the room next door. Do *not* let them speak to each other under any circumstances."

"Got it, boss," Tyler said, hopping to his feet.

"Keep Mann there until we arrive. And don't you talk to him, either. Let him stew."

"Will do. How long will you be?"

Logan grimaced as he hobbled around to face the door. The Incident Room had never looked quite as large before. "As long as it takes, son," he replied. "As long as it takes."

CHAPTER NINETEEN

THE PLAN WORKED PERFECTLY. BY THE TIME LOGAN had limped his way down to the interview room—having politely declined Dave's offer of a shot of his wheelchair— Reverend Mann was a paranoid wreck, simultaneously demanding to know why Kerry Philip was there, while claiming to have no real connection to her.

"She said she had some information for us," Logan said, once Tyler had been sent back upstairs, and the formalities with starting the recording were all out of the way.

"What? What kind of information? About what?"

Logan looked at Ben, and both men shrugged. "We're detectives, son," Ben said. "No' mind readers. I'm sure we'll find out in due course."

"Unless you've got some idea?" Logan pressed. "What could she possibly want to tell us? Any clue?"

The Reverend sat on the fence for a few seconds, not wanting to commit either way, until finally he gave a shake of his head. "I don't know."

"You know her, though, right?"

"She's... She comes to the church, yes."

"Why?" Logan wondered.

"What do you mean, 'why?'" Mann asked. "Because she believes in God's word."

"But why your church, specifically? She lives in Drumnadrochit, right?"

"Yes. I mean... I believe she does, yes."

"So, why not go to church closer to home?"

"She never... I don't know. I didn't ask."

"Well, rest assured that our colleague will be asking her that right now. That, and a whole lot more." Logan pursed his lips into a razor-thin smile. "Sure there's nothing you'd like to say on the matter? Before we hear it from elsewhere?"

Mann opened his mouth, looked from Logan to Ben and back again, then closed it again. "I don't know," he said, after a pause. "I didn't ask."

Logan opened his folder and slid a photograph across the table. It was the one showing Lois and Ruby on a boat out on Loch Ness that he'd taken from the house. At his first glimpse of it, the Reverend drew in a sharp breath and averted his gaze.

"Look at them, Gareth," Logan said.

"I... can't."

"Why not? What do you see when you look at them?" Logan pressed. "Do their faces remind you of what you did?"

"No!" Mann yelped, slamming his hands on the table. His glare was hot and fierce as it fixed on Logan, then cooled as he relented and looked down at the picture on the table between them.

A sob caught at the back of his throat. His fingertips traced over the face of his daughter, like he could sweep her wind-blown hair out of her eyes for her.

"Lois hated that day," he said in a throaty whisper. "Ruby enjoyed it, but Lois hated every minute."

"She looks happy enough," Logan said.

"Yes, well. She was always good at putting a face on things," the Reverend said, and there was a hint of something like an accusation in it. "But she said it was awful. It was one of those Loch Ness cruises, but the boat was a shambles. Overcrowded, smelly, dirty... She wasn't impressed. Got her money back in the end. Tore strips out of the owner, from what she..."

He picked up the photograph and regarded it, a series of parallel lines forming on his brow.

"Wait."

"What is it?" asked Ben.

The Reverend set the photo down and pointed to a man in the background. He was leaning on a railing with his back to the camera, but his head was turned enough to give a glimpse of his face.

"Lord. Of course! Why didn't I think about that?" the Reverend whispered. "Will Strand."

"Will Strand?"

"Yes! Will Strand! He's another of the reasons she hated the boat trip so much." Mann jabbed a finger repeatedly against the man in the photo. "That's Will Strand."

"And?" Logan asked. "Who's Will Strand when he's at home?"

"Will. William. Strand. He lives locally. He's been coming onto Lois since Ruby was going to playgroup. Before then, actually. But that's when it started getting out of hand."

"Out of hand in what way?" Logan asked.

"Just... I mean, he wasn't violent. Nothing like that. He's... nice enough. He just... he has his problems. And he can get a bit, I don't know, creepy I suppose. Kept coming onto her. Inviting her out for a drink. Saying how good she looked. Sending her flirty messages implying what he'd like to do with her. Completely inappropriate stuff. I had a word, but he just laughed it off. Said she'd got the wrong end of the stick, and that he wasn't interested in her like that. But it kept happening. Got worse, if anything."

Logan listened for the scratching sound of Ben's pen on on his notepad to stop before continuing. "Did you ever report it?"

"No, I..." the Reverend's brow furrowed for a moment, then his eyebrows exploded upwards. "Yes! Yes, we did! I didn't want to cause a fuss, but Lois insisted. She spoke to someone on 101. Apparently an officer came out. Presumably, they spoke to Will, because it stopped after that. He didn't say a word to her after that. Hasn't since, to the best of my knowledge."

"Wait a minute. Strand?" Ben asked. He flicked back a page in his notebook. "Any relation to Elizabeth?"

"How do you know Elizabeth?" Mann asked.

"We spoke to her outside the church. Big fan of yours," Ben said.

"Yes. Well. Elizabeth is lovely. That's one of the reasons I didn't want Lois to call the police on Will. To spare Elizabeth any embarrassment. She had such a difficult time last year. Lost all her life savings to... well, a dodgy investment, I suppose. And, it isn't her fault her son's... the way he is. Will is... difficult. For a variety of reasons. I believe he's on the spectrum, also, which likely doesn't help."

Logan could practically hear the frown forming on DI Forde's face.

"What, the games thing?" Ben asked.

"Jesus Christ, Detective Inspector. Showing your age there. The autistic spectrum, no' the bloody ZX."

"Oh. Right. Aye," said Ben, hastily making a note.

"The harassment. When did all this happen?" Logan asked, turning back to the Rev.

"Three... four months ago?" Mann replied.

"You asking us or telling us?"

"Sorry. Telling. Three or four months."

"And there's been nothing from him since?" asked the DCI. "He didn't try to speak, didn't make any accusations or threats?"

Reverend Mann shook his head. "No. Nothing like that. Or nothing I'm aware of, anyway. I'm sure Lois would have said. She'd tell me if something like that happened. But he used to be obsessed. You need to speak to him. Ask him where he was. Find out if he did it!"

"We'll look into it," Logan told him.

It was Ben who jumped in with the next question. "She'd have told you, you say? So, trusting relationship, was it? The two of you, I mean. Discussed things like that, did you?"

"Of course we did. Yes," Mann said, but the hesitation before he answered arguably said more than the words themselves did. "She was my wife. We told each other everything."

"Come on. Not everything, Gareth. Nobody tells their wife everything," Logan said, scoffing at the very suggestion. He removed a piece of paper from his folder and slid it across the table. "Mind telling us about the numbers highlighted in yellow?"

The Reverend peered down at the paper. His eyes darted across it, left, right, up, down, like he was trying to make sense of it.

Or trying to avoid looking too closely.

"It's a printout of all your most recent phone calls," Logan explained. "Including two on the day your wife and daughter were murdered. One before you say you went to the house, and one shortly after you say you left. Mind telling us whose number that is?"

Mann said nothing. His fingers tapped anxiously at the corner of the paper, like he was beating out some secret distress signal via Morse Code.

"The number's Pay As You Go. No record of who owns it. We've looked through your phone, hoping that would enlighten us. The number's stored, but with no name. No identifying features at all, in fact, just that number."

Gareth continued to look down at the page in silence. Logan pressed on, regardless.

"Here's something we found interesting. The printout clearly shows that several calls were placed and up to thirty text messages were sent *every single day* to that number over the previous few months, but the records of all of that have been deleted from your phone. Gone. Kaput. Almost like you didn't want anyone finding out about them." Logan pulled a face that suggested this made no sense. "If your relationship was so honest and open, Gareth, why hide who you've been in touch with? Obviously, whoever it is, they're very important to you."

"I... It's... As part of my job, I have to make myself available to—"

"Your wife knew what your job was, son. Don't insult us by trying to say those were work related," Logan warned. He took the paper back, produced his own phone, and sat it next to the page. "You a gambling man, Gareth? Because, I'd be prepared to put money on a wee hunch of mine. I'll bet that if I call that number now, a phone's going to ring in the next room."

He picked up his phone and thumbed the screen awake. Reverend Mann's gaze followed his movements the entire way.

"What do you think, Detective Inspector Forde?" Logan asked, beginning to dial the number on the keypad. "You taking that bet?"

"Aye, I'll take it," Ben said, watching the other man closely. "I mean, I'm sure Reverend Mann here wouldn't be so stupid as to no' just admit it. If I was him, and you were sat here about to dial that number, and I knew the owner of that phone was sitting on the other side of that wall..." His gaze flitted briefly to the wall at Mann's back. "Well, I wouldn't be backwards about coming forwards. Let's put it like that. It'd look pretty bad for me, if that were the case."

"Like you had something to hide," Logan suggested.

Ben agreed with a nod. "Exactly that. To the casual observer, it'd look like I had something to—"

"OK! OK, yes," the Reverend blurted. "Yes, it's Kerry's number. Alright? We were just... It wasn't..." He sighed. There was no avoiding the fact—the game was well and truly up. "We were... We were seeing each other."

"Seeing each other?" Logan asked. "In what sense?"

"In a..." Mann sighed again, heavier this time. He looked to the ceiling. There was something apologetic in it. "In a sexual sense."

Logan rested his elbows on the table, interlocked his fingers, and pressed the palms together.

"Well, Gareth," he said. "Now we're finally getting somewhere."

SINEAD SAT AT HER DESK, the phone handset cradled between her shoulder and her ear, her fingers flitting effortlessly across her computer keyboard.

"No, it's not here," she said. "Is it a file or a link?" She listened for a moment. "No, it's definitely not here, then. What inbox did you send it to?"

At his own desk, Tyler spun slowly in his chair, walking himself around in circles with his feet. A few more evidence bags had been dropped in—the knife that had been found in the drain being the most interesting by far—and Dave was in the process of cataloguing and checking them in.

Tyler watched him for a while, half-listening as Sinead continued to question whoever was on the other end of the line. From what he could gather, they'd emailed something to the wrong account, and she was now getting them to resend it to the correct one. She obviously had it well in hand.

He stopped circling for a moment and clicked 'refresh' on his own email. He was waiting for a few updates from different departments, but wasn't expecting them for hours yet. There was probably plenty he could be getting on with in the meantime, but he'd skipped breakfast and his rumbling stomach was making it difficult for him to concentrate.

The Big Board drew his attention. With a final spin in his chair he got up, crossed to it, and looked it over.

Sinead's layout was just as organised as DS McQuarrie's had always been, but in a very different way. She bunched related information together in clusters, with spaces between each cluster so the board looked a bit like a map of the Orkneys, or some other cluster of islands.

Bridges of red thread ran between the islands, crisscrossing as they connected the various printouts, photographs, Post-Its and the like with counterparts elsewhere on the board. Sinead had never done the Big Board training course that DS McQuarrie had attended, and had unashamedly based her style on 'the way they did it on telly.'

She'd searched Inverness for red string to link the various bits of evidence together, but had been forced to settle for a big ball of red wool from Magpie Wool and Crafts out on Old Edinburgh Road.

Tyler took a few moments to look over the board. Logan had taken a photo of the victims in with him to the interview, which had left a space in one of the clusters. The DC idly traced his finger along the length of wool that connected the space to a photograph of the Reverend Mann. He was in full 'cool young minister' mode, proudly showing off both his dog collar and a semi-acoustic guitar that he held with a confidence that suggested he at least knew a chord or two.

"Christ. He's one of those," Tyler muttered, before giving the wool a *twang* and turning away.

Sinead was still on the phone. Her conversation had become just some noises of agreement now, and the odd, 'uh-huh.' Tyler wandered past his desk, wiped some dust off the top of his monitor, then stopped by the Exhibits desk.

"You a religious man, Dave?" he asked, picking up an evidence bag and turning it over in his hands.

"Me? No," Dave replied. He plucked the bag out of Tyler's grasp and set it back on the table in front of him. "You?"

Tyler shook his head. "Nah. Used to go to these, I don't know, religious club things in the summer holidays."

Dave regarded him curiously. "Eh?"

"As a kid, I mean. Not now."

"Oh. Right. Aye."

"They'd always make them sound dead interesting. They'd come into school on the last day of term, and be all like, 'We've got games, and music, and cakes. As much Kia-Ora as you can drink.' Made it sound brilliant." Tyler blew out his cheeks. "Then, you'd go in, and they'd be like, 'Right. We've got them. Shut the doors.' And one of them would crack out a guitar and start giving it all..."—he closed his eyes, mimed playing the guitar, and sang—"'Jesus is my spaceship, let's ride Him through the stars!'"

Dave frowned. "That's a new one on me."

Tyler ignored the comment, his face scrunching up in distaste. "Meanwhile, we were all like, 'Aye, very good, mister. Are we going to play Ker-Plunk now, or what? And where's them French Fancies you promised us?'"

"Sounds like the experience left quite an impression," Dave remarked.

"Total con," Tyler concluded, visibly disgusted by the whole affair. "Total waste of bloody time."

Over at her desk, Sinead jumped to her feet, spat a hurried, "Aye, got it, thanks," into the phone, then slammed it back into its cradle. She clicked her fingers in Tyler's direction, and pointed past him to the door. "Go get DCI Logan and DI Forde," she instructed. Leaning back, she stared, wide-eyed, at her computer monitor. "They both need to see this. Now."

CHAPTER TWENTY

Sandra Atwood loved her son with every fibre of her being, but by fuck, he could be a right pain in the arse sometimes.

He'd been a pain in the arse yesterday afternoon, when he'd had a hissy fit about his daddy being off-shore for another week.

He'd been a pain in the arse during the night, when he'd insisted there was a scary man hiding under his bed, and made her check and double-check half a dozen times during the wee small hours.

He'd been a pain in the arse when he'd spilled his cereal all over the floor thirty seconds before they were due to leave for nursery, and had been an even bigger pain in the arse when he'd come home demanding that they get out his crayons, glue stick, and—Christ have mercy—the big tub of glitter, so he could finish the art project he'd started during that morning's session.

Somewhere deep down, she knew it wasn't his fault. Not really. It was easy to blame him, of course, and she did so on a regular basis. But he was three years old, full of energy, and—although she'd never had any official confirmation—almost certainly crammed to the brim with ADHD.

Her exhaustion didn't help any. If she'd had a good night's sleep, she could deal with most things. His flights of fancy. His crashing around the living room like a bulldozer. His complete emotional meltdowns whenever she didn't butter all the way to all four corners of his toast. With a good night's sleep, she could handle all that without batting an eyelid.

Today, all she wanted to do was shake him by the shoulders and scream, "Get a fucking grip! It's just toast, you little shit!"

She wouldn't, of course. She'd save that until he was asleep, and her face was buried sufficiently deep in a pillow that her shouting wouldn't waken him up.

He was upstairs now, apparently looking for one particular crayon that was vital to the artwork he was in the process of creating. He'd described it as, "Blue, but not *blue*, just blue. Like *blue* blue."

She'd gone to his room, searched his art box, and come down with the only four crayons that could be conceivably described as 'blue.' The wee bastard had rejected all of them.

At which point, she'd sent him upstairs to find the bloody thing himself.

That had been ten minutes ago. She could still hear him rummaging around, although it sounded more like he was dragging everything out of a toy box, rather than checking through art supplies.

God, what a pain in the arse.

"Simon? Sy?" Sandra called from the bottom of the stairs. "What are you doing?"

Upstairs, in his bedroom, Simon Atwood lost his grip on his toy box, then jumped back just as it toppled sideways onto the floor, spilling out hundreds of toy cars, three-fifths of a *Thomas the Tank Engine* train set, and a Batman action figure with its trousers missing.

"Nuffing," he called back, guilt dripping from every syllable.

"You're meant to be getting your crayon," came the reply. "Not taking your toys out."

"I'm not!"

"You definitely bloody are," his mum said, although she mumbled it quietly, like she hadn't wanted him to hear it. When she next spoke, her voice was louder. "Just find your crayon and come down, OK, sweetheart? You can get toys out after lunch."

"OK, Mummy!" Simon said, picking up one of the cars and clutching it to his chest like it was the most valuable item in the world. "Be there soon!"

His art box wasn't really a box at all. It was a large plastic tub filled with paper, pencils, paints, pens, and anything else that could conceivably make or receive a mark. Going through all that would take a while, so he settled for standing over it and peering suspiciously down, like the tub was using his blue crayon as bait, and the moment he reached a hand in, he'd be dragged down and swallowed whole.

"Blue crayon?" he asked, in a light, sing-song sort of voice. He idly drove his car up one arm, making a low *chugging* noise that suggested a full service and oil-change was long-overdue. "Come out, come out, wherever you are."

Creak.

At the sound of movement, Simon gasped. He stepped back from the tub, then in closer, then back again until he was exactly the same distance away from it as had been when he started.

"Hello?" he whispered apprehensively. "Blue crayon?"

The creaking came again. Louder than before. Simon shifted his gaze from the toy box to the edge of his bed. Shadows gathered below it like storm clouds. Heavy. Thick. Oppressive.

He wanted to shout his mum, to call for her, to hear the *thump* of her running up the stairs, and to feel the immense sense of safety and contentment as she carried him away in her arms.

But she'd seemed so tired last night. So angry. So annoyed. He'd been sure there had been someone under the bed, but she'd checked again and again, and had finally snapped at him not to be so stupid.

He didn't want to be stupid. He didn't want his mummy to think he was, either.

And so, still holding onto the car, Simon Atwood got down onto his hands and knees and peered into the darkness below his bed.

Behind him, a door opened.

CHAPTER TWENTY-ONE

Sinead sat at her desk, Logan, Ben, and Tyler looming behind her as she hovered her mouse pointer over the play button on the video file.

"So, there were no CCTV cameras around the house, as we know," she said. "But it was a wild night. Rain, high winds..."

"The usual, then," Ben remarked.

"Aye, but worse. A neighbour's car was parked at the entrance to the cul-de-sac. It's got a dashcam fitted—one of those ones that activate if the car gets knocked or bumped. Or, in this case, walloped by a big gust of wind."

Logan bent down to get a closer look at the screen. "It got something?"

"It did, sir," Sinead confirmed. "The driver checked the footage after the door-to-door. The camera recorded over forty short clips over the course of Sunday evening. Including this."

She clicked the play button. The view was from inside a car, through a windscreen marbled with rain. Daylight was clinging on by its fingernails, the thick layer of cloud blanketing the street in a murky grey gloom.

About thirty or forty yards away, where the street ended, stood the house where Lois and Ruby Mann had been murdered. The lights were on, but the curtains were open.

"Nothing's happening," Tyler pointed out.

"Hold on," Sinead told him, then she pointed to the screen. "There."

A man strode past the car from behind, walking away from the camera, his head down to shield himself from the rain. He turned back, just briefly, to check the coast was clear before stepping out onto the road, and they all caught a glimpse of the white collar around his neck.

"Is that Mann?" Ben asked. Logan confirmed it with a nod, his eyes laser-targeted on the man on the screen.

"What time was this?" he asked, not wanting to glance away even long enough to check the time stamp.

"Four thirty-seven," Sinead said.

"Fits his story," said Ben, joining Logan in leaning down to watch the footage more clearly.

Feeling left out, Tyler did the same, and both senior detectives turned briefly to look at him when his head appeared in the narrow gap between theirs.

"Alright?" Tyler asked, smiling a little uncomfortably. "This is a bit close, isn't it?"

"Depends if you're planning to make a move on either of us," Ben said. At which point, Tyler straightened up again, and all eyes went back to the screen.

Reverend Mann was standing outside the garden gate, not yet making any move to go inside, despite the weather.

"What's he up to?" Logan wondered.

"Can't really see, sir," Sinead told him. "On the phone,

maybe? The rain makes it hard to tell, and then..." She pointed at the screen again just as the video cut out. "... camera goes off."

"Bollocks," Logan muttered.

"Don't worry, there's more," Sinead said. She minimised the video window, then clicked over to a folder containing four other files.

Before she could click on any of them, the door to the Incident Room flew open, and DS Khaled came running in, slightly out of breath.

"You're here. Good. Got a bit of a breakthrough," he announced between huffs and puffs. "Kerry Philip and Gareth Mann." He pushed back his shoulders and pushed his chest out a little, building up the moment.

"Were having an affair?" Logan guessed.

Hamza deflated again. "Eh? Shite. I mean, aye, sir," he said. "Been going on for a while. Did Mann tell you?"

"He did," Logan confirmed.

Hamza looked down at the notepad he had clutched in his hand. "Right. Well, that's... good."

"Keep up, Detective Sergeant," Tyler teased.

Hamza extended a middle finger, then joined the crowd around Sinead's desk. "What have we got?"

"Dashcam from the night of the murder," Sinead explained. "We've just seen Mann heading for the house. This one is from just over an hour later."

She hit play on the next file. Up flashed an almost identical video to the previous one. Same blurry windscreen, same angle, same house at the end of the same street.

"Look. The downstairs window," Sinead said, as a gust of wind briefly cleared the view through the glass.

Two adults—one male, one female, Logan thought,

although it was hard to tell for sure—stood framed in the downstairs window. There was no sound on the recording besides the rattling of the rain on the car roof, but it was clear from the hand gestures that the people in the house were having a stand-up row.

"Someone's no' happy," Ben observed. "Fits with his story again."

Logan checked the time stamp. "Assuming that's Lois Mann, we know she was alive at quarter to six, then."

Something about the video had just started to nag at Logan when it came to an abrupt end. Sinead closed the window down and moved onto the next one. This one was from after six. It was only a few seconds long, and immediately showed Reverend Mann at the front of the car, having apparently bumped into it with one of the black bags he was carrying.

The windscreen was a little clearer than it had been, and gave a reasonably clear view of Mann's face as he readjusted his grip on the bags and went marching past the car, out of the camera's view.

Behind him, at the house, the curtains of the downstairs window were jerked closed by a blurry, backlit silhouette of what was almost certainly a woman.

"There we go, then," Ben said. "His story fits. Timing's are right, and she's still alive in the house when he leaves."

"Assuming that's Lois Mann," Logan said.

"Even if the timings match up, there's no saying he didn't go back," Tyler added.

Logan angled the screen a little to reduce the glare from the lights. "Show me Mann again, will you?"

Sinead scrubbed back through the video until she reached a clear shot of the Reverend.

He doesn't have the shiner," Logan said, indicating Mann's eye.

"It wouldn't appear right away," Ben reasoned.

"No, but given the size of the thing now, I'd expect to see something there. Some mark. There's nothing." Logan gave a little wave to Sinead to indicate he was finished with the clip. "I think he's lying about her hitting him with the shoe."

"Hold on," Sinead said. "There's one more video you need to see."

With a series of mouse clicks, she brought the last file up on screen. "It's really brief, and you can't see much. I had to watch it a few times until I picked up on it." Without touching the screen, she circled an area of the street on the still frame with the end of a pen. "Watch this bit. This is from just before nine."

She clicked the play icon. The footage was darker, and a light had come on just ahead of the car. The video shook, a particularly violent gust having rocked the car and roused the camera.

As they all watched, a man dressed in black came scampering around from the back of the house right where Sinead had drawn her circle in the air. He had a hood up, and his head down, and walked at a fair old clip.

The footage stopped then, the man just a blur of black on black.

"Who's that?" Ben asked, squinting as he tried to make out details that weren't there. "Is that Mann?"

"I don't think so, sir," Sinead said. She held a pen horizontally, lining it up with the top of the figure's head. "See where the pen meets the lamp post? I did the same with Mann in the first video when they both cross the same point on the street. This guy's a fair bit taller."

"We don't have footage of him heading to the house?" asked Ben.

"No, we only get him coming away, sir."

Logan straightened, rubbed his chin, and briefly regretted losing the beard, then bent down again. "Go back to that second video," he instructed. "The one of the arguing."

He waited for Sinead to make all the necessary clicks, then they all stood in silence until the short clip had played almost all the way through.

"There. Stop," Logan said, and Sinead scrambled to click the pause icon. He leaned in closer, angling his head to avoid the reflected glare of the overhead lights. "Jesus Christ," he muttered. "Look at the window."

The other men all bent down, so their heads were lined up next to Sinead's.

"You look like you're posing for an album cover," Dave remarked, briefly glancing up from his work.

"What am I looking for?" Ben asked. He pulled on his glasses, decided they made everything significantly worse, and removed them again. "I see a couple arguing. Presumably Gareth and Lois."

"No' that window," Logan said. He pointed to the upper floor of the house. "That one."

He gave everyone a moment to study the image, and watched them as the pennies began to drop. "Bloody hell, boss," Tyler remarked. "Is that...? Is there someone up there?"

"Aye, looks like it."

"Where?" Ben demanded, narrowing his eyes and scrunching up his nose. He put a hand on Sinead's shoulder. "Can you zoom in and enhance it?"

"*Zoom in and enhance it?*" Logan tutted. "Aye, and maybe we can get the infra-red function turned on at the same time."

Tyler grinned. "Yeah, what do you think this is, boss? Blade Runner?"

Logan and Ben both fixed him with matching glares, and the smile fell away as quickly as it had turned up.

"We, eh, we can actually zoom in on this software," Hamza said. Sinead took her hand off the mouse, letting him take over.

"What was that you two said?" Ben asked, pushing an ear forward and looking between Logan and Tyler. "'Sorry,' was it? 'You were right, and we were wrong.' Was that what I heard?"

"Aye, in your dreams, maybe," Logan muttered.

They all waited for Hamza to finish zooming in on the top window. The already blurry image was now little more than a smear of light and shadow, but with a bit of imagination, it was possible to make out the outline of a man in the upstairs window.

"By my reckoning, that's Ruby's room," Logan said. "Which begs the question—if both parents are down in the living room..." He prodded the screen with the tip of a finger. "...then who's the big man upstairs?"

CHAPTER TWENTY-TWO

EVERYONE KNEW WHAT THEY HAD TO DO. LOGAN HAD barked out orders, hammered them home with snaps of his fingers and pointed glares, then gone sweeping out of the Incident Room like a bear desperately in need of some Paracetamol.

It had, Tyler had happily remarked, been just like old times.

"Miss Philip?" Logan said, assembling some sort of smile for the young woman on the other side of the interview table.

There was something fairy or elf-like about her, with a slender face and short hair that she'd dyed a shade of reddish-purple. She looked up at him through a messy fringe and rearranged her features into something that passed for a smile.

"It's Mrs, sir," Hamza told him, before pointedly adding, "She's married."

"Oh. Right," Logan said. He extended a hand for her to shake. "Detective Chief Inspector Jack Logan."

"Kerry," she told him. "Uh, I mean, you know that, but Kerry. Call me... You can call me Kerry."

"Thank you," Logan said. "DS Khaled tells me you've been very helpful, so I don't want to keep you back much longer."

He pulled out a chair and lowered himself onto it, doing his best not to let on about the burning pain it brought to his hips and thighs.

"But I wonder if you could answer just a few more questions?"

"Detective Chief Inspector Logan will join us in a few minutes," said Ben, taking his seat across from Reverend Mann. "I brought you a cuppa in the meantime. Thought you could probably do with it."

He clonked the mug down on the desk and slid it over so it was within the younger man's reach.

"Thank you," the Reverend said, gratefully accepting it. He took a sip, then wrapped his hands around the mug, welcoming its warmth.

"Alright?"

The Reverend nodded. "Lovely, thanks."

"I looked for biscuits, but there was nothing worth writing home about," Ben said. "Found a box of Jaffa Cakes at the back of a cupboard, but the Best Before is June last year, so horsed them straight in the bin. Wouldn't want to poison you."

Mann smiled thinly. "Very kind of you. I take it you're 'good cop,' then?"

"Ha! I'll take that," Ben said, raising his mug as if in toast.

"Truth is, though, most of us are the good cop. DCI Logan comes across as a surly big bugger, but... Well, he is. But he's not the bad guy, Gareth. He's just been around them too long. And he just wants to get justice for Lois and Ruby."

"I didn't do it," the Reverend said, emotion choking him and turning his voice into a whisper at the mention of their names. "I didn't kill them. I couldn't. I could never... I just couldn't."

"We're getting to the bottom of it, son," Ben told him. "Evidence has come to light that, well, it's given your story credibility, let's just say."

Mann's shoulders heaved, and he looked down into his mug, hiding his tears.

"You're alright, son. You're alright," Ben soothed. "Drink your tea, and you'll be fine."

"Sorry. Sorry. It's just... the thought of them. Of someone doing..." He sniffed and drew a sleeve across his eyes. "I should've been there. I should've been there to look after them."

Ben sipped at his own tea, not really tasting it. "Aye. Well. Can't change the past, eh?" he said. "Much as we might like to." He inhaled a swirl of steam from the mug. "And you can't be everywhere. No one can. Things happen. Terrible things. And you wish you could have done something to stop it. You... you hold yourself responsible. When you shouldn't, son. You really shouldn't."

He took another swig of tea, swirled it around in his mouth, then swallowed and recited his next words from memory.

"'But we also glory in our sufferings, because we know that suffering produces perseverance; perseverance, character; and character, hope.'"

Reverend Mann raised his eyebrows, surprised and impressed. "Romans Five," he said. "You're a Christian?"

Ben looked mildly embarrassed by the suggestion. "I don't know what I am, in all honesty. But recently I've found it... helpful. My, eh... My wife passed away just under a year ago."

"Oh. I'm so sorry," said Mann, and everything in his voice and in his expression said that he meant it. "What was her name?"

Ben paused with his mug halfway to his mouth, the steam swirling up from the hot liquid's surface. He came to a decision, gulped down another mouthful, then returned the mug to the table.

"I'm sorry, I shouldn't have mentioned anything," Ben said. He glanced back at the door. "I'm sure DCI Logan will be joining us shortly."

A LOW WHISTLE escaped through Tyler's teeth, prompting Sinead to roll over in her chair to see what he'd found.

She scanned his computer screen, which showed a completed Incident Report dated from a few months previously.

"What have we got?"

"William Strand. The fella the boss asked me to look up. Lois Mann reported him for harassment back in May," Tyler said. "He'd been following her about, calling, texting... Jesus, he wrote her letters."

"Definitely a stalker, then," Dave chipped in from his corner.

"I know, right? I mean, who else writes letters these days? Stalkers and weirdoes."

"I write letters," Sinead said.

Tyler patted her reassuringly on the hand. "You're a woman. That's allowed."

"Oh, well that's a relief," Sinead said, rolling her eyes. She turned her attention back to the screen and read through the report. "Uniform spoke to him."

"No official caution or anything, though."

"Which is weird, because..." Tyler flicked to another report. "He's got a history of it. She'd reported him a month earlier. He'd come up to her and her daughter on some boat cruise thing, and wouldn't leave them alone. And it's not just her, either..."

Another click. Another report.

"He's done it to other women, too. One in Inverness, one in Invergarry. They had a word with him, he said he wouldn't do it again, and that was it."

"No further action taken?"

Tyler shook his head. "Not that I can find. Going by the reports, the mother seems to do most of his talking for him. She must be helluva persuasive."

Sinead budged Tyler aside and clicked through the open files. She skimmed them, scrolling with the mouse wheel as her eyes flitted left and right.

"I've read through them. There's not a lot more in there." Tyler pointed out.

And he was right. The reports were brief and largely unremarkable. The pattern was more interesting, though.

"With the first woman it was just texts and letters," Sinead said. "He stopped contacting her after being spoken to. The next woman, he started phoning at home. Presumably got her number from the phone book."

"The phone book? What was he, a time traveller?" Tyler asked.

"They still do the phone book," said Sinead.

"Well, I haven't seen them knocking about. Dave?"

Dave looked up from his work. "Yes?"

"Phone books."

"What about them?"

"Do they still exist?"

Dave's broad brow furrowed. "Is this a philosophical question?"

"What? No," Tyler said. "Do you still get phone books?"

With one carefully aimed finger, Dave pointed to the phone book on the next desk over from where the Detective Constables were both sitting. "Yes," he said, then he turned his attention back to his paperwork.

Judging by his face, Tyler tried to come up with some sort of pithy comeback, failed dismally, and turned his attention back to Sinead and the screen.

"Sorry, you were saying?"

Sinead smirked as she continued. "So, first texts and letters, he stops when he's given a warning. Then, he finds someone else to obsess over, and this time, he starts to phone. Again, he's spoken to, and it all seems to stop."

"Right," Tyler agreed.

"But, with Lois Mann, he doesn't just phone and text, he approaches her in person. Repeatedly. And, after he's given a warning, he doesn't stop. Not until he's spoken to a second time, at least."

"It's escalating," Tyler realised. "He's getting bolder."

"The question is," said Sinead, clicking the 'Print' icon at the top of the on-screen report. "Did he get bold enough to kill?"

"Dun-dun-*duuuun!*"

Both Detective Constables rotated their chairs to look in Dave's direction.

"Sorry," he said, his mouth curving into something that was part smile, part grimace. "That was probably inappropriate."

TYLER INTERCEPTED Logan between interview rooms, rattled off everything they'd found out about Will Strand, and provided the DCI with a bundle of printouts.

"I want you to go talk to him," Logan instructed. "Casual, though. Find out his whereabouts on Sunday. Get a feel for him. You know the score."

"Right, boss. Will do."

"Oh, and Tyler?" Logan said, calling the DC back before he could go more than two steps. "Don't fuck this up."

"You can count on me, boss."

"Aye. Well." Logan sucked in his bottom lip, then spat it out again. "On second thoughts," he said, "take Sinead."

DCI LOGAN ENTERED the interview room that currently held Reverend Mann, and took a seat beside DI Forde.

"So, what did I miss?" he asked.

"Oh, not a lot. The Reverend and I were just having a chat about religion, really," Ben replied.

"Sorry I missed that. Sounds fascinating," Logan said,

sarcasm oozing from every word. "You know what else has got me fascinated, though, Gareth?"

"What?" asked the Reverend, visibly apprehensive about what the DCI might be about to say.

"Bryan Philip. Kerry Philip's husband," Logan said. He pointed to the Reverend's black eye. "The man who gave you that big shiner there."

Mann wrapped his fingers tightly around his mug and clutched it to him, like he might be able to somehow hide behind it.

"See, Detective Inspector Forde, Mrs Philip next door has been very helpful to the investigation, unlike the Rev here. Turns out they've been seeing each other for quite some time now. In fact, she left her husband six months ago, after she and Gareth agreed they were going to end their existing relationships, leave it a month or so, then announce they'd started seeing each other. Mrs Philip went through with it. Held up her end of the deal. But you didn't, did you, Gareth?"

"It was... It was easier for her. They both knew it wasn't working. For me, it was more difficult, I—"

"She put up with your excuses for months, but then finally gave you an ultimatum, didn't she, Gareth? Tell your wife, or she would," Logan continued. "And what was the date of that ultimatum, Reverend?"

Mann's reply was little more than a mumble. "Sunday."

"Sunday," said Logan. He slapped a hand on the table, underscoring the word. "The day your wife and daughter just happened to be murdered. That's one hell of a coincidence, is it not?"

"I did what she asked! I broke up with Lois. I ended it!" Mann cried. He set his mug down on the table, his hands shaking too much to safely hold onto it. "I did what she said!"

"And then, you went around to hers, didn't you? You got in a taxi, and you went to Kerry Philip's house."

Mann opened his mouth as if to protest, but Logan shut it down.

"We got the phone records from the church, Gareth. You called for a taxi at half-seven. We can check where it took you like *that*." Logan clicked his fingers with a loud *snap*. "So, I'd think very carefully before lying to us."

"Alright. Alright, yes. I went to see her," Mann said. He sat forward, propping his elbows on the table and holding his head in his hands. "I phoned her. After, I mean. To say it was done. That I'd broken it off with Lois. I expected her to be happy, but she was... distant. I don't know. Just... something felt off."

"So, you went round," Logan said. "Your mobile says you were at the church. Why didn't you take it?"

"I suppose... habit. I'd always leave it if we were meeting up somewhere. Was terrified the location tracking would give me away if Lois ever went poking about in it."

"You could've turned the location tracking off," Ben said. He was fairly certain this was the case, although he wouldn't have the first bloody clue as to where to start.

Mann shook his head. "That'd have rung alarm bells. She was always suspicious. Even before Kerry and I..." He swallowed back his shame. "Even before."

"What happened when you got to her house?" Logan asked, in the tone of someone who already knew precisely what had happened, but wanted to hear it from the horse's mouth.

The horse in question shifted around in his seat for a

while, before eventually replying. "He was there. Bryan. Kerry had apparently texted me, warning me not to come over, but... Well. I didn't have my phone. She, uh, she came to the door, and I told her that I'd left Lois. That I was hers now. That we could be together." He smiled, but it was a mask to hide his upset. "And, well, what do you know? Bryan heard all of it. He... Let's say, he didn't take it well."

"He chinned you," Logan said.

"He did, yes. But, I don't want him charged. I don't want the..." He sighed as the utter pointlessness of what he was saying fully occurred to him. "The scandal."

"Aye, I think we can safely say that particular genie's already out of the lamp, Gareth," Logan told him. "Front desk has been fending off calls from the press all day. 'Man of God Murders Family.' That's a juicy headline right there."

"I'm not... I didn't..." Mann sat back in his chair, still holding his head. He bumped his elbows together a few times, like he was trying to fend off a complete mental breakdown, then let his hands drop into his lap. "I think... I think I should have a solicitor."

"Oh, now you want a solicitor, Gareth?" Logan asked. "Why now? What's changed?"

"I just... It feels like you're railroading me."

"You'll know when I'm bloody railroading you, son," Logan told him, his face darkening. "Who was upstairs?"

The Reverend glanced to the ceiling, either seeking guidance from God or trying to see through to the floor above. "Upstairs?" he asked. "Where?"

"At your house. The night Lois and Ruby were killed. Who was upstairs?"

Gareth looked to Ben for support. Or an explanation,

maybe. Something that would help him answer the question, anyway.

"Ruby, I suppose? She'd have gone to bed around—"

"While you were arguing. You and Lois. In the living room," Logan barked, cutting him off. "There was a man upstairs in Ruby's bedroom. Who was it?"

The reaction from the minister would have been very difficult to fake, Logan knew. The mention of some unknown man lurking in his daughter's bedroom dilated his pupils and made his breath catch at the back of his throat.

He grabbed for the table, like he was desperately in need of some sort of anchor to hold him here. To stop him falling through the floor and into whatever murky abyss lay beneath it. Two tears ran down his cheeks and dripped from his chin, perfectly in unison the whole way, like synchronised divers on a quest for Olympic gold.

"I don't... I don't know. What man? When?" he wheezed. "Who? What are you talking about? I don't know what you're talking about!"

"You're alright, son. Take it easy," Ben said.

"Take it easy? *Take it easy*? How can I take it easy?" Mann demanded. "You're wasting time with me in here when you know the person who killed my wife and daughter is out there! Right now!"

His voice was becoming louder and more shrill, as grief knotted his features and churned up his insides. Nothing that had been said before had hit him as hard. He'd known his wife and daughter were dead, of course. He'd been in no doubt of any of it.

But the mention of a man lurking up there... In his daughter's bedroom. Hiding.

Waiting.

That was the thing that did it. That was what opened the floodgates.

That was the thing that finally broke him.

"Oh, God, why?" he pleaded, sobs wracking his whole body, his gaze fixed beseechingly on a sky he couldn't see. "Not my Ruby. Please. *Please*. Not her. Not my little girl."

CHAPTER TWENTY-THREE

Down at the station's reception, Hamza had just finished thanking Kerry Philip for her time, when his phone beeped to signal an email had been received in the team's shared inbox.

He read it while he waited for the lift, and was still reading it when he almost bumped into Tyler and Sinead as they stepped out of the elevator.

"Alright, Ham?" Tyler asked. He'd referred to the newly-appointed DS as 'Sarge,' for a while, until, during a particularly heartfelt late-night conversation, Hamza had told him to cut it out, because it felt far too bloody weird.

This, of course, had made Tyler double-down and exclusively address him as, 'Detective Sergeant Khaled, *sah!*' for the next twenty-four hours, before switching back to all the old abbreviations, nicknames, and affectionately-intended insults.

"What?" Hamza asked. "Oh. Yeah. Sorry. Seen the email that just came in?"

Tyler shook his head. Sinead whipped out her phone and prodded it into life.

"The hair sample found in the cupboard in Ruby's room? Doesn't belong to either parent."

"Oh!" Tyler ejected. "Well, I mean... That's good, isn't it? If we find who it matches, that'll most likely tell us who our man upstairs is. Right?"

"You can't get a conclusive DNA match from hair, can you?" asked Sinead. "Not unless the root's attached."

"Also, no saying when it was left there," Hamza said. "Could've been there for a while."

"Pretty sure it was recent," Sinead said, not looking up from her phone.

"Where does it say that?" Hamza asked, peering down at his own.

"Hmm? Oh, no. It doesn't. But, if you look back at Palmer's original report, given the position where it was found, he reckons it was a recent addition."

Tyler shot Hamza a warning smile. "She'll be after your job soon, mate. I'd watch your back."

"Sample was from a Caucasian," Sinead said, reading from the email. There were annoyingly very few bits of information that could be gleaned about a person from a single strand of hair, but race was one of them.

"Given the racial diversity of the Highlands, that narrows the list of suspects down by about one percent," Hamza remarked. "Still, I guess it's me off the hook, at least."

"Diesel," said Sinead. She realised this made no sense whatsoever out of context and clarified. "There's traces of diesel or some kind of fuel in the hair."

"What, like, absorbed from the environment?" asked Tyler.

"Well, I doubt he was drinking it," Sinead replied.

"You never know up here," Tyler said.

None of them could argue with that. While in uniform, Sinead had encountered more than one individual whose choice of tipple came in one-litre bottles with a skull and crossbones on the label and a child-proof safety cap on the top. She'd even once helped to shut down a house party where over half of the guests had picked up their carry-outs from the paint supplies aisle at B&Q.

Still, it would take a pretty steady diesel drinking habit for it to show to such an extent in someone's hair. And, if that were the case, they were unlikely to be alive enough themselves to murder anyone.

"Where you headed to?" Hamza asked, slipping his phone back into his pocket.

"Off to talk to Will Strand," Tyler said.

DS Khaled looked blankly back at him.

"He's had a couple of warnings for stalking Lois Mann," Sinead explained. "And harassing two other women."

"He lives with his old dutch," Tyler said. "Think you met her. Elizabeth Strand?"

"The wifey outside the church? Oh, well, in that case..." Hamza patted Tyler on the upper arm and grinned at both detective constables. "Good luck!"

ELEANOR EDWARDS HATED WAITING. *Hated.* It.

As far as she was concerned, if you arranged a time to do something, then you stuck to it. It was just manners. Common decency. Even more so if you were meeting a friend, and you were the one who'd arranged the bloody thing in the first place.

"Chanelle. Get off the wall," she snapped, taking a draw on a *Lambert and Butler*. "I'm warning you."

A few feet away, a chubby four-year-old with two pierced ears and an attitude completely ignored said warning, and carried on teetering along the low wall outside the garden, holding onto the saggy wires of the fence to stop herself falling off.

Eleanor unlocked her phone, checked if she'd got a reply to her message, then blew out her smoke and her annoyance in one big puff. "Fuck's sake," she muttered, before raising her voice to a shout. "Sandra! Chop-chop! Fucking Bookbug!"

The was no movement from the house. The curtains were open upstairs and down, so they were awake, at least. Could they have left already? They'd better fucking not have. She'd gotten out of her pyjamas for this. Given Chanelle a bath and everything. If Sandra had pissed off to the library without them, Eleanor would be raging.

"Totally fucking *raging*," she said, stabbing a finger into Sandra's face on her phone, summoning her number from the device's memory. She clamped the phone to her ear, waiting for it to start ringing. "Chanelle. Off the wall. I'll no' tell you again."

With a look of unrestrained contempt, Chanelle jumped off the wall, landing on the flats of her feet with a *thack* that was presumably meant to sound more impressive than it actually did.

"Fix your face, you wee cow," Eleanor snapped, then she held a hand up to silence her already silent daughter as the handset began to *burrr-burrr* in her ear.

It took four or five rings before she heard Sandra's phone blasting out a tinny version of Pink's *Beautiful Trauma* from within the house. The living room window was open a crack —a compromise Sandra had reached with her boyfriend over his concerns about their son and passive smoking—and the music could clearly be heard through it.

Both it and the *burr*ing in Eleanor's ear stopped as Sandra's phone went to voicemail.

"Fuck's sake, Sandra. Come on. I'm outside waiting!" Eleanor hissed, after the default greeting invited her to leave a message.

Then, she squashed a thumb against the button that disconnected the call, grabbed the protesting Chanelle by the hand, and marched on up to the house's front door.

She knocked twice, opened the door, and went barrelling inside. "Sandra? You seen the time?" she called. "This fucking Bookbug thing's on in five minutes."

The house swallowed the words and replied with a hushed stillness.

Pulling her daughter along with her, Eleanor threw open the door to the open-plan living space and kitchen. "Come on, you lazy cow. This was your idea, not—"

The words dried in her throat, choking her. Silencing her. She heard Chanelle gasp, felt her chubby hand tightening its grip.

And, when her eyes fell on the shape on the floor, Eleanor Edwards covered her daughter's face.

And screamed.

"WANT HALF A TWIX?" Sinead asked.

Tyler frowned. "Can I no' have a whole Twix?"

"No, because then I'll have to eat a whole Twix, too."

Tyler regarded her with very little expression on his face, unclear as to why this might be considered a problem.

"And I don't want a whole Twix," Sinead explained. "I just want half a Twix."

This made very little sense to Tyler. A Twix, as far as he was concerned, qualified as a chocolate bar, in much the same was a Wispa, Aero, or Cadbury's Dairy Milk did. Buying a bar of chocolate, then only eating half of it, seemed pointless.

Nobody in their right mind would ever eat half a Curly Wurly, for example, so why eat half a Twix? Just because they were split into two distinct sections didn't mean you were only meant to eat one of them. It was just done for the sake of convenience.

"Well, just buy one and eat half of it, then," Tyler suggested. This, as far as he was concerned, solved the problem.

Sinead, however, disagreed.

"I'm not going to go carrying half a Twix around for the rest of the day, am I?" she said. "And I'm not going to bin it."

"Definitely don't bin it," Tyler cried, visibly appalled by the very suggestion. "Tell you what," he said, spying an opportunity. "I'll have one-and-a-half Twixes. And don't say I'm not good to you."

"Gee, thanks. You spoil me. You really do," Sinead told him as she dropped two Twixes into the basket alongside a triple pack of cheese-themed sandwiches, a bottle of water, and a can of Irn Bru.

Will Strand had so far proven elusive. The address they had for him was his mother's, but the house had been empty when they'd arrived, and neighbours had said she'd headed out a couple of hours before to pick up the newspapers and a few messages from the wee shop at the petrol station.

Neither of the neighbours on either side had seen Will for a few days, although they said he came and went quite rarely, and kept, 'funny hours.'

When pressed for more details, both neighbours said he mostly kept himself to himself, but they'd sometimes see him heading out for a walk at ten or eleven at night.

"Even in winter," the old woman living in the bungalow on the left had added. "*Especially* in winter, in fact, although maybe you just notice it more then, I suppose. But, aye, he's an odd fella that one, right enough. Very odd. I don't know how Lizzie copes. But, where are my manners? Will ye no' come away in for a wee cuppie of tea?"

The tea declined, and Elizabeth's house checked front and back, Tyler and Sinead had set out to retrace her steps, and had taken the opportunity to grab lunch at the petrol station.

It was one of those multi-purpose places that you found dotted around the Highlands, offering everything from hot sausage rolls to prescription medication; disposable barbecues to midge hoods; an eclectic range of stuffed toys to an even more diverse selection of pornographic magazines. This place did it all.

Petrol was also available, albeit almost as an afterthought.

Fort Augustus was almost bang-on halfway between Inverness and the Fort, and anyone who travelled the road regularly was familiar with that petrol station. This was partly because of the range of goods it offered, and partly because of its close proximity to the public toilets.

If you stopped to buy fuel, you did so begrudgingly, and

only out of necessity, knowing full well that it would have been cheaper where you were coming from, and also where you were headed.

It was close to the toilets first, a cracking wee shop second, and the fact that it sold petrol was very occasional a welcome, if expensive, bonus.

The woman behind the till smiled warmly when Tyler set the basket down. She was in her early fifties and had the look of a runner about her—skinny and wiry, and with a face that had served its time getting blasted by wind and rain.

Granted, that rain-blasted look was par for the course across most of the Highlands, but runners usually had it worse, every other bugger more sensibly choosing to get indoors or cower under a brolly during the worst downpours.

"Get everything you need?" she asked, taking the sandwich from the basket and scanning it.

"We did, thanks," Sinead said, shaking out the little foldable shopping bag she kept attached to her car keys. "We were wondering, though, has Elizabeth Strand been in this morning?"

"Lizzie?" The attendant paused, mid-scan of a Twix, and looked both detectives up and down. "I don't know. Why? Who's asking?"

Tyler produced his warrant card and held it out for the attendant to see. She regarded it suspiciously, like it might be a fake.

"We think she might have some information that could be useful," he said. "She was chatting to a couple of our colleagues recently, and was very helpful."

"Is this about Lois and Ruby?" the attendant asked. There were a few other people in the shop, but all too far away to hear the conversation. She lowered her voice, anyway. "Did he do it? Reverend Mann? Did he kill Lois and that poor little girl?"

"We're pursuing a number of lines of inquiry," Sinead said, pitching her voice somewhere between 'bright and breezy' and 'officious bastard who might well sling you in the jail.' "Nobody has been charged with anything at this stage."

It was very clear from her face that this was not the juicy gossip the attendant had been hoping to hear. "Oh," she said, dropping the Twix into Sinead's bag and reaching for the bottle of water. "That's good."

"So...?" Sinead prompted. "Elizabeth Strand?"

"She was in earlier," the attendant said. "Getting her papers and milk, I think." She scanned the water with a *bleep* and placed it in the bag. "And asking about Billy."

"Billy? You mean Will? Her son?" Sinead asked.

The attendant nodded, and carried on scanning.

"Why was she asking about him?"

"Well, he's meant to be working, isn't he?" the woman replied. "Due in yesterday for his shift. No sign."

"He works here?" Sinead asked. "Will Strand works here?"

"Part-time, yeah. Sixteen hours or so. Not usually on the checkouts, though." The attendant nodded out through the front window at the rows of fuel pumps all lined up there. "He mostly deals with the fuel deliveries. You know? The petrol and the diesel."

LOGAN WAS JUST CONSIDERING WRAPPING up the interview when the voice of Detective Superintendent Mitchell came crackling over the room's speaker.

"DCI Logan. A word."

Logan and Ben both turned in surprise to the mirror that lined one wall of the interview room. They'd had no idea that anyone was in there. That was the whole point of the set-up, of course, but while it was standard for the person being interviewed not to know who was on the other side of the glass, it was generally expected that those doing the interviewing would be aware.

Logan turned to Ben and made a vague gesture in the direction of the recording controls. "I think we're about done here for now, anyway," he said, standing up. "Thank you for all your help, Gareth. I appreciate that none of it could've been easy for you."

Reverend Mann gawped up at the much taller man. "What? You mean... I can go?"

"You can, yes," Logan said. "DI Forde—Ben—will help ensure you have everything you need."

"I want to see them," the Reverend said. "Lois and... and Ruby. I want to see them. Is that possible?"

"It's... possible," Logan conceded, although the look on his face made it very clear he didn't think it was particularly advisable. "Ben will discuss all that with you."

Logan put a hand lightly on DI Forde's back and looked down at him, an eyebrow raised. Ben nodded to confirm he would take care of it, then Logan said a brief farewell to the minister, with a promise to follow-up with him soon, and left the room.

The outer door to the observation room was open and waiting for him. He closed it behind him, then opened the inner door and stepped into the half-darkness.

Detective Superintendent Mitchell stood with her back to the window, her hands crossed behind her like a soldier standing at ease. On the other side of the glass, Ben and Gareth Mann were still talking, although the audio feed had been turned down, so it would require some pretty adept lip-reading to work out what they were saying.

It would be mostly waffle, Logan knew. Ben would be keeping Mann talking for a few minutes, just in case the DSup had called him away to deliver some devastating new evidence that would expose the Reverend as a liar and send the interview in some new, unexpected direction.

A couple of minutes would do it, then Ben would assume no such revelations were coming, and the once prime suspect could assume the role of grieving father and husband.

For now, at least.

"Everything alright?" Logan asked, getting straight to business.

"Not remotely, no," Mitchell said, and everything about her—every intonation, every line of her face—told Logan this was serious.

Christ. What had he done this time?

"We've got another one," she said. "Young mother and her son. Dingwall. Pathology and Scene of Crime are en route. Details—what little we currently have—should be in your inbox."

"Shite. Same M.O.?" Logan asked, patting down his pockets as he tried to find his phone.

"That's for you to ascertain, Detective Chief Inspector," Mitchell told him, a hint of reproach in there somewhere.

"Right, aye," Logan said, finally tracking his phone to his left trouser pocket. He took it out and checked the inbox. "Bloody press is going to get wind of this. We'll need to—"

"I've already started to put together a statement."

Logan glanced up from his screen, frowning. "What, before passing the news on to me?"

Mitchell tapped the side of her head. "Up here. While waiting for you to get your finger out. It's called multi-tasking, Jack. You should really look into it."

"Sounds a bit too much like hard work," Logan remarked, his gaze returning to his phone. "Jesus. A three year old?"

"I don't like the way this is going, Detective Chief Inspector," Mitchell said, her lips drawing back over her teeth in distaste. "I want it dealt with. Gone. Find whoever's responsible, and do it quickly. You can have any resources you need."

"*Any* resources?"

"That's what I said, yes," the Detective Superintendent replied. She held up a finger, silencing Logan's next question before it could make it out of his mouth. "With the exception of a new car."

LOGAN WAS CROSSING the car park when he heard his name. Or a stab at it, at least.

"Uh, Inspector... Chief Logan?"

It took him a moment to place the Welsh accent, then a moment more to find the owner. Gwynn Dugdale, the postman who'd spotted Lois Mann's body through the living room window, was standing with one foot on the ground, and one still in the driver's footwell of a Vauxhall Astra so clapped-out it almost made Logan reevaluate the Fiesta.

Almost.

Gwynn gave a nervous little wave and held up a plastic-wrapped package.

"Found the parcel," he said, as Logan approached. He waggled it for emphasis. "It got returned to the depot, right enough. Was a bit of a panic to find it, but we got there."

"That's great, Mr Dugdale. Thank you."

The packaging of the parcel was a dark purple postage bag, the colour of an old bruise. It had been placed inside a clear plastic bag, presumably by the Royal Mail, and sealed at the top. Logan had a prod and a squeeze at it when Gwynn handed it over, like a kid at Christmas trying to figure out what his presents were.

"Feels like clothing," he remarked.

Gwynn nodded enthusiastically. "There's a company name on the back of the packaging. A label thing. I looked them up." His face suddenly took on a worried expression, like he shouldn't have just admitted that. "Just... I mean, I just Googled the name. That's alright, isn't it?"

"It is. Very industrious of you," Logan said, setting his mind at rest. "And?"

"T-shirt company," Gwynn said. "Down south. Stuff from independent designers, mostly."

"I see," said Logan, his interest in the package waning somewhat. He wasn't sure what he'd expected, or how he'd hoped it might impact the case, but a t-shirt was unlikely to prove helpful. He tucked it under his arm and fixed Gwynn with a look that was half 'much appreciated' and half 'get the hell out of my way, I'm in a hurry.' "Well, thank you for handing it in, Mr Dugdale. Was there anything else?"

"No. Yes. No." Gwynn muttered something chastising below his breath, then tried again. "I was just... We were all wondering. We heard Reverend Mann was taken in. And, well, we just can't believe it."

The postman lowered his voice and glanced around the

car park, like he was the one about to reveal some major bit of gossip.

"Did he do it? Was it really him?"

"I'm afraid I can't discuss an ongoing case, Mr Dugdale," Logan told him. "However, I'm sure Reverend Mann won't mind me telling you that he's being released without charge. It's going to be a difficult time for him, and I hope the community rallies around. Maybe you could help make that happen?"

"Me?" Gwynn spluttered. "I mean... I could try, but—"

"Excellent. Thank you," Logan said, cutting off any objections. "He's going to be in a bad way. He'll need all the help he can get."

"Right. It's just... I'm not going to be down the road for a couple of days. Thought I'd check into a hotel up here. Go to the cinema. Do some shopping. Clear the head." He indicated through one of the rear windows of his car. A rucksack was jammed in behind the driver's seat. "That's alright, isn't it? If you need me to head back down, I can. But, you've got my number..."

"No. That's fine, Mr Dugdale. If we need you, we can get hold of you. Enjoy your stay."

"Thanks, I just thought it'd be nice to get—"

But Logan was already walking again, his long legs striding him across the car park, the package still jammed in between his arm and his ribcage. "Sorry, excuse me," he said, not looking back. "There's somewhere I need to be."

CHAPTER TWENTY-FOUR

THE MOMENT OF ARRIVAL AT A MURDER SCENE WAS always a confusing one, filled with conflicting emotions.

On the one hand, it killed you. Not all the way, of course. Just a little. Sometimes, not even enough that you'd even notice. Each scene was a draw on a cigarette. A single drop of poison. Not enough to finish you off in one go, but over time it killed you, all the same.

On the other hand, that moment of turning onto the street, seeing the cordon tape, and the Uniforms, and the bustling figures in the white paper suits was when Logan truly felt most alive.

Those were the moments when he knew, deep in his core, that he was in the right job. The right place. The right time. The moments when he knew he could make a difference. Right a wrong. Bring peace to some poor bastard's ghost.

He'd been away for almost a year. This was his first murder scene since then as Senior Investigating Officer.

And, as he heaved himself out of his undersized car, it felt like he'd never left.

"You. Aye, you. With the glaikit look on your face," he said, jabbing a finger in the direction of a uniformed constable who had been leaning on a fence, idly staring into space.

The officer's face registered his surprise and annoyance at being spoken to in such a way.

"Excuse me?" he said, striding across to intercept the newcomer. "This is a crime scene, you need to turn around right now, and—" He shifted gears when Logan produced his ID, his back straightening and his downward-sloping eyebrows rising in surprise. "Good afternoon, sir. Constable Windram, uh, reporting for duty. Sir."

"You're already on duty, son," Logan reminded him. "You might want to try looking like it." He pointed to the cordon that had been set up across the middle of the street like the finishing line of a marathon. "Get that shifted further down the road. I want it set up on the other side of that house. It's far too close."

"I, uh, I thought putting it here was better, sir," Windram explained. He indicated a junction running off at a right angle from the road they stood on. "That way, it blocks anyone coming along the street *and* round that corner."

"Is there a shortage of bloody tape, or something?" Logan demanded

"Sir?"

Logan turned and made a series of sweeping motions with an outstretched finger, practically painting his instructions in the air. "One across there, another across the entrance to the side road. Got that?"

"Right, sir. Yes. Will do."

"Good. It's no' rocket science, son. And get onto your pal over on the other side," the DCI continued, looking past the throng of police vehicles to where another cordon had been set up. "Get them to push further along the street, too. If the press turns up, I want them kept out of my way. Preferably, out of my sight. Got that?"

Windram snapped off a nod. "Got it, sir."

"Right. And, a word of advice, son. When you're standing there, at least try and appear interested, eh? And, if you can't do interested, I'll settle for awake. That clear?"

The constable's cheeks reddened. "Very clear, sir," he confirmed.

And then, with a grunt, Logan went marching off in the direction of the house.

If you didn't count the Uniform who'd first responded to the call, and the paramedics who'd no doubt trampled all through the place soon afterwards, Logan was the first on the scene.

After getting suitably gloved up and slipping his feet into a fetching set of plastic blue shoe coverings, he entered the house for a wee poke around.

An adult female lay half in the kitchen, half in a small dining room that was barely large enough to accommodate the four-seater table contained within it. There was no door separating the rooms, just an archway, and the body was wedged in against one side of it, an arm folded awkwardly below the torso.

She was on her back. Eyes open. Vomit clogging her nose and plastered down one side of her face.

Her skin was a blueish-white. The colour of cold. There was a puddle of water on the click-vinyl flooring of the kitchen, and the dining room carpet squelched faintly beneath Logan's foot as he tested it.

It took him only a few seconds to spot the murder weapon. It wasn't a jug this time, but a plastic basin—the kind generally found in a kitchen sink. It lay on the floor in the dining room, an inch or two of water still sitting at the bottom.

There was no blood this time. No knife wounds. No pretence at suicide. She'd been drowned on dry land—in her own house—just like Lois Mann.

Logan briefly regarded the various rooms he passed through as he headed for the stairs, but didn't take much of them in. Modern. Bit untidy. Plenty of money on the go. There'd be time enough to get a fuller picture later.

After he'd seen the boy.

His name was Simon. The woman who had called emergency services had given it. She was a friend of the family or something. He'd talk with her soon. Find out what she could tell them.

After he'd seen the boy.

The stairs were covered in an incredibly thick, soft carpet like someone was paranoid about falling down them. It muffled Logan's footsteps, so only the crinkling of the bags on his feet could be heard as he padded slowly up to the floor above.

Simon's room was easy to identify. His name had been painted onto the fascia around the frame. Three times, no less—once across the top, then again vertically down each side. The styles were all different—stencil, bubble writing, and something more futuristic. They'd all been painted by the same inexpert hand, but with great care and attention.

Logan briefly contemplated checking in the other rooms

first. Just a quick peek. Just a few moments to prepare himself, that was all.

But, no. That would be a cop-out. He could check the other rooms later.

After he'd seen the boy.

"Right, then," he said to himself, then he fixed his gaze on the half-open door at the end of the landing, and began the long, lonely walk towards it.

THEY FOUND Elizabeth Strand sitting on a bench outside the church. She was knitting and sucking on a Mint Imperial like her life, and the lives of all those she'd ever loved, depended on it. The rattling of the mint against her teeth and the clicking of the knitting needles sounded like some sort of jazz percussion as Tyler and Sinead approached.

"Mrs Strand?" Tyler asked.

The DCs had agreed that Tyler would do most of the talking this time, given that women of a certain age tended to respond well to him. He put this down to his cheeky grin and winning personality. Sinead put it down to their failing eyesight and diminishing critical faculties.

Whatever the explanation, though, there was no denying that it got results.

Usually.

"Who's asking?" Elizabeth demanded, raising her head to glare at the couple while her hands continued to knit and purl uninterrupted.

Tyler watched hands, needles, and wool flying for a moment, as if hypnotised by the movement, then cranked up his smile and turned on the charm.

"Sorry to bother you, Mrs Strand. I'm Detective Constable Neish, but you're more than welcome to call me Tyler. This is Detective Constable Bell."

"Sinead," the other DC offered.

"I'm sure you're well aware of the recent tragedy," Tyler continued, his face suitably solemn and grave.

"Of course," Elizabeth replied. "What of it? Has Reverend Mann been found yet?"

"We, uh, we're not at liberty to say," Tyler told her.

The knitting paused, mid-stitch. "So that's a 'yes,' then. Did he do it? Did he kill them?"

Tyler's smile faltered just a little. "I'm afraid we're not at liberty to say that, either," he told her. "Investigations are ongoing. You know how these things are."

"Why would I know how 'these things are?' What are you suggesting?"

"I'm... No, I'm not suggesting anything," Tyler assured her.

"You'd better not be suggesting anything," Elizabeth warned. She switched her attention to Sinead. "He'd better not be suggesting anything."

"He isn't. He's—"

"I've never been in trouble before in my life. Not so much as a parking ticket," Elizabeth said, steamrolling over the rest of Sinead's reply. "So, no, young man. I don't 'know how these things are.' I don't have the faintest clue."

Her knitting resumed, but the smooth, flowing motion had been replaced by something much jerkier and more violent.

Sinead flung a sideways look in Tyler's direction, prompting him to get on with it. He opened his mouth, let it form the shape of various vowels and consonants without ever settling on any of them, then gave Sinead a nudge with an elbow.

Detective Constable Bell gave a little tut, before stepping into the hole in the conversation that Tyler had vacated.

"To be honest, Mrs Strand, it's not you we're looking for," she said. "It's your son. William."

The old woman muttered sharply as she dropped a stitch. "Drat!" She sighed, still not looking up, and began fiddling with the tips of the needles. "I don't know where he is. But he has nothing to do with... what happened."

"I'm sure he doesn't," Sinead agreed. "But, we'd like to have a word with him so we can—"

"Are you deaf?" Elizabeth spat, slamming her knitting down into her lap. "Will has nothing to do with what happened. Nothing. I just told you. I just said that."

"And, as *I* said, I'm sure you're right, and he has nothing to do with it," Sinead said, keeping her tone just on the right side of affable. "But, either we can have a quick word with him to clear up one or two things, or we can have half a dozen uniformed officers start the search for him at your house, in full view of the neighbours. Either one's fine by us, really. Whichever you'd prefer."

Elizabeth looked from one detective to the other, then stuffed her knitting into a small tartan bag that had been sitting at her feet, alongside her milk and other shopping she'd picked up at the petrol station.

"I honestly don't know where he is," she admitted. The confrontational tone had left her voice, and she somehow came across as much older without it. "He's... I haven't seen him in a few days. That's why I've been coming here every day, really. I thought, maybe, if I could get in and say a prayer. If… if Reverend Mann could offer some guidance… He's always been so good to me. So kind."

"When did you last see William?" Sinead asked.

Elizabeth pursed her lips and rolled her tongue around inside her mouth like she was trying to keep her teeth in place. She stared past the Detective Constables at the church behind them, tears nipping at her eyes.

Sinead sat on the bench beside her and spoke softly. "Mrs Strand? Elizabeth? It's very important that we speak to your son. Can you remember when the last time you saw him was?"

The old woman, who was getting older by the second, nodded, but it took her several more seconds to wrestle a reply through her unwilling mouth.

"Sunday," she said, in a voice that was barely a whisper. "I last saw him on Sunday." A tear broke through her defensive barricades and rolled down her cheek. "The day that Lois and Ruby were murdered."

CHAPTER TWENTY-FIVE

HE WAS SO SMALL. THAT WAS THE FIRST THING THAT struck DCI Logan as he stood in that doorway. So small, so vulnerable.

So dead.

While Ruby Mann had been in bed when she was attacked, Simon had been awake. Given the position of the body, he'd been lying on the floor, playing with some chunky plastic toy cars with dogs as drivers.

He still had one of the vehicles clutched in a tiny hand. It was blue, and the dog sitting in it was dressed like a police officer.

Had he been holding it, or had he grabbed for it during the attack, hoping it could somehow protect him? Come to his rescue? Whatever the reason, he'd clung tightly to it throughout his ordeal.

"You poor wee bugger," Logan whispered into the thick, soupy silence of the room. And then, because he felt that wasn't enough, he added: "I'm sorry."

Simon had been strangled. Shona would be able to

confirm when she turned up, of course, but it didn't take a medical degree to know the signs, just a depressing amount of past experience.

Capillaries had burst all over his face, hundreds of branching red lines turning his skin into a roadmap of suffering and pain. His eyes were so bloodshot they were almost two balls of pure crimson.

His mouth was open and his tongue lolled out like a dog's on a hot day. His t-shirt had flopped up over his neck, but Logan didn't need to see the bruising to know it existed. There were no ropes or straps lying around, so the killer had probably used their hands. A quick look at the bruises would be able to confirm, but he didn't feel the need to do that, quite yet.

Christ knew, the poor lad's body would be put through enough. Let him be, for now.

His gaze shifted away from Simon, searching for something else to fix on, but there was nothing particularly noteworthy about the bedroom. Nothing except the cupboards.

Two of them, built side by side into one wall of the room. The door on the right was closed. The one on the left was ajar and showed a thin, shadowy strip of the contents.

Logan nudged the door open a little more. There were three large built-in shelves inside holding towels, curtains, bedsheets, and the like. There was potentially enough room for someone to hide, as the shelves didn't come all the way to the door. It'd be tight, but manageable.

Returning that door to its starting position, he carefully pinched the very top and bottom of the long metal handle of the other cupboard, avoiding any parts that anyone else was likely to have touched.

This didn't give him much of a grip, and the door resisted

for a few seconds, before finally relenting and springing from the frame.

Logan hissed and drew back, fist clenching, when he saw the face of a man grinning at him from inside the cupboard.

No, not a man. A clown.

He relaxed when he realised the face was printed onto the lid of a board game box. It was someone called 'Mr Tumble,' apparently.

"Arsehole," Logan muttered in the box's general direction, then he considered the available space inside the cupboard.

Simon had a lot of toys. A *lot*. He also had a filing system that could best be described as 'haphazard'. The inside of the cupboard was a densely packed mound of fire trucks, teddies, building blocks, action figures, and a jumpy-ball-thing shaped like the planet Saturn, which looked like a bloody deathtrap.

There would be no room for anyone to hide in a cupboard like that. Not unless they were a particularly limber dwarf with a high tolerance for having jaggy bits of plastic poking into many of their more sensitive areas.

Logan closed the door again, offered the body of the boy on the floor an apologetic look, then headed for the door.

He stopped there, just out on the landing, but didn't turn back.

"We'll get him, son. I promise you that."

By the time the DCI returned down the stairs, a man with a face like an angry wee pug was marching up the path towards the house, his white paper suit crinkling as it rubbed together at the thighs.

"Oh, great," Logan muttered, as Geoff Palmer pushed open the front door. "The cavalry's arrived."

Elizabeth Strand's house was pretty much exactly as Tyler and Sinead had both privately expected it to be. It was reasonably sized, but fussy and cluttered so the rooms seemed smaller than they actually were.

A large bay window in the living room looked out onto the Caledonian Canal, but a faded net curtain blocked most of the view, and a small army of porcelain dolls stood as deterrents against anyone who might try getting close enough to peer through the yellowing mesh.

All four of the room's corners had tall, narrow units standing in them, each one crammed with ornaments and knick-knacks. Four more porcelain dolls, all dressed in Victorian style, stood atop the corner units, watching over the room with their painted eyes.

Probably planning how they were going to kill everyone in it, Tyler reckoned. The creepy wee bastards.

While Tyler kept an eye on the dolls, Sinead was getting down to some good old-fashioned polis work. Partly, this involved drinking tea. The other part was right now focused on listening to Elizabeth, and occasionally prodding her in whatever direction was most likely to draw out something useful.

They'd been over most of Will's school career at this point. He'd been quiet as a mouse in primary school, but had found confidence after the move up to secondary.

"Too much bloody confidence, I used to think," Elizabeth said. "Always talking back. Always with an *opinion*."

The way she said the word suggested she was perfectly happy that her son had opinions of his own, provided they were in complete alignment with hers. Evidently, this had not been the case in William's teenage years, and their relationship had become strained as time went on.

"Not enough for him to move out, though?" Tyler asked. He was fiddling with a little ornamental well on the mantelpiece, carefully winding the little wooden handle that raised and lowered a bucket the size of a child's thimble.

"We got past it. As he grew older, we agreed more and argued less," Elizabeth said, watching the DC closely. "Would you mind not touching that? It was my grandmother's."

Tyler gave the handle one last turn, then left the ornament be. Sinead shot him a very deliberate look, then dragged her eyes to the empty space on the couch beside her.

For once, Tyler got the message right away and came to join her. Unlike Sinead, who was perched on the very front of the settee, he sat back, and was immediately consumed by the cushions.

"Fuck!" he ejected, as everything from his thighs to his kidneys sank into the gap between the seat and its back. "Sorry, I mean... Oops."

He wriggled himself forward, pushing with his hands. The spongey cushion filling was determined not to make life easy, though, and it took him several seconds of manoeuvring before he could get himself into some semblance of a dignified sitting position.

"Comfy couch," he said, once he'd finally extracted himself from its clutches. He perched on the front, like Sinead, supported by the wooden frame, and lifted the ornate china cup and saucer from the glass coffee table. "This mine, is it?"

"You said you didn't want any," Elizabeth reminded him.

Tyler paused with the cup almost to his lips. "Oh. Aye."

He set the cup and saucer down again in silence, then watched as Elizabeth picked it up and took a sip.

"I can make you some, if you like?" she said, but in a way that heavily implied she'd never forgive him if he said yes.

"No, no. I'm grand," Tyler insisted. "I'd only be peeing all the way back up the road."

Silence hung over the room for a few moments, the ticking of two different clocks on two different walls the only sound.

"Right," Elizabeth said, having presumably gone over a few other possible responses before settling on the one least likely to continue that particular conversation. "Fair enough."

Sinead smiled patiently. "Sorry, Elizabeth. You were telling us about you and Will's relationship?"

"Master and skivvy?" Elizabeth said, only half-smiling. "No. That's not true. Although... feels like it, sometimes, right enough. I'm forever doing his washing, ironing, making his dinners, a piece for his work. I don't mind, of course. Mother's job, isn't it? That stuff. I bet your mothers still run after you pair, don't they?"

Tyler knew that one would've stung Sinead, but if it did, she didn't show it. Not on her face, anyway.

Out of sight of the old woman, Tyler put a hand in the small of Sinead's back, and felt her lean her weight against it for support.

"That's what we're for," Elizabeth continued. "And, do I wish he'd moved out? Yes. But for his sake, not mine. I love having him here. I'll always love having him here. I just wish he'd settled down, you know? Found someone nice. Kind. Someone who'll look after him, after I've..."

She took another swig of her tea and smiled, not quite meeting either detective's eye.

"Well. You know."

"He's never had a serious relationship, then?" Sinead asked.

"Will? No. Not for want of me trying, mind. I'm always trying to set him up with people. At church. In town. Some-times, and this is silly, I'll give you, if I see someone nice in the paper—the local paper, I mean—I'll cut it out and show him it. 'Here,' I'll say. 'What about her?' He's never inter-ested. And, I mean, you could probably get the number, couldn't you? Off the paper, if you rang them?" She gave a slow, sad shake of her head. "But, no. He never tries. He's never interested. Ungrateful, that's what he is. Ungrateful."

"I'm, eh, I'm sure he appreciates everything you do for him," Sinead said.

Elizabeth closed her eyes and smiled for a moment, clearly embarrassed about what she'd said. "Sorry, you must think I'm desperate to get rid of him. I'm not, honestly. I just... I want him to be happy. To find someone, like I found his father, God rest his soul."

Her gaze went to an old black and white wedding photo-graph on one wall. The movement appeared reluctant, though, like it knew the thing it alighted on would be painful.

"It's not good to be alone," she said. "It's important to have someone. Don't you think?"

"Aye," said Sinead, feeling the warmth of Tyler's hand supporting her. "I do."

CHAPTER TWENTY-SIX

LOGAN STOOD IN A FINE MIST OF RAIN, DRINKING COFFEE from a paper cup. He was usually a tea man, but the only place to get a hot drink nearby was the petrol station, which had one of those *Costa Express* machines that seemed to be popping up everywhere.

He'd instructed the Uniform who'd been hand-selected for the task—mostly on account of being the first officer Logan had spotted after leaving the house—to bring back the plainest, blackest variant of the drink as it was possible to get.

What he'd returned with had been the opposite of both those things. The machine, it transpired, did not do 'plain'. The coffees it offered were one scoop of ice cream away from being a milkshake, and Logan glanced disparagingly at the plastic lid between each grudged sip.

"What's a nice guy like you doing in a place like this?"

Logan turned to find Shona Maguire standing behind him, the rain matting her hair to her head. She carried a large backpack over one shoulder, and wore a heavy waterproof jacket that was doing a much better job of keeping the rain off than Logan's overcoat was.

"I enjoy the atmosphere," Logan told her.

"How's the legs?"

"Well, they've stopped feeling like they're on fire," the DCI replied. "So, that's something."

"You did well," Shona told him. "I thought you'd drop out well before the top."

"Drop dead, more like," Logan said. "It was a close-run thing, let me tell you."

Shona looked past him to the terraced house at the centre of all the action. A haze of rain surrounded the place like a thin fog, giving it a vaguely supernatural appearance.

"What have we got?"

"Similar to the last one. I mean, near-identical," Logan said. "Mother and young son. He was strangled, I'm thinking. Up in his bedroom."

"And the mother?"

Logan sucked in his bottom lip. He didn't want to say it out loud. Not if he could help it. If he said it out loud, it cemented the connection. Created the link. Saying it out loud meant there was no way to avoid discussing the implications of what it meant.

"Drowned," he said, then he kept right on talking in the hope it stopped the next question. "I mean, you'll be the best person to know for sure."

"Oh. Bloody hell. So... are you thinking serial killer, then?" Shona asked.

Damn. And there it was.

"I mean, I know it's early days, but two near-identical double killings just a couple of days apart with the same

M.O. That's got to be the same killer. Right?" Shona continued.

"We try not to make assumptions like that until we have all the evidence," Logan said. A sigh found its way out from somewhere deep inside him. "But, it's looking like the most likely explanation, aye. Cause of death was never given out to the press. If this is the same—if that woman has been drowned—then either the same killer is responsible for all four murders, or we've another leak that's in sore need of plugging."

Logan wasn't sure which he'd prefer. Or, if it even made a difference.

"Hate to say it, but looks like we won't be hitting the hotspots of Nairn on Sunday," Shona said.

"No. Doesn't look like it," Logan agreed. He tutted and shook his head. "Inconsiderate lot, these murdering bastards. Never a thought for anyone else's plans."

Shona reached into her bag and produced her phone. "That reminds me. I'd better text Olivia and let her know our movie night's off tonight."

Logan watched her tapping at the screen. "I can have a word with her, if you like? Get her to stop coming over."

With a final flurry of taps, Shona finished the text. There was a *whoosh* from the phone as the message went flying into the electronic ether.

"It's fine. I don't think she has anyone else to just hang out with. Her mother's useless."

"She doesn't mention anything, does she?" Logan asked. "About Bosco's old business?"

"No. Not a thing," Shona said, looking a little surprised by the question. "As far as I know, once Bosco was locked up, that was her involvement over."

Logan nodded. "Right. Good," he said, although he wasn't entirely convinced. Bosco may have played the big man, but he was just one of many links in one of the many chains that had been bringing drugs into Scotland for decades. Those who were in, in whatever capacity, rarely ever got the chance to get all the way back out again.

Olivia was just a kid, but to the people further up the chain, that just made her all the more useful.

"If she does mention anything, let me know, will you?" Logan asked.

"Of course. Aye."

A figure appeared in the open doorway of the house, dressed head to toe in white, and looking a bit like a podgy ghost. Geoff Palmer shot a look of irritation out at the world, then spotted Shona and made a sharp beckoning motion with one gloved hand.

"Oh. Your man's calling," Logan told her.

Shona groaned out a low laugh. "I was about to go in, too. I feel I should stay here as a matter of principle."

"Too bloody right," Logan said.

"Shit. He's coming over," Shona whispered, fixing a smile on her face as Palmer came thundering up the path. "Geoff! There you are. DCI Logan was just filling me in."

"Oh, he bloody wishes," Palmer spat, shooting a look of disgust at the detective that bounced right back at him. "You do know we've got two dead bodies in there, yes? You know we're waiting on you before we can proceed?"

It was, Shona had to admit, a pretty fair point. She conceded it with a nod, shoved her phone back into her bag, then flashed Logan a farewell smile. "Talk to you soon."

"Aye. I'll give you a ring," Logan said, making damn sure that Palmer heard. "We'll get that wee getaway rearranged."

He felt the heat of Palmer's glare and chose to just smile genially back at him as Shona hoisted her bag onto her shoulder and headed for the house.

"Everything alright, Geoff?" Logan asked.

Palmer's words were a low, cold hiss. "I thought we agreed...?"

"Agreed what?"

"She's off-limits!"

Logan shrugged. "Apparently, nobody thought to tell her." He placed a hand on Palmer's shoulder. The weight of it almost buckled the smaller man's legs. "Still, plenty more fish in the sea, eh?"

Palmer wrenched himself out of the DCI's grip. "Now, listen here—" he began, before Logan cut him off.

"You do know you've got two dead bodies in there, yes?" he said, indicating the house with a tilt of his head. "You know they're waiting on you before they can proceed?"

A few seconds passed, in which Palmer wagged a finger and made a variety of noises that sounded like the first syllable of several potential responses.

But then, having failed to come up with anything suitably scathing, he turned and went storming up the path. It would've been a far more impressive exit had his paper suit not been chafing at the thighs, forcing him to exit to a soundtrack of crinkling and rustling.

Logan was enjoying the moment when it was rudely interrupted by a uniformed constable. "Uh, sir?" she said. "Bad news, I'm afraid."

"What now?" Logan asked, turning towards her. "Not another body, is it?"

The young constable shook her head. "Worse, sir," she said. She jabbed a thumb back over her shoulder in the direction of the cordon tape fifty yards along the street. "The press is here."

CHAPTER TWENTY-SEVEN

THE DOOR TO WILL STRAND'S BEDROOM WAS LOCKED. There was no actual locking mechanism built into the door itself, but at some point in the past he'd drilled a hole in the frame and added a small sliding lock and padlock combo.

"Like I said, I don't mind you going in, but I don't have a key," Elizabeth explained.

They were all huddled in the narrow L-shaped landing at the top of the stairs. The house was one-and-a-half storeys high, and the slant of the roof intersected the top of the wall beside Tyler's head, forcing him to lean sideways.

"Are you sure, Mrs Strand?" Sinead pressed. "It would be really useful if we could get a look inside."

"I wish I could help, dear. I really do," Elizabeth said. "But he takes the key with him. Won't even let me in to tidy up. I haven't been in there in years."

"And he doesn't have a spare lying around? Sinead asked. "We want to help your son. We really do. But, to do that, we need to have a look in there."

The floorboards squeaked as Elizabeth shifted her weight

from one foot to the other, her hands wringing together. "I just... I don't think he'd like anyone poking around in there. He's a very private person. Very private."

Tyler pursed his lips. "Look, I didn't really want to say this, Mrs Strand, but our concern is that Will might be in there. Maybe in need of help."

Elizabeth's eyes went to the door, suddenly all wide and worried.

"What? No. Oh, no!"

"Do you maybe have a screwdriver?" Tyler asked. "We can pop this lock off and just make sure he's not in trouble?"

Elizabeth pushed past Sinead and rapped her bony knuckles on the door. "Will? William? Are you there?"

The silence that followed did nothing to prove Tyler wrong. "It could be serious, Mrs Strand. We don't have much time."

The old woman was halfway down the stairs before she replied. "I've got a wee screwdriver set in the kitchen. I'll get it!"

Sinead waited until Elizabeth had thumped down the last few steps and gone dashing towards the kitchen before she spoke.

"You don't really think he's in there, do you?"

Tyler shook his head and smirked. "Nah. I mean, maybe, but I doubt it. That was just what you'd call reverse psychology in action." He winked. "Stick with me, kid, and you'll learn a thing or two. Think of me as your own personal Yoda."

"Aye, well," Sinead snorted. "I always thought you were a bit of a Muppet. I think it was just normal-direction psychology, too. And *of course,* he's not in there."

Tyler frowned. "How can you be so sure?"

Sinead pointed to the lock. The lock on the outside of the door.

It took Tyler a few seconds to understand, and a fraction of that time to come up with a cover story for himself.

"Yep. Exactly. Hoped you'd spot that," he said. "Full marks, Detective Constable."

Before Sinead could reply to that, Elizabeth came hurrying up the stairs again, a small plastic tub clutched in both hands.

She was out of breath when she reached the top and thrust the container out for Tyler to take without uttering a word.

"Thanks," the DC said, peeling the lid off the tub. A variety of tools, mostly all ancient and in bad shape, lined the bottom of the box.

Selecting the smallest screwdriver, Tyler nudged Sinead aside and set to work removing the screws that held the slide lock in place.

"Should I call an ambulance?" Elizabeth asked, her breath returning in a series of rasping wheezes.

"Let's just see if we need them, first," Sinead said. "It's possible that he isn't in there."

"Then where is he?" asked the old woman, and there was a rising panic in her voice. "If not there, then where?"

"We're going to do our best to find out. I promise," Sinead assured her. "If he's not here, then hopefully we'll find something that tells us where he might be."

"He's not a bad boy," Elizabeth said, although it wasn't immediately apparent who she was trying to convince. "He's not a bad boy, he just... He must be so lonely. So lonely."

Tyler gave a triumphant little cheer, then set the lock

he'd removed on top of the gloss-painted bannister beside him.

"You might want to hang back," Sinead warned Elizabeth, as Tyler pushed open the door to Will's bedroom.

A smell rolled out that forced DC Neish to withdraw a pace. For a moment, he considered the possibility that maybe Will Strand *was* in that room, until he remembered the lock he'd just removed.

Of course, they'd assumed Will had locked it himself. What if he hadn't? What if Elizabeth had locked him in? He glanced back at her, just briefly, not wanting to draw her attention.

God, could she have done it? Could she have committed the murders? Could she have done away with her son, then gone to Lois and Ruby's house and—?

"He's not in there," said Sinead, peeking around the door frame.

Elizabeth pressed the flat of a hand against her chest, like she was trying to force her heart back in. "Oh, thank the Lord," she whispered, sagging against the bannister.

So, 'no,' was the answer to his question, Tyler decided. Elizabeth Strand almost certainly wasn't the killer.

"Mind if we open the window in here?" Sinead asked, stepping into the room. "It's a bit... stale."

'Stale' was too kind a descriptor for the odour in the room. The air was thick with the smell of tobacco and cannabis, sweaty socks, dirty dishes, and bedsheets that likely hadn't been changed in several months.

A laundry basket stood in one corner, its contents having spilled out over the sides so they lay in little heaps on the floor around it.

A pair of skid-marked boxer shorts hadn't made it as far

as the basket, instead, getting caught on the corner of a fifty-inch TV that was surrounded by overflowing ashtrays and empty beer bottles. Four different games consoles lay on the floor, cables tethering them to the TV like spacecraft attached to their mothership.

The walls were covered in the same old-fashioned floral wallpaper as much of the rest of the house. Evidently, it wasn't to Will's tastes, because he'd elected to hide most of it behind several large glossy posters, mostly of perky, smiling, dead-eyed young women with their tits out. Four of them—a full fifty percent—straddled motorbikes, or lay draped across the bonnets of sports cars.

"Look at the state of this place," Elizabeth said, bustling into the bedroom behind the detectives. "I've been telling him to bring me his washing for months now."

"It'd be better if you didn't touch anything, Mrs Strand," Sinead said, but Elizabeth was already bending to retrieve something from the floor by the unmade single bed.

"Why's there a big pile of socks here?" she wondered. She ran the material through her fingers. "And why's this one all crinkly?"

Tyler side-eyed Sinead, but said nothing.

Elizabeth seemed to pick up on the thought, regardless, and immediately dropped the sock back onto the pile.

"Oh," she said, brushing her hands together. She looked around the room in disgust, then shook her head. "I'll be downstairs," she said. "You two can do what you like. I give you my full permission."

She was barely out of the room when Sinead cracked open the window, and gratefully inhaled the swirl of fresh air that billowed the half-shut curtains.

"God. Stinks in here," she remarked, just in case Tyler's

nose had stopped working. She turned and came eye-to-nipple with one of the women on the wall. "He's a class act, right enough."

"Shit!" Tyler said. It was more an exclamation of surprise and wonder than of dismay. "His computer's open."

Sinead spun around to find Tyler bent over a shoddy, shoogly desk. A small flatscreen monitor stood like an obelisk on top of it, surrounded by empty mugs and sweetie wrappers. The screen was currently displaying a slightly stretched image of the actress, Megan Fox, bent over a car in tight denim shorts, in a scene from the *Transformers* movie.

There were several icons layered down one side of the image, and as Tyler moved the mouse an arrowhead white pointer darted around the screen accordingly.

"Probably didn't bother password protecting it since he had the door padlocked," Sinead said, picking her way through the dirty laundry and other debris until she joined Tyler at the desk. "Can we go through it?"

"You heard his mum. She gave her permission."

"Well, yeah, but can she give permission for us to go through his stuff?"

"It's her house," Tyler reasoned.

"But, it's his room. His computer," Sinead countered.

Tyler thought about this for a few seconds, then shrugged. "Fuck it," he said, and he slipped onto the seat, opened a browser window, and clicked on the 'History' tab.

CHAPTER TWENTY-EIGHT

IT WAS FAIR TO SAY THAT YOU'D BE HARD-PRESSED TO find any big fans of the local or national press in the ranks of Police Scotland. Certainly not among those working on the front lines, anyway.

Granted, the media had its uses. It could be invaluable, if used correctly. The problem—at least, as far as most of the polis was concerned—was journalists themselves.

Logan didn't tend to like making generalisations, but he was prepared to go on record to say that they were all bastards. Individually and collectively. Every last one of them. Utter, total, absolute bastards.

This was not some bias on his part. It was not an unreasonable conclusion to have drawn. They had proven themselves bastards time and time again. He'd given them ample opportunity to demonstrate some other side to themselves— some non-bastard side that they kept buried deep down—and they had consistently disappointed him.

Bastards. That's what they were. Every single one.

He had made a point of shouting most of this at them as

he'd gone storming over to the cordon tape. It was important, he thought, that they knew where he stood, and he'd made sure to make the rant sufficiently foul-mouthed that there was no possible way they could quote him on any of it.

It was mostly the local bunch there at the moment—the Highland News, the Inverness Courier, the Press & Journal —but there was a BBC van parked down the street that Logan very much did not like the look of.

"What can you tell us about what happened?" asked one of the journalists.

He was a particularly scrawny specimen, and almost jumped out of his skin when Logan barked, "Fuck all," at him in his less than dulcet tones.

"We've heard—" another of the bastards began, but he, too, was quickly shouted down.

"We'll release a statement when we've got something to say, alright? I'll personally make sure you three are the first to know. So, you can either stand around here getting soaked to the arse, or you can piss off back to whatever holes in the ground you crawled out of, and wait for us to phone you."

There was some shuffling and general uneasiness at that. Logan looked across their faces, pausing at each one to drill into it with his stare.

"So, what's it to be?"

Nobody said anything. Not right away. There was a bit of vague mumbling, some more shuffling, and then the woman from the P&J piped up.

"I'll, eh, I'll hang off here. Thank you."

The two men made some agreeing noises and nodded.

Logan hadn't really expected anything else. He'd hoped for it, of course. He'd hoped they'd pack up and clear off, and sit waiting by their phones for a call that would never come, but he knew they wouldn't. He wasn't that lucky.

"Fine. Your call," he said. "But you'll stay behind the cordon. Agreed?"

They were all quick to confirm that. Of course they would. No problem. They'd stay out of the way.

"Good. Right, then," Logan grunted, before spinning on his heels and marching back in the direction of the house.

He stopped, just briefly, to talk to a Uniform on the way.

"Shift that cordon back another thirty or forty feet, will you?" he said. "Ideally, try to make sure that lot end up ankle-deep in a big puddle."

The constable appeared to enjoy the idea, and tapped his forehead in salute. "On it, sir. It'll be my pleasure."

By the time Logan got back to the house, Ben's car was pulling up. DI Forde and DS Khaled climbed out, shot reproachful looks at the sky, then hunkered their heads in lower between their shoulders in an attempt to stop the rain finding its way down their necks.

"What've we got, Jack?" Ben asked, carefully positioning himself in close at Logan's side, effectively using him as a windbreak and rain shield.

Logan explained the situation, telling the other detectives what he'd seen in the house, and bringing them both up to date.

That done, he left Hamza to start dishing out orders to the Uniforms. He'd co-ordinate the door-to-door, see if any of the neighbours had seen or heard anything, and try to trace any CCTV or other video footage that might be available.

Getting footage from a residential street like this was unlikely, but the dashcam clips from Fort Augustus had proved it wasn't impossible.

While Hamza set off to put all that in place, Logan remained rooted to the spot. He couldn't look at the house without his eyes being drawn to that top window. The boy's bedroom. Was Shona going over him now, he wondered? Doing her preliminary checks before taking the poor wee bugger back to Raigmore to cut him open?

"I want this bastard, Ben," he muttered. "I want him bad."

"Aye. We'll get him," DI Forde said.

They stood in silence for a while longer, listening to the static hiss of the rain as it rattled off every surface. More and more Uniforms were arriving on the scene, Hamza immediately taking ownership of them and giving them their orders.

"You spoken to the friend yet?" Ben asked. "The one you said found her?"

Logan shook his head. "Not yet."

"Well..." Ben ran his sleeve across his eyes, wiping away some of the rain that was determined to temporarily blind him. "Fancy it?"

Logan considered the house again. His eyes returned to the room upstairs.

"Aye," he said, with a sigh of resignation. "Why not?"

"Right, I've found something," Tyler said.

Sinead, who had been cautiously poking around in Will Strand's laundry basket with the end of a plastic *Star Wars* lightsaber, was more than happy to return to DC Neish's side at the computer.

"Not more porn, is it?" she asked.

"No. I mean, aye. I found plenty more of that, but didn't

think you'd be that interested in seeing it." He looked up at her, and she could almost see the lightbulb coming on above his head. "Or... are you interested in...?"

The expression on her face did her answering for her. The bulb fizzled out again.

"No. No, thought not," Tyler said, turning back to the screen.

"So, what have you got?" Sinead asked. "Besides a head full of dirty thoughts, I mean."

Tyler grinned mischievously, but otherwise managed to keep it professional. "Browser history was exactly what you'd expect the browser history of a forty-year-old man living in a room like this would be. Lot of porn, as I say. He also visits several movie news and reviews sites, reads a lot about cars, and has three different profiles on Twitter, all fan accounts for stuff, with a combined follower total of two-hundred-and-seven."

"A real winner, then."

"Just getting started," Tyler replied. "He's on Reddit constantly, and from what he writes and upvotes there, it's pretty clear he's racist, homophobic, and crazily misogynistic. Really doesn't like the woman who plays *Captain Marvel*, if you believe what he says in his posts, and yet his porn search history very much begs to differ."

"No real surprises so far, then."

"Here's one for you. I think he has cancer," Tyler revealed. "Or, I think he thinks he has cancer, at least. He's been Googling various symptoms. 'Bleeding arse,' being the main one."

"God, he's well up to speed on all the proper medical lingo, then, eh?" said Sinead.

"I mean, he should be. By the looks of it, he's been

researching it all for a while. Weight loss, abdominal pain, various unpleasant toilet-related scenarios I won't trouble you with the nitty-gritty details of. The arse bleeding."

"Doesn't sound like he's in great shape."

"Physically or mentally," Tyler said, clicking to another tab. This one showed the Google search results for the search phrase, 'How to kill yourself'.

"Jesus," Sinead whispered, her eyes scanning the page.

"Plenty more where that came from, too," Tyler told her. "He's signed up to half a dozen subreddits about suicide, and one or two on euthanasia. He's posted a few messages in the past saying he's going to kill himself, but people have usually talked him down."

"People being nice on the internet. Seriously?" Sinead asked. "Wonders will never cease."

"I said 'usually'. Last week, he put up a post saying he was going to do it, and a couple of people called him out as an attention-seeker. They shared links to his previous posts, and it all got a bit primal from there."

He clicked through a few tabs until he found the post, then scrolled down so Sinead could read.

"'Just fucking hurry up and do it, then, you sad little basement-dwelling incel mommy's bitch.'" She nodded, satisfied that her view of the world had been restored. "Aye, that's more in line with what I was expecting, right enough."

"That was Thursday last week," Tyler said. "He didn't reply."

"And he's been missing since he went out on Sunday morning."

"Correction. He *was* missing," Tyler said. He minimised the browser window, opened the email, and presented the screen with a, "Ta-daa!"

Sinead squinted at the screen. Will Strand's account was crammed with emails, over three thousand of which—according to the little counter at the side—had not yet been opened.

"What am I looking at? His inbox?"

Tyler tutted and double-clicked one of the subject lines, his big reveal ruined. "Shite. Thought I'd left it on the screen. There."

It was a booking confirmation from Airbnb. Seven nights, starting on the Sunday he'd gone missing. The Sunday Lois and Ruby Mann had been murdered.

"He's booked a trip away? That's some timing," Sinead remarked.

"Not exactly away," Tyler said, scrolling until he found the address of the accommodation Will had booked for the week. "By my reckoning, that's about five minutes' walk from here." He turned in the revolving chair. "Fancy a wee stroll?"

THEY TOOK the Fiesta when they went to talk to Eleanor Edwards.

Partly, this was so Hamza would have Ben's car available in case he needed to rush off anywhere before the others got back. Mostly, though, it was because Logan had decided that if he had to endure the bloody thing, so should everyone else.

"Is this a present for me?" Ben asked, shifting the purple parcel off the passenger seat and onto his lap as he got in the car.

"Shite, no. Forgot all about it," Logan said, turning the key in the ignition. The engine whined pitifully into life, and some annoying bastard of a buzzer immediately alerted them to the fact that they didn't have their seatbelts on. "Better do what it says, or it'll only get worse." Logan sighed, reaching for his belt.

Once they were both strapped in and secured, Ben turned his attention back to the package. He turned the clear bag containing the parcel over in his hands as Logan drove off along the street, and read the name and address on the back.

"Lois Mann?"

"Postman who found the body was delivering it. He took it back to the van by mistake. They just found it at the depot today."

"So, it hasn't been in the house?"

"No," Logan confirmed.

He gave a wave to the officer who unpinned the cordon tape for him to get through, then floored the accelerator and headed straight for the puddle beside what was now a growing knot of journalists.

To his immense annoyance, the Fiesta didn't have the required torque to get him up to speed quickly enough, and the tyres failed to generate the arc of water spray he'd been hoping for.

God, he hated this bloody car.

"We can open it, then," Ben said.

"Knock yourself out," Logan told him.

Ben spent the next minute or two trying to open the top of the Royal Mail bag without damaging it, then he gave up and forced a thumb through the plastic, instead, and tugged on the hole until it was wide enough to remove the contents.

The purple postage bag was made of much thinner plastic and came with a clearly-marked 'tear zone' that made the whole thing spring open with one firm tug.

As suspected, there was a t-shirt inside. It was an eye-watering shade of shocking pink, with black print on the front.

Ben unfurled the shirt, and Logan tore his eyes off the road for long enough to read the message on the front.

"'Gareth Mann shagged Kerry Philip,'" Ben read. He turned the shirt around to check the back, then read the print on the front again. "Bloody hell, that's specific. How on Earth did she find one that said that?"

"I'm going to go out on a limb and assume she had it custom-printed," Logan explained. "Hell of a coincidence, if not."

"You do that, can you? Get t-shirts printed?" Ben asked.

"Aye. Plenty of places online do it. I'm sure there's even somewhere in that Victorian Market place."

Logan indicated left and pulled into the early-evening traffic that was slowly chugging its way along.

Meanwhile, his mind was racing. Lois Mann had known about the affair prior to her death. Days prior, at least. Possibly weeks. She'd gone to the trouble of having a t-shirt printed, presumably as part of some big reveal she'd been planning. Some way in which she had intended to expose Gareth and Kerry's relationship, humiliating them both in the process.

"It's big, isn't it?" Ben said, still holding the shirt up. "That'd never fit her, would it?"

Logan took his eyes off the road for long enough to confirm that for himself. Ben was right, the t-shirt was a medium, possibly a large. Lois Mann was smaller. This thing would've been hanging off her.

"Check for a delivery note," Logan suggested.

Ben folded the t-shirt to the best of his limited ability, then had a rummage around inside the packaging until he produced a sheet of A5 paper with dot-matrix style printing on one side.

He read silently for a few moments, before a guttural, 'Hmm,' at the back of his throat announced he'd found something interesting.

"What is it?" Logan urged.

"Order name and address doesn't match the delivery," Ben said. "Lois Mann didn't order this t-shirt."

"What? Who did?"

"Bryan Philip," said Ben, and Logan almost lost his grip on the wheel. "Kerry Philip's husband."

CHAPTER TWENTY-NINE

Tyler and Sinead had both driven past St. Benedict's Abbey countless times in the past, but neither had paid it any more attention beyond a cursory thought that it looked quite nice, and that they should swing by and have a closer look at some point.

It had been built back in the 1800s, used for over a century as a Benedictine monastery and school, then—after reams of sexual abuse allegations made parents somewhat reluctant to send their offspring there—the monks installed a gift shop and opened the place up to tourists.

It didn't last.

In recent years, the place had been bought by a property developer and turned into luxury apartments. It was only while strolling past the giant chess board in the courtyard, and peeking in through the windows at the lavish swimming pool, sauna, and steam room, that the detectives grasped quite how luxurious the apartments must be.

There were few buildings Tyler would describe as 'breathtaking.' Architecture was never really his thing. Don't get him wrong, he enjoyed a good episode of *Grand Designs* as much as the next man, but he tended to enjoy the failures more than the successes.

For him, it wasn't about the buildings so much as it was about seeing some smug rich bastard spunking three-quarters of a million on some glass and concrete eyesore that they'd never get to live in.

But here, though? Standing in one of the abbey's courtyards, surrounded on all sides by the towering stone walls, stained glass windows, and what his limited architectural vocabulary could only describe as 'twiddly bits,' Tyler's breath had officially been taken.

"Pretty stunning," Sinead remarked, sharing the same impression of the place.

"Aye, well, it's the closest I'll ever get to going to Hogwarts, that's for sure," Tyler said, mesmerised by the balconies and balustrades.

Sinead patted him on the arm. "Don't you sell yourself short," she told him, then she pulled open a heavy glass door, leaned inside, and had a peek in both directions. "I reckon it's this way," she announced, although quite what she was basing this on, Tyler didn't know. "Follow me."

Tyler had no idea where the apartment was that they were looking for, so he followed obediently behind Sinead, marvelling at how the inside of the building somehow managed to be even more impressive than the outside.

The corridors were all high ceilings, curved archways, and tiled floors. They reminded Tyler of movies and TV shows he'd seen set in old universities that he'd never have been able to afford to go to.

Tall church windows appeared around every corner, and at the top of every flight of steps, each one offering some new glimpse at the spectacular scenery the building was set in. Views out onto Loch Ness were the most common, and the detectives stopped once or twice to watch the boat tours go cruising past.

"Wasn't a monk the first one to ever see the Loch Ness Monster?" Tyler asked. "Yonks ago, like? In, I don't know, the fifteen hundreds, maybe?"

Sinead's reply was a less than helpful shrug and a blank expression.

"I think it was," Tyler said. "I wonder if he came from here?"

"Not unless he was living here three hundred years before they built the place," Sinead said.

"Oh. Aye. Fair point," Tyler conceded. He ran a hand up the smooth stone that formed the window surround and gave it a pat like he was congratulating it on a job well done.

Sinead watched him, curiously.

"You're acting weird," she said.

"Hm? Oh." Tyler let his hand drop back to his side, then turned away from the window. "Sorry. Just think this place is pretty cool. Imagine living here. I wonder what it costs? How amazing would it be to live here? Us, I mean."

Sinead stumbled, just briefly, over that last part, before steering the conversation in a more pressing direction.

"Pretty amazing, right enough. But, you know, we might have a murderer to catch or a suicide to stop. We should probably crack on with that."

Tyler conceded that, on balance, those things probably took priority. He let Sinead lead the way again, until she finally stopped outside a set of heavy wooden doors with black iron ring-handles and hinges.

"God, even the doors are cool," Tyler muttered.

"This is it," Sinead said, checking the number against the details she'd jotted down in Will Strand's bedroom. "Now, remember, we don't know his emotional state."

"Or if he's alive," Tyler added.

"Yes. Or if he's alive. Good point," Sinead said. "Assuming he is, though, probably best if I do most of the talking until we figure out if he's suicidal or not."

"Why?" Tyler asked. "What are you trying to say?"

"Just that... you're sometimes not the most tactful. That's all."

"I bloody am!" Tyler protested, but before he could object further, there was a *thump* from somewhere on the other side of the door.

Sinead knocked. She used her knuckles first, but the wood was so thick and heavy that it made very little noise, while simultaneously hurting like a bastard. She tried again, this time rapping the iron door knocker that had been fixed in place specifically for the purpose.

"Mr Strand? William?"

There was another thud. A gasp.

"Mr Strand, we know you're in there. This is the police. Can you open the door please?"

"G-go away."

His voice was a pained sob. Muffled.

"We can't go away, Mr Strand," Sinead said, keeping her voice light and cheerful. "Your mum asked us to check on you. She's really worried about you. Maybe you could let us in so we can have a quick word, eh?"

"No. P-please, just leave me alone," he said, then there was a loud *ker-ack* and he let out a whimper, like an animal in pain.

"Mr Strand?" Sinead rattled the door knocker again. "Will? Are you OK?"

Silence followed.

"Shit," Sinead spat. She tried turning the ring handles, but the doors were firmly locked. "Damn it."

"Aye, well, I'm glad you're the one doing the talking," Tyler told her. "Great work so far."

"I think he's hurting himself," Sinead said, stepping aside. "You'll have to kick the door in."

"No' bother," Tyler said. Stepping back, he drew in a few sharp breaths, then sprang forward and fired a kick at the height of the doors' locking mechanism.

The impact made pain explode in his foot, then simultaneously in his knee and hip as the vibrations shot up through his leg and went rattling through the rest of his skeleton.

"Nope, that's not going anywhere," he announced, immediately knocking the idea on the head. He grimaced as he returned his foot to the ground, and tried very hard not to scream.

"He might be dying in there! Try it again!"

"Fuck off, *you* try it again!" Tyler yelped. "It's like kicking a brick wall!"

Sinead spun around and slammed the heel of her hand against one of the doors. "Will? Will, can you hear me? You need to let us in! Will? Mr Strand?" she called, sounding more and more desperate with each lack of response.

Tyler groaned. "Right, out of the way, then," he said, pinning his arm to his side and pointing his shoulder. "Maybe this'll work."

Sinead stepped aside, and Tyler ran. At the last moment, he launched himself into a flying leap, hitting the doors with everything he had.

Unfortunately, everything he had was not even remotely close to enough, and he emitted a strangled, 'Urmf!' sound through his nose as he knocked all the air out of his lungs, bounced harmlessly off the doors—or, harmlessly for the doors, at least—and landed in a heap on the floor.

"Nope. Right the first time," he wheezed, heaving himself back to his feet. "Completely impossible. Don't know what I was thinking there."

He put a hand on his lower back and clicked something into place. From the way his eyes widened, even this small act hurt. A lot.

Clearly, brute force wasn't going to be the answer. Sinead brought her face closer to the door and tried to push the panic from her voice. "Will, my name's Sinead. Sinead Bell. I'm a detective constable. I... I know things aren't great right now. I know you're probably scared, and that you're hurting a lot. But just... talk to us, Will. Tell us what we can do to help. Don't let us go back to your mum with bad news, eh?"

There was no response. No sound from within the room.

"Will? You still with us?"

Again, no reply came.

"Damn it. Kick it again," Sinead urged.

Tyler had just started to make his feelings on that matter very clear when they heard the squeaking of a floorboard on the other side of the door, and Sinead held up a hand to silence the other DC.

"Will? You there?" she asked, turning back to the doors. "We'd really love to talk to you. Come on, open up, and we can have a chat, eh? You know what they say about a problem shared, and all that. It'll do you good to—"

One of the doors opened suddenly and sharply. A

woman stood there, dressed from head to toe in black leather, with various openings showing off those parts of the body that were usually the most likely to be covered up.

Her head had been shaved on one side, and bleached so blonde on the other that it was almost silver. On the shaved side, most of her scalp was covered in a tattoo of two demons doing something to each other that was presumably meant to be pleasurable, but looked far from it.

"Vot?" she demanded, in an accent that immediately conjured up images of vampires in Tyler's mind.

"Uh…" Sinead looked the woman up and down, briefly wondered how the hell she was able to stand up in those heels, then met her eye again. "We were looking for Will Strand. We were… concerned for his welfare."

"His welfare, it is fine," the woman said. She teetered to one side on her heels and indicated the room behind her. "See? Fine."

The ginger-haired man in the room behind her did not look particularly fine. He was naked, aside from a large baby bonnet that had been tied to the top of his head. He, himself, had been tied face down to a glass table in the centre of the room, his wrists bound together beneath the top.

A leather strap was fastened across his mouth, jammed in between his teeth so he was biting down on it. Tears ran down his cheeks. His other cheeks, at the far end of the table, glowed like they were red hot, and the detectives spent several seconds staring silently at the assortment of whips, paddles, clamps, chains, and other assorted torture items that had been neatly set out on one of the room's two expensive-looking suede couches.

"Uh…? You alright there, Mr Strand?" Tyler asked.

From his position, face-down on the table, Will Strand

raised a thumb that the detectives could see through the glass. "I'm thine," he managed to lisp through his gag.

"Good. Well, in that case, you've got five minutes to get your clothes on," Sinead said, producing her warrant card and holding it up for both occupants of the room to see. "You and us need to have a *very* serious chat."

CHAPTER THIRTY

ELEANOR EDWARDS HAD BEEN SHAKEN BY THE SIGHT OF her friend's dead body. Logan knew this, because she'd told him four times now, each time holding a hand out flat to demonstrate the way it still trembled.

"Couldnae believe what I was seeing. Just couldnae believe it. Shook me, it did. Just really shook me up," Eleanor said, her accent far more of the Gorbals than of the Highlands. "She held the same hand out for the fifth time. "See?"

"It must've been a real shock," Logan said. He'd said variations on this a few times now, and was rapidly running out of new ways to sling the same few words together.

They'd already gone over the details of the discovery. How Eleanor had been waiting for Sandra to join her and her daughter for the monthly Bookbug session at the library. How Sandra hadn't answered the phone when Eleanor had called. How Eleanor and her daughter had gone inside, only to discover...

"Aye. You can say that again. It was a shock, alright," Eleanor said. She held the same hand out once more, shook her head at the way it wobbled up and down, then returned it to her lap and gave it a comforting squeeze with the other hand. "Couldnae believe it. Just couldnae believe it."

From elsewhere in the house, there came the *clang-clang-clang* of metal walloping against metal.

"Chanelle! Come on tae fuck! Gonnae quit that?" Eleanor shouted.

The clanging continued. Eleanor glared at Logan and DI Forde like this was entirely their responsibility. "Is someone going to tell that uniformed lassie who's meant to be keeping an eye on her to get her to stop with the fucking clanging? I swear, my head's going to burst."

Ben made the move before Logan could, practically bouncing off the couch and onto his feet. *The bastard.*

"Aye, I'll go have a wee word," he said, successfully freeing himself from the remainder of the conversation.

"Cheers," Eleanor said to Ben's back as he left. She turned back to Logan, massaging her temples with her fingertips. "I'm just... I'm stressed out to fuck. Look. See that?"

She held the same hand up in the same position. Again. Logan watched it shaking. Again. He nodded, but this time didn't pass comment.

"Did Sandra have any enemies you were aware of?" he asked, trying to bring some sort of focus back to the interview.

"Enemies?" Eleanor asked, her face contorting itself into a scowl. "She wisnae fucking Iron Man. Why would she have enemies?"

"I mean any jealous ex-boyfriends, people she's fallen out with. That sort of thing," Logan clarified.

"No. I mean, aye. Probably. I mean, I don't know her that well—we just really got to know each other through the kids' stuff at the library—but we've all got people we've pissed off and fallen out with, don't we?"

Logan couldn't really argue there. His list was longer than most.

"Anyone in particular you can think of?" Logan urged.

"No. No one she ever spoke about," Eleanor said, then she turned in her armchair and shouted at the door. "I thought you were going to get her to stop wi' the fucking clanging?"

Ben's reply was fraught with frustration, which pleased Logan no end. "Trying!"

The clanging continued, unabated.

"Was she a swimmer?" Logan asked.

"The fuck's that meant to mean?" Eleanor asked, glaring at him like he'd just tried to proposition her.

Logan replayed the question in his head, trying to figure out if there was something inappropriate in it that he'd missed the first time. If there was, he was damned if he could see it.

"I mean, did she swim?"

"Swim? What do you mean, 'swim'?"

Was it him? Logan thought. Was he the one somehow misunderstanding? As far as he could tell, the question was pretty straightforward.

"I mean, did she regularly use the swimming pool, go swimming outdoors...? That sort of thing."

"The fuck's swimming got to...?" Eleanor muttered, then she sighed heavily, like a teenager who didn't like whatever was being asked of them. "No. She didn't go swimming, as far as—" She pressed her fingers to her temples and glared out into the hallway, where the cacophony continued. "See that *fucking* clanging?" she hissed, before getting back to the question. "I don't think she went swimming, no."

"What about boating? Did she go yachting, canoeing, kayaking? Anything like that?" Logan asked, even though he wasn't entirely sure what the difference between two of those examples actually was.

"Have you got a toddler?" Eleanor asked him.

Logan shook his head. "No. No, I don't."

"Aye, well, see if you've got a toddler? You don't spend your days romping about on the fucking lake. You spend it scraping *Weetabix* off the kitchen table and trying to go for a shite without company."

"So that's a 'no' to the kayaking, then?" Logan asked.

"As far as I know, she didn't do any of that, no," Eleanor confirmed. "No swimming, no yachting, no fucking... paragliding, or bungee jumping, or anything else. She spent all her time chasing after Simon, and—"

And that's when it happened. There was almost always a point when it did. Logan had seen it countless times on countless faces. That moment when it hit them. When it finally sunk in. When they were finally confronted by the enormity of what had happened.

Sometimes, it was so subtle, you almost missed it. A tightening of the lips. A flash of something in the eyes. A reddening or a paling of the skin as the blood flow either climbed steeply or plummeted rapidly.

Other times, it was practically a performance. How many times had he sat there awkwardly while a witness fell to the floor and writhed around in some grandiose display of grief? How many packets of tissues had he distributed? How many hands had he held?

Eleanor's reaction was closer to the former, thankfully.

She slumped back in the armchair like a puppet whose strings had all been cut, and Logan could watch her attitude evaporating before his eyes, but there was no wailing or gnashing of teeth.

She just fell silent. Through in the kitchen, the clanging noise finally stopped as if in sympathy.

"God," Eleanor finally whispered. "Simon. Someone killed him. Someone proper actually killed him, didn't they? Both of them."

"I'm afraid they did, yes," Logan confirmed.

"Will you get them? You'll get them, won't you? That's what you're there for, isn't it? That's your whole point."

"We'll do everything we can," Logan told her.

There was a squeak of a floorboard out in the hall, and Ben appeared in the doorway. "Finally got her to stop," he said. His hair was sticking up on one side, and he was dabbing with a bit of kitchen roll at a jammy hand print on the belly of his shirt.

"It's fine," Eleanor said, turning in her chair. She looked along the hallway behind him to where the kitchen door stood half-open. "Tell her she can make as much noise as she likes."

Ben stopped dabbing at the stain, his jaw dropping open. He looked imploringly at Logan, who was trying very hard not to look smug.

"If you could pass that message on, Detective Inspector," Logan said. "While Miss Ellen and I finish up here."

"Fine." Ben glowered at the DCI, scrunched up the paper towel, then turned on his heels. "I'm sure she'll be delighted."

And with that, he plodded back along the hallway, through the kitchen door, and once more unto the breach.

CHAPTER THIRTY-ONE

WILL STRAND WAS DRESSED NOW. THIS WAS A considerable improvement. At least, from the detectives' point of view.

After getting dressed, he'd rejected Tyler's suggestion that he should sit down while they spoke, choosing instead to stand, shifting his weight gingerly from foot to foot, and occasionally giving one or both buttocks a tentative rub.

It was only when the woman, who'd introduced herself as Tatiana while Will had been getting dressed, had barked out an order for him to sit that he'd reluctantly obliged.

He was propped up on one of the two couches now, a cushion beneath him, and a couple more supporting him on either side. There was some candle wax stuck to his forehead and a couple of deep red welts on his neck.

Tyler and Sinead separately concluded that they weren't going to ask about either.

Rather than wait to be asked to leave, Tatiana had elected to go for a shower, leaving the two DCs alone with the cowed, shrunken Strand.

"It's not illegal, you know?" he said, jumping in before either of them could ask any questions. "We're both consenting adults. There's nothing wrong with it."

"Never said there was, Mr Strand," Tyler replied.

"Did you pay her, though?" Sinead asked.

Strand went through several stages of panic in about a second and a half. "No. I mean... I haven't..."

Sinead silenced him with a wave of a hand. "It's fine, Mr Strand. Your whole..." She gestured at the whips, chains, and other bondage equipment "...thing isn't why we're here."

"Oh, shit!" Strand sat upright, then grimaced at the pain it brought. "It's not Mum, is it?"

"Your mother's fine. This isn't about her," Sinead said.

"It's about Lois and Ruby Mann," Tyler told him.

Both DCs shut up then, and paid very close attention to how Strand reacted.

Not a lot, was the answer.

"What about them?"

"You know them, then?" Sinead asked.

"It's Fort Augustus. Everyone knows everyone," Strand pointed out.

"You were in contact with Lois, weren't you?" said Tyler, flipping open his notepad. "Even though she repeatedly asked you not to."

"That was a while back," Strand replied, shifting his weight from one aching arse cheek to another. "I haven't spoken to her in yonks. Why? What's she said?"

"You were spoken to by our colleagues on two separate occasions concerning your harassment of Mrs Mann," Sinead said. "Why didn't you stop after the first time?"

"It wasn't *harassment*," Strand protested.

"That's what she called it in the reports," Tyler pointed

out. He glanced down at his notes. "She said you were a 'weirdo stalker,' in one statement." He winced. "That must've been hard to hear, Will. Was it?"

"What? No! That wasn't hard to... Actually, I hadn't heard that. 'Weirdo stalker'? Seriously, that's what she said? 'Weirdo stalker'? Huh." He chewed on his lip and bumped his fists against his knees for a few moments, visibly wrestling with something. "Look, I wasn't stalking her, OK? We had... a thing."

Sinead raised an eyebrow. "A thing?"

"Yes. Like... You know. A romantic thing."

"What kind of romantic thing?" Tyler asked.

"She wanked me off in the car park."

Tyler snorted out a laugh of sheer surprise, tried with moderate success to disguise it as a cough, then snapped his head down like he was suddenly fascinated by the notepad balanced on his knee.

For the next few seconds, the only sound in the room was the hissing of the shower next door.

"I've got photos," Strand said. "On my phone. I can show you. I can show everyone, if she's going to start saying I'm harassing her again." He smiled shakily. "Not that I was ever harassing her before."

"We'll maybe take a look later," Sinead said.

Tyler coughed again, repeatedly cleared his throat, then sat up straight. "Sorry. Wee frog there," he explained, tapping the spot where his neck met his chest. "So, to be clear, you're saying you haven't been in touch with Lois Mann recently?"

"No! If she says I have, she's lying. Your lot told me to stay away, I stayed away. Whatever she's telling you, it's shite."

"Lois Mann and her daughter, Ruby, were murdered on Sunday evening, Mr Strand," Sinead told him.

Strand stopped shuffling around and became still. Frozen.

"You what?" he said, some time later. "Sorry, what?"

"They were murdered," Sinead said again.

"Ruby? As in... the kid?"

Sinead nodded. "Both of them."

"Jesus Christ," Strand whispered, running his hands back through his hair and clamping his fingers around his skull. "Murdered? Like, actually properly murdered? Like, *murdered* murdered?"

"Where were you between the hours of 6 p.m. and Midnight on Sunday, Mr Strand?" asked Tyler.

Will frowned, like he didn't understand, then leaned back when it hit him. "Wait. You think I did it?"

"Did you?" Sinead asked.

"No! No, of course, I bloody didn't! Why would I? Jesus Christ! Is that why you're here?"

"We're looking into all avenues of investigation," Tyler said.

It was something he'd heard DI Forde say before and thought it had sounded dead professional. He'd made a mental note to use it himself in future. Although, now that he had, he couldn't help but feel it sounded better when the older man had said it.

"Well, you're looking into the wrong avenue here, I can tell you," Strand snapped. "You want to know where I was on Sunday night? Here. That's where I was. I was right here. Right where you're sitting, in fact, getting a figging from Tatiana."

Tyler and Sinead both briefly regarded the couch they

were sitting on, even more briefly wondered what 'getting a figging' involved, then tried to put it all from their minds and pressed on.

"I don't suppose you happen to have any evidence of that, Mr Strand?" Sinead asked.

"Evidence? Like what? I didn't check-in or anything, just picked up the key, so there's no paperwork, if that's what you mean," Strand said. "Tatiana was here, though. She'll tell you."

"With all due respect to your... lady friend," Sinead said, glancing at the bathroom door. "You could've arranged for her to provide a cover story. We don't know that she wouldn't lie to protect you."

"Protect me?" Strand scoffed. "Have you seen the state of my arse? The last thing she wants to do is protect me."

"Still. I'm afraid it doesn't get you off the hook, Mr Strand," Tyler said. He stood up, keen to put as much distance as possible between himself and the sordid acts that had been committed on that couch. Whatever they were. "I think it's best if you come back to the station with us, and we can discuss it more thoroughly."

"What? No. There's no need to—" Strand began to protest, then he exhaled and sagged against the cushions propping him up. "Fine. You want evidence? I've got evidence. I can prove I was here all day."

He blushed. Considering that he hadn't blushed while strapped to the table with a baby bonnet strapped to his head, and his buttocks red raw, this made both detectives more than a little apprehensive about what was to come.

"But I'm warning you," Strand said, shuffling himself up off the couch and onto his feet. "It's not for the faint of heart."

A FROWN FORMED at a glacial pace on DI Forde's forehead, continued down his face like a cold front on a weather map, then eventually arrived at his mouth as a question.

"Ginger?" he said. He extended an index finger and vaguely mimed inserting it into something. "Up the arse?"

"Very much up the arse, boss, aye," Tyler confirmed.

Ben's frown only deepened at this confirmation. He lowered himself onto the edge of his desk, like he was concerned he might fall over.

"But... but *why?*"

"Beats me, boss, but they call it 'figging,'" Tyler said. "Apparently, they do it with radishes, too."

"Radishes?" Ben spluttered, as if this was somehow worse. In some respects, it was. He wasn't a fan of ginger, but he did enjoy a nice radish. Or he used to, at any rate. Now, he'd always be viewing them with suspicion. "Not at the same time, surely?"

Tyler turned to Sinead for confirmation. "What are you looking at me for?" she asked. "I don't bloody know."

"Probably not at the same time, boss, no," Tyler said. He shuddered, a whole-body vibration that rattled through him from head to toe. "I mean... not that we saw, anyway."

"But why radishes and ginger? Why those two vegetables specifically?" Ben asked, determined to get to the bottom of it.

"Ginger's not a vegetable, is it?" asked Hamza, who had been listening in from his own desk.

Ben turned to him, suddenly even more confused. "Isn't it? What is it, then?"

"Is it a fruit?" Tyler guessed.

"Of course, it's not a bloody fruit," Ben said. He raised his eyebrows at Hamza. "It's not a fruit, is it?"

"No, I think it's just, like, a root, isn't it? Of a plant?"

"Oh," said Ben. He mulled this over for a moment. "So, why are people putting it up their arses?"

"That, I don't know, sir," Hamza replied. "It's a new one on me."

From over at the Exhibits desk, Dave chipped in with a suggestion. "Probably gives off a burning sensation, doesn't it?" he said. "If it's peeled, like."

"Was it peeled?" Ben asked, looking back at Sinead and Tyler. He had his glasses perched on the end of his nose and was peering over the rim, his whole face a mask of confusion.

"It was, sir, yes," Sinead confirmed.

Ben tilted his head back, his eyes moving from side to side as he played through this slightly revised scenario in his head, still trying to work out the benefits of it.

"That's worse, isn't it?" he eventually concluded. He looked over at Dave. "Why is that a good thing? Why would you want that?"

"Peeled ginger up my arse? I wouldn't," Dave said, scrunching up his face. "Not my cup of tea at all, that. I was just saying, that's what they're into, isn't it? Pain, and that."

"What about a radish?" Tyler asked. "Is a radish a vegetable?"

Ben ignored him, but seized on the radish thing. "Why would you shove a radish up there?" he asked Dave, like he was now the fount of all knowledge on such matter. "What's the point in that?"

Dave puffed out his cheeks. "Not sure. They're a bit peppery, aren't they? Radishes? Maybe that?"

Ben contemplated this some more, then shook his head. "The dirty bastards," he muttered.

The door to the Incident Room swung open, and Logan entered. He stopped when he saw the look on Ben's face.

"Shite. What now?" he asked. "What is it? What's happened?"

"Some boy's been sticking ginger up his arse," DI Forde explained.

Logan blinked. This was not the response to his question that he'd been expecting. In fact, if he'd been asked to write a list of a hundred responses he had been expecting, the one he'd actually been given would not have featured anywhere on it.

"Sorry?" he said, reasonably confident that he must have misheard.

"He wasn't actually sticking it up his own arse, boss," Tyler clarified. "Someone else was doing it for him."

"What do you think of that?" Ben asked.

"I think you lot have got too much bloody time on your hands," Logan said, resuming his walk across the room. "Where's this coming from?"

"Will Strand, sir. Elizabeth Strand's son," said Sinead.

"The stalker. Aye, what about him?" Logan asked.

"He was face down on a couch in an Airbnb most of Sunday," said Tyler.

"What, sleeping?"

"No. Getting ginger shoved up his arse," Ben added, unwilling to let it go. "And maybe radishes, we're not sure."

"In other words, boss, he's got an alibi."

"Bollocks. How tight is it?" Logan asked, then he jumped in with a clarification as Tyler's face lit up with glee. "His alibi, I mean. No' his arse."

"Because, that'll be hanging in tatters, by all accounts," Ben remarked.

"It's solid, sir," said Sinead, carefully picking her words to avoid any other accidental detours into innuendo. "Whole thing was livestreamed on a BDSM fetish site. Timestamps match, and you see a clock a couple of times with the actual time on it."

"Do you?" asked Tyler. "I didn't see that?"

"That's because you were staring at... events, and I was looking anywhere else but."

Tyler turned to the others. "It was like a car crash, that was all," he explained. "You don't want to look at it, but your eyes won't let themselves be dragged away."

Sinead raised a hand to shoulder height, like a pupil trying to get the attention of a teacher. "To be clear, my eyes let themselves be dragged away just fine."

"Don't suppose you asked him where he was yesterday?" said Logan, slumping into his chair.

"According to Strand and his... lady friend, they haven't left the room all week, boss," Tyler said.

"Why? What happened yesterday, sir?" Sinead asked.

"There's been another one," Ben told her.

"What, a murder?"

"Double. Mother and her kiddie. A boy this time. Over in Dingwall. Husband was off-shore. He's on his way back."

"Shite," Tyler muttered. "Same killer, we think?"

Logan nodded. "She was drowned. Report just came in from pathology. Big basin of water poured into her when she was down on the floor."

"What about the boy, sir?" Sinead asked.

"Strangled. Bare hands. The one bit of good news is we managed to get a partial print from his neck."

He glanced away for a moment, looking out through the window at the lights of the now darkened city on the other side of the glass. The traffic had thinned along Longman Road, most sensible folk having headed home long before now.

"Sad fucking state of affairs when we consider that 'good news,' eh?" he remarked, then he shook his head and turned back to the team. "No matches yet. We can take Will Strand's prints and rule him out, but sounds like he's not our man."

Hamza leaned so he could see past his monitor, and looked over at the Big Board. "So, where does that leave us, sir?" he wondered.

Logan's response was largely an unenthusiastic one. "We need to get ahold of Kerry Philip's husband. He sent her a t-shirt that shows he knew about Kerry's affair with Gareth Mann a good week or so before Lois and Ruby were murdered."

Hamza nodded slowly. "Meaning...?"

Logan shrugged. "Meaning... I don't know. He didn't let on to Kerry that he knew. Not until Gareth turned up and he lamped him one. At least, that's what Kerry's telling us."

"You think she's lying, Jack?" Ben asked.

The DCI let out a sound that was midway between a sigh and a groan. "I'm not sure it matters. Maybe she is. Or, maybe he just didn't tell her he knew. Either way, what does it give us? I've picked at it, but I can't get it to unravel into anything bigger. He knew about the affair. So what? Why would that make him kill Gareth's family? I get sending the t-shirt—he wants everyone to know about the relationship. He wants to expose the betrayal. But murdering the only other real victims of the affair? That's a big jump I can't nail the landing of."

"Want me to work it up on the board, sir?" Sinead asked.

Logan shook his head. His chair creaked as he stood up. "No. Go home. Get some rest. We'll sleep on it and tackle it fresh in the morning. I know it's Saturday, but I'll need you all back in bright and early."

"Aye, no bother, boss," Tyler said. He reached for his jacket, which he'd draped over the back of his chair. "But the tattie scones are on you."

"I think I'll hang off another half an hour, sir," Sinead said. "If that's alright? I just want to get my notes updated."

"I've had the digital forensics report through," Hamza added. "I'll have a quick scan through that, and print off anything that might be useful. I need to check in with Uniform, too, to see how the house-to-house went in Dingwall."

Tyler set his jacket down again, and did an admirable job of not looking too disappointed. "Right, well, sounds like I'm on tea and coffees, then."

"You're all mental," Dave remarked. His watch gave a *bleep-bleep* and he immediately jabbed the button that turned his monitor off. "That's me," he announced, wheeling himself backwards away from the computer. He waved cheerfully. "See you all on Monday!"

"Aye, see you then," DI Forde said. "Who's filling in over the weekend?"

"Buggered if I know, sir," Dave replied, with a shrug of his big shoulders. He backed his chair into the doors, nudging them both open. "Bye for now!"

With a final backwards push, he disappeared through the doors, letting them swing closed with a faint *whum*.

"There's a man with the right idea," Logan said, gathering up his coat. He yawned. Five o'clock that morning suddenly seemed like a very long time ago. "Come on, Detective Inspector," he said. "Let's leave these youngsters to it."

CHAPTER THIRTY-TWO

HE COULD HEAR THEM. UPSTAIRS. LITTLE THUMPING *footsteps. The squeaking of a bed being bounced on. Giggling. Whispering.*

And then, a groan. A mutter. A thud of feet swinging down onto the floor.

The bitch was awake. The vicious, soulless cow who had helped ruin him was up and about. He could hear her grumbling and muttering away, no doubt regretting the choices that had brought her here. That had made her life this endless trudge through drudgery.

Serves her fucking right.

He hadn't seen her name on the list, but she was one of them. One of those bitches. One of those liars.

One of them.

He crept through from the living room to the hall, following the creaking of her as she moved from room to room above.

At the door to the kitchen, he stopped, listening as a corresponding door upstairs was thrown open, and the bitch-cow roared at the two ungrateful little bastards that had come slithering from her womb a few years earlier.

"It's nearly midnight!" *she bellowed.* "Come on, cut the capering. It's time to bloody sleep!"

The offspring mewled and moaned their pathetic objections. Pleaded and begged, but found only deaf ears.

"Come on. Into your beds. The pair of you," *the bitch-cow commanded. Her voice was harsh. Angry. Bitter and twisted, just like she had proven herself to be when she'd systematically torn down his whole life. When she had ripped apart everything he'd worked so hard for, and laughed while she did it.*

She'd joked. They'd all joked. Them and their words, and their lies, and their stares. They'd ruined him. Ruined everything. They'd killed every chance he had of happiness.

It was only right that he was returning the favour.

The first one had been hard. Messy. He'd overthought it, and tried to hide what he'd done.

He hadn't tried to hide it the second time, though. That one had been better. Cleaner. Infinitely more enjoyable.

The third time would be better still. And from here, he'd just keep on improving.

He entered the kitchen, still listening to the voices overhead. The words were soothing now. Kinder.

Anger coiled his intestines like a snake about to strike. She could *be kind, then. She* could *be gentle. Thoughtful. Compassionate. Considerate. To know that she had the capacity to be all these things just made everything she'd done to him that much worse.*

Either she was a monster then, or she was lying about being one now. Either way, she had to be stopped.

She had to be punished.

They all did.

As the bitch-cow sang a lullaby above him, he opened a kitchen cupboard, and found himself a jug.

CHAPTER THIRTY-THREE

Logan should've been in bed long before now, he knew, but the armchair was comfortable, and his legs kept asking for five more minutes.

The pain that had been radiating through every joint and muscle had faded as the day went on, but he could feel it creeping back in now, and was already dreading what his legs would be like come the morning. He should probably have iced them. Or massaged them.

Amputated them, maybe.

They'd swung in by the twenty-four-hour Asda on the way back to Ben's. It had been Ben's idea, his principled stance on all-night supermarkets apparently not coming into play when he was a bit peckish and needed to pick up toilet roll.

Both men now sat sprawled in chairs across from each other, the cardboard and plastic wrappers of their pre-packed sandwiches strewn on the coffee table beside a couple of empty crisp packets, and half a bag of *Minstrels*. Most of the remainder of the bag had spilled across the table and onto the floor, but neither man had the energy nor the inclination to pick them up.

It was hardly a feast fit for a king, but you got used to such slim pickings on the job. Especially on days like these.

"God, imagine what herself would have to say about that being our dinner," Ben remarked, indicating the food debris.

"She'd have approved that we got them cheap, though," Logan said. "I mean, aye, technically they were a minute out of date, but..."

"Tasted fine."

"Tasted fine," Logan agreed.

Ben chuckled. "Aye, she'd an eye for a bargain, right enough?"

"Who did?" Logan asked.

The DI wasn't going to get caught out that easily. "You know fine bloody well who," he said, not making eye contact.

He leaned his head back against the high armchair and closed his eyes, signalling he was done with that particular topic.

Logan didn't have it in him to pursue it any further right now. "Here," he said, switching conversations. "Meant to ask. Was Hoon in the Special Forces?"

Ben opened one eye. "Bob Hoon?" He opened the other eye, but kept his head against the chair's high back. "Eh, aye. I think maybe he was. I know he was ex-military, anyway. Why?"

"No reason," Logan said. "Just hadn't heard."

"Aye, well, he was never exactly forthcoming with information about himself, was he? Not really someone you wanted to spend much time chatting to."

Logan grunted his agreement. "This is very true."

They sat in silence for a while, Ben closing his eyes again,

Logan staring, unseeing, at the ceiling. Body and mind were both utterly bloody shattered, but he already knew he wouldn't sleep. Not tonight. There was too much whizzing around inside his head. Too many questions without answers. Too many things still to figure out. Too many mysteries that needed to be solved.

He was missing something. He had to be. Some connection between the victims. The significance of the drowning. Something obvious. It was there like an itch he couldn't quite reach. It niggled away at him, and while the whispers of it were fairly quiet now, they would be a deafening roar come the middle of the night.

The water. The choice of victims. It wasn't random. Far from it. If he could connect those, he'd be getting somewhere. If he could connect those, maybe he could stop it from happening again.

But that wasn't it, he thought. That wasn't the thing that was worming away at him. That was something else. Something smaller, but potentially just as significant.

He closed his eyes, hoping it would come to him, that there would be some flash of inspiration or insight. There was something he wasn't getting. Something he had missed.

When he opened his eyes, the room was in darkness. A blanket covered about as much of him as any one blanket could.

He checked his watch. It was just after three. He thought about getting up and heading to bed. Thought very hard about it.

Just five more minutes, his legs suggested.

And Logan closed his eyes again and drifted off into a shallow, fitful sleep.

It had taken Logan a full five minutes to get into Ben's car at the house, and almost seven to get back out at the other end of the short trip. Every part of him felt like it had seized up during the night. Even his toes hurt, and Tyler's near-joyous cry of, "Bloody hell, boss, you're walking like the Tin Man from *The Wizard of Oz*," as he waddled into the Incident Room did nothing whatsoever to improve his mood.

"Tea," Logan replied through gritted teeth.

"Aw, come on, boss, have a heart," Tyler said. He looked particularly pleased with himself at that one, and shot an approval-seeking grin at Sinead and Hamza, who were both already at their desks.

"Sorry about him, sir," Sinead said. "He's been necking the Red Bull since the early hours."

"What? You've no' been here all night, have you?" Ben asked.

"We got a bit of sleep between us," Hamza said, although the bags under his eyes didn't lend the statement much credibility. "We just got caught up in everything."

"You're bloody idiots," Logan said, although there was no real venom behind it. He looked over at the Big Board, which had been almost completely revamped. "Anything new come in?"

"One or two little bits from the door-to-door," Sinead said. "Nothing major. But I wanted to get it all set out for us on the board." She shrugged. "I can't help but think—"

"That we're missing something," Logan concluded. "Aye. I know what you mean." He cocked his head, listening. "Hang on. Is that the kettle boiling I hear?"

Tyler listened for a moment, before grasping the meaning. "Oh. Were you actually wanting tea, boss? Didn't think you were being serious."

"Since when did tea become a joking matter, son?" Logan asked. "Of course I was being bloody serious."

"Right, boss," Tyler said. He gave a double thumbs-up and started for the door. "On it, boss."

"I'll have a coffee, if it's going," Hamza called after him.

"Tea for me," Ben added.

Tyler groaned, cursed himself for not being fast enough, then turned to face the room. "Fine," he said, taking out his notepad. "But tell me it all again."

Once everyone's orders had been given, and Tyler had set off to get the drinks organised, Logan grimaced his way out of his coat and winced on over to the Big Board.

"Suffering, sir?" Sinead asked.

"Aye, you can bloody say that again," Logan muttered, scanning the changes and updates Sinead had made during the night.

"Still, be worth if it means passing the bleep test."

Logan didn't turn to look at her. "Be lucky if I can pass a tying my shoelaces test, the way I'm feeling right now." He tapped a note that was pinned next to Will Strand's name. "He had a sexual relationship with Lois Mann?"

"Sort of, sir, aye," Sinead confirmed. "Or he's claiming to have had, at least."

"She wasn't sticking ginger up his arse was she?" Ben asked.

"No, sir. She, eh... manually pleasured him in the church car park."

Ben's lips thinned in disapproval. "I mean, I suppose that's better..."

Sinead quickly pressed on before anyone got bogged

down by that particular detail. "We told him we might call him in to talk about the relationship, but given that his alibi's pretty watertight, we didn't think it was worth bringing him in yesterday."

"Aye, good call," Logan told her. He glanced over the rest of the board. There was a lot of information on there that hadn't been there when he'd left the night before. Sinead had done well. "What's new and exciting?"

"A lot new, sir, not a lot all that exciting," Hamza said. "Got a report on the information from Sandra Atwood's phone. Doesn't look like she knew Lois Mann. Neither woman was in the other's contacts, at least, and they'd never emailed each other. No shared contacts at all, actually."

Logan winced. Damn it. That could've been a quick win. One mutual friend with a history of violence would've opened up a new avenue of investigation—something they were sorely needing right now.

"Any connections at all?" Ben asked.

"A tenuous one. They're both active on Mumsnet," Hamza said. "But then, so are a hundred-and-nineteen million other people, and there's no sign they've ever directly interacted on it yet."

"Yet?" Logan asked.

"When I say they were both active, I mean they've posted and commented thousands of times each, sir. There's a team going through their comments now, trying to cross-reference, but it's not going to be quick. I'm going to help out when I can."

The door swung open. Logan turned, expecting to find Tyler struggling with an assortment of paper cups, but instead got a wave from a broad-shouldered man in a wheelchair.

THE BIG MAN UPSTAIRS   271

"Alright?" Dave asked.

"Thought you were off until Monday?" said Ben.

"Aye. Well," Dave replied, smiling in a way that made him look just a touch embarrassed. "Thought you'd all be here, and maybe I could help. Not like I've anything better to do."

Logan gave him a nod. "Good to have you here, son," he said. "There's plenty to be cracking on with."

"Ever used Mumsnet?" Hamza asked, turning in his chair.

"Funnily enough, no," Dave said, wheeling himself over to his desk. "But, let me guess, I'm about to start?"

"Not quite yet," Logan said. He was back looking at the board again, studying it, taking it in. He had been hoping to see the thing they'd missed. The thing that had been niggling away at him. But, it wasn't there. Whatever it was, they were still missing it. "I want all eyes on this bloody thing," he continued, indicating the board. "We're going to go over the whole thing again from the start."

CHAPTER THIRTY-FOUR

ONCE TYLER HAD RETURNED WITH THE TEAS AND coffees, then been guilt-tripped into going back to get one for Dave, they all took their seats in a semi-circle around the Big Board, with Hamza leading the walkthrough.

They started with the Mumsnet activity from Lois Mann on the day she'd died. She'd responded to dozens of posts about cheating husbands, going so far as to fully empathise with one woman, and write a short rant about how all men were bastards.

From that, they agreed it was almost certain that she knew of the affair between the Reverend Gareth Mann and Kerry Philip. But, if so, then why hadn't she let on that fact to Gareth during their argument later?

And the Mumsnet activity had been from that same day, which suggested she'd only just found out. Given that this was the same day that her husband had planned to end their marriage, was this just coincidental timing, or something more?

They knew from the t-shirt he'd tried to send her that the still unaccounted for Bryan Philip had known about the affair. Had they spoken about it? Had they planned some big confrontation based around the t-shirts? Some joint public humiliation of their cheating spouses?

"That might explain why Lois didn't let on she knew," Sinead ventured. "If she and Bryan Philip were planning doing some public shaming, she might have bit her tongue so as not to ruin the big reveal."

It was possible, they all agreed. It was also the only workable theory they had on that part, so Hamza made a note of it and stuck it to the board.

Sinead then got up, moved it to a more appropriate spot, and sat back down again.

There were some things they couldn't account for. The bruises and carpet burns on Lois Mann's hands and knees. She'd been hitting something, hammer-strike style. The floor, presumably, if the injuries had been sustained at the same time.

"Grief?" Ben suggested. He didn't make eye contact when they all turned to look at him. "People who're grieving, or... you know, upset, they might fall to the floor and hit it like that. You know, theoretically."

Logan nodded slowly. "Shona reckons they were from a day or two before she died."

"Maybe that's when she found out about the affair, boss," said Tyler. "Had a wee breakdown to herself, then pulled it together on Sunday and went on Mumsnet then."

"Could've been looking for ways to get her own back on him," Hamza said.

"Or, more likely, just getting reassurance that she wasn't

the only person who'd ever been cheated on by their partner," Sinead countered. "We don't just jump straight to
revenge, you know?"

"That's reassuring," Tyler said with a grin. It disappeared
like a fox down a hole when he caught the look from Sinead.
"Not that I'm planning to..." His voice died in his throat, and
he turned back to the DS standing up front. "Sorry, Ham,
you were saying?"

They took their time over the next few links in the chain.
They were, after all, the most significant.

Reverend Mann had come home on Sunday afternoon,
intending to tell his wife that their relationship was over. An
argument had followed, during which someone—a man—had
been caught on video upstairs in Ruby Mann's bedroom.

The Reverend had left the house just after six that evening.
Another man had been recorded leaving the house around nine.

Logan sat forward in his chair, his fingers running up and
down over his mouth and chin. The niggling had become a
pneumatic drill now, boring into the base of his skull. Whatever he was missing, it was here somewhere.

But, Hamza was already moving on, and the DCI didn't
want to disrupt the flow of the recap, in case it helped something else click into place.

After Reverend Mann had dropped his belongings at the
church, he'd headed to Kerry Philip's house in Drumnadrochit, where he'd received a solid wallop to the coupon from
her husband, Bryan.

Back in Fort Augustus, approximately around the same
time (although, this was an educated guess) the killer had
disposed of his knife down a drain a six minute walk away
from the house where the murders had taken place.

"We get anything from the knife?" Logan asked.

A print would've been nice. A print and an engraved name, even nicer. Sadly, neither had been present.

"Weird looking knife, isn't it?" Tyler said, studying the photo of the weapon that Sinead had stuck to the board. "Why's the blade that long and thin?"

"Some sort of kitchen knife, isn't it?" said Ben. "Like a... I don't know. A chef thing."

"You think?" asked Sinead. "I'm not sure. The handle looks a bit rubbery for something that would be used in a kitchen."

"I mean, like, the big professional kitchens," Ben said. "Like, an industrial thing."

"It's for fishing," Dave said. He looked around at them all when they turned his way. "It's a fillet knife. I thought we all knew that?"

"Fishing?" Logan said, suddenly perking up.

Fishing meant water. Other than a shared love of Mumsnet, water was about the only thing that connected both adult victims.

"So, what, we're looking for a fisherman?" Tyler asked.

"Not necessarily a professional, or anything," Dave said. "They're pretty common. My old man used to take me out sometimes, and we used a knife like that. Not as long, like, but otherwise pretty much the same. It's for cleaning the fish."

"Fishing. Drowning," Ben muttered, clearly thinking along the same lines as Logan. "Is there something there?"

"Maybe, aye," Logan said.

His eyes zig-zagged across the Big Board, following Sinead's lines of red wool. There, in the centre of it all, was a blow-up of the photograph of Lois and Ruby Mann that they'd taken from the crime scene.

The photo of the two of them together.

On a boat.

Logan half-expected to feel the buzzing niggle intensify again then, but it didn't. This was a new train of thought, certainly, but it wasn't connected to whatever it was he'd missed.

"The boat trip," he remarked, drawing everyone else's attention to the photograph. "Who runs that? Do we know?"

There was silence, and shrugging, and not a lot else.

"I could probably find out, sir," Sinead said. "Reverend Mann might be able to tell us. I could give him a ring."

"Do that," Logan said, still focused on the photograph.

Eleanor Edwards had said that Sandra Atwood sometimes went on day trips to Fort Augustus with Simon.

Boat trips, maybe?

On *that* boat?

"The hair found in the cupboard in Ruby Mann's room. There were traces of diesel, weren't there?" Logan asked.

"That's right, aye," Dave confirmed. "I logged that."

"Will Strand works at the petrol station in Fort Augustus, boss," Tyler said. "Hair colour doesn't match, though."

"And we already know it wasn't him," Ben said. "He was busy getting bits of ginger shoved—"

"We're well aware of how Mr Strand was spending his evening, Detective Inspector, thank you," Logan said.

"Too aware, if anything," Tyler remarked, his face taking on the sort of haunted expression usually reserved for soldiers returning from the trenches in old World War I photographs.

"Some boats use diesel. Right?" Logan said. "Or, some variation of it? Marine diesel, or something?"

"You asking us or telling us?" said Ben. "I've got no idea."

"I've got the report saved," Dave said. "I can go through the lab stuff, and try to make heads or tails of it. Might be something useful in there."

"Get on that," Logan told him. "If there's no joy in the report, you or Tyler can call them up."

"You think the boat's significant, then, boss?"

"I don't think anything yet," Logan replied. "But we're not exactly swamped with leads here, so it's worth digging into."

"Not getting any answer from the reverend, sir," Sinead said, covering the mouthpiece of her phone with one hand. "Will I leave a message?"

Logan shook his head. "No. Better done in person, anyway."

"I'll head down, if you like?" Ben suggested, already getting to his feet. "Still feel guilty about everything we put him through in the interview. Might get a chance to apologise."

"We were doing our jobs, Ben," Logan reminded him.

"True, aye. But doesn't hurt to say sorry once in a while," Ben replied.

"That a Bible thing?" Logan asked.

Ben gave a single chuckle. "No, just a decent human being thing," he said, pulling on his coat.

"Aye, well. I wouldn't know about that," Logan muttered.

"You keep telling yourself that, Jack," Ben told him. He turned away from the team and headed for the door. "I'll call as soon as I have anything."

Hamza waited for the doors to swing closed, and for

Dave to finish wheeling himself over to his desk, then he gently cleared his throat and got back to the recap.

"Right then," he said, with a glance down at his notes. "Moving on..."

HE COULD HEAR THEM. *Up there. Whispering. Giggling. Sharing their secrets and their filthy, filthy lies.*

They were above him. On the bed. One on the top bunk—he'd felt the frame shake as she'd climbed the ladder—and one below. Too far apart for him to get them both without one having a chance to scream. Too far apart for him to strike quite yet.

But he was nothing if not patient. He'd proved that at the last two places. He could wait. He could linger. Thanks to their bitch of a mother, he had all the time in the world.

A bare foot dangled down over the side of the bed. He lay there, face down, watching it swinging back and forth, back and forth, back and forth. So close, he could reach out and grab it, pull the child under. Be the monster under the bed.

But, no. Too risky. He'd got the last one right by being patient, and he was going to get this one right, too. If he kept getting them right, he could carry on until the mission was done. Until they'd all been paid back.

Each and every one of them.

Above him, the children began to sing. Some half-remembered Disney song, the vocals descending into low, uncertain muttering during the verses, before rising triumphantly—if tunelessly—during the chorus.

He closed his eyes and listened. He had no other choice. Not right now.

But soon, he would.

Soon, he'd make his move.

Soon, he'd silence them both, and the bitch downstairs, too.

And nobody connected to this family would ever feel like singing again.

CHAPTER THIRTY-FIVE

Reverend Mann was standing out on the front step of the church, dressed in a short-sleeved black shirt that could've done with a quick press, when DI Forde pulled up in the car park. The minister was scrubbing at the double doors with a hard brush, soapy water running like tears down the wood's grooves and grain.

"Everything alright there, Reverend?" Ben asked once he'd made his way over to the church entrance.

It was a silly question, really. The evidence was right in front of him that, no, everything was not alright. Despite his best efforts, Reverend Mann had been largely unsuccessful in removing any of the eight letters that were scrawled in bright yellow paint across the doors.

MURDERER.

Mann greeted him with a thin-lipped smile, and two empty voids where his eyes should have been. "Hello, Detective...?" His brow furrowed as he struggled to recall the rest of the rank.

"Inspector. But Ben's fine. You've had trouble, I see."

"Yes. Unfortunately so," the Reverend said, casting the door a sideways glance. "It's true what they say, I suppose. A lie is halfway round the world before the truth has its boots on. Evidently, someone heard word of my arrest, but not my release."

"I'm sorry about that," Ben told him. "I'm sure there's a suitably pithy Bible quote about gossip, or bearing false witness, but I'm drawing a blank. So, we'll settle for, 'Some people are right arseholes.'"

"Ha!" Mann said, although it was nothing like an actual laugh. "I couldn't possibly comment."

"Well, we'll put out a statement today. Make it very clear that you had no involvement in... What happened."

"Thank you. That would be very much appreciated," said the minister, with a gracious nod of his head.

On the surface, he appeared perfectly calm, despite everything that had happened. Ben knew better, though. He knew that look. He'd seen it in the mirror every day for months now. If the eyes were the windows to the soul, then Reverend Mann's were wide open, and the view through them was of something damaged and soiled.

"If you've another brush, I can give you a hand," Ben suggested.

"That's a very kind offer. But—to use a particularly appropriate phrase—this is my cross to bear," the Reverend said. He placed his brush into the bucket of soapy water at his feet and rubbed his hands together in a vague attempt to dry them. "Have there been developments?" he asked. He took a deep breath, steadying himself. "I mean, I presume that's why you're here?"

"Uh, yes. Not directly related to Lois and Ruby, though,"

Ben said. "There's been another attack. Very similar circumstances."

Mann placed a hand on the door and leaned on it, supporting himself. "Oh, no. No. What, here in town? Who? When?"

"In Dingwall," Ben said. "A young woman and her son. Does the name Sandra Atwood mean anything to you?"

Reverend Mann shook his head. "No. No, I can't say it does."

"As far as we can tell, there's no obvious connection between Sandra and your wife," Ben explained. "Other than them both being members of the same website."

"Let me guess, Mumsnet?" Gareth chuckled drily, recalling several past conversations. "She was always on that thing. Day in, day out. That, endless online shopping, and TripAdvisor. You know, the review site?"

"Heard of it. Never used it," Ben replied. He paused for a moment, bracing himself for the next part. "Cause of death was also identical. As you know, Lois was drowned. Same with Sandra."

The Reverend's face had lost all of its colour now. He stood there, one hand on the door, his head shaking tiny fractions left and right, like it was trying to stop him asking the question he didn't want to know the answer to. But, he had to know. He had to.

"And... the child?"

"The boy was... He was strangled," Ben said.

Mann's hand became a clenched fist against the door of the church. He rapped his knuckles against it, hard and slow, like he was checking to see if anyone was home. Apparently, nobody was.

"Oh, God," he whispered, the dark hollows that were his

eyes somehow finding it in themselves to produce a light smir of tears. "Why is this happening? What's going on?"

"We're working very hard to find that out," Ben told him, then it was time to broach the real reason for coming. "The photo of your wife and daughter that we took a copy of. On the boat."

Mann sniffed and wiped his eyes on a bare forearm. "Yes. What about it? Do you need another copy?"

"No. No, nothing like that. We were just wondering, do you remember the boat company the trip was with?"

The Reverend's eyebrows bunched together in a knot above his nose. "The boat company? Why? What's that got to do with anything?"

"Probably nothing at all," Ben said. "We're just hoping to trace the owner."

"But, why? Do you think they were involved?"

"No. Nothing like that. We'd just like to check a few things with them," Ben said, keeping it as light and breezy as he could. "Do you remember the name of the company?"

Mann's eyes looked up and to the side, like he was physically searching his memory banks for the information. "Uh, no. No. Sorry, I don't. There are always a few of them. Tourists can't get enough of them. Think they'll get to see the monster, I suppose. I think it shut down soon after Lois and Ruby took their trip, though. I remember her being quite pleased."

"Pleased?"

"She hated the trip. Said it was unsafe. Complained, actually. Got her money back."

"Aye, I think you mentioned that at the station. But, you don't know the name of the company?"

"No. Sorry."

"Would it be on a bank statement, or other correspondence somewhere?" Ben pressed.

"She paid cash, I think. There might be something on her computer, I suppose, but your people still have that, so you'd be better placed to know than me."

Ben jotted a note down in his pad. "We'll check. Anything she mentioned about the owner? The crew on board?"

Reverend Mann gave a resigned little shrug. "I'm afraid not. She could be... opinionated. She launched into these little rants on a regular basis. I have to confess, I was often only half-listening. Sometimes, not even that. If she mentioned anything about them, then it probably went in one ear and out the other."

Ben watched a flicker of something dart across the other man's face. "You just remember something?"

"No, I just... It makes me realise. I never listened. Not really. Not to them." He looked up at the church. "I come here every day, and I listen to people telling me their problems. Sharing their concerns. A friendly ear, that's one of the things I pride myself on."

A smile came fleetingly, then was gone.

"And yet... Lois. God, Ruby, even. They'd talk, and I'd nod along. But I so rarely listened. Actually listened." He let out a long, slow sigh. "Honest answer? She did tell me all about the cruise. She's bound to have. I just didn't hear her. I just nodded along to her rant, and let it all wash over me."

He ran a hand down the door, his fingers coming away yellow and wet.

"I didn't murder her, but I think... I think I may have been killing her for years."

Ben could only shake his head. "Don't be too hard on

yourself, son," he said, the words coming slowly and hesitantly. "After... *my wife* died. I blamed myself. Actually, I blamed everyone. But mainly myself. And I spent every night lying awake, combing over every wrong I did to her. Every time I snapped after a long day. Every time I moaned at her. Every time I didn't pick up on the fact she was hurting over something. A million things. More, even. I thought... she deserved better, you know? Better than me. Better than what I'd been able to give her." His voice dropped a handful of decibels, and his eyes glazed over a little, his gaze now fixed somewhere in the past, rather than here in the present. "And a damn sight better than what happened to her."

"I'm so sorry," Mann said.

Ben cleared his throat and snapped back to the here and now. "The point is, it's natural, son. We all do it. None of us is perfect. And the Big Man..." He pointed to the sky. "... doesn't expect us to be. So, don't be so hard on yourself, eh? Learn the lessons, and try to do better in future."

Mann nodded slowly, contemplating this.

"Sound advice."

"Maybe," Ben said. "We'll see. If anything else comes back to you, Reverend, then please just give us a call. You still have my card?"

"I do."

"Good. Day or night, if there's anything you can tell us, just ring."

"I will. Thank you," Mann said, then his face fell when he saw Elizabeth Strand come marching towards him, a look of thunder on her face. "Oh dear," he muttered, bracing himself as the old woman swept right past Ben and came to a stop at the bottom of the step.

"Reverend," she said, her face fixed in a scowl.

"Elizabeth."

"I'm horrified. Utterly horrified," Elizabeth spat. "I mean, it's a sin. An absolutely bloody *sin*!"

Mann managed a smile. "Look, I know what you may have heard, but—"

"And you'll never get it off with soapy water."

The Reverend blinked. "I'm sorry?"

"This filth," Elizabeth said, indicating the graffiti. "Turps is what we need. White Spirit. Lucky for us..." She reached into her bag and produced a bottle full of clear liquid. "...I came prepared. Just let me go in and get my coat off, then you and me will get rid of this in no time."

"Elizabeth, I—"

"Elizabeth nothing. 'This is my commandment, that you love one another as I have loved you.' Ring any bells?"

Gareth nodded gratefully. "One or two. Thank you."

"Right, then. No more arguments."

Elizabeth paused to give DI Forde the curtest of curt nods, before barging past the minister and into the church.

"Well, looks like I'm leaving you in good hands," Ben chuckled.

"Yes. She's quite the force of nature."

The two men said their farewells, then the Reverend reached back into the bucket and took out the brush. He was two good scrubs in, and Ben was a quarter of the way back to his car, when Mann stopped.

"Detective Inspector?"

Ben turned. "Yes, son?"

It took a few seconds for the Reverend to fully form the question in his head before he could ask it out loud. "Does it get easier? Does the pain fade?"

For a while, Ben said nothing as he gave the question the consideration it deserved.

"Hopefully," he eventually replied. "I'll let you know."

Then, with an almost imperceptible nod, he turned and headed for his car, leaving the Reverend to carry on his labours.

LOGAN SAT at his desk in the Incident Room, a finger poised on a mouse button, his eyes fixed on the computer screen. Gareth and Lois Mann were arguing. A man was upstairs. Twenty years of polis experience was telling the DCI that this was important. Something significant was happening in one of those videos. His subconscious had picked up on it, but was keeping its cards close to its chest.

The rest of Hamza's recap had gone over everything they already knew, touched on the new information from Shona Maguire's post-mortem report, and confirmed that, as of yet, there was no match for the partial print found at the second murder scene.

After that, they'd discussed next steps, Logan had dished out the orders, and they'd all returned to their desks to start working their way through their individual To-Do lists.

Dave was the first to report back, having the advantage of his head-start.

"The results on the fuel. Inconclusive, if I'm reading this right," he said, gesturing to his screen. "Nothing to say it's from a boat."

"But nothing to say it isn't?" Logan asked.

"No. In fact, it's listed as one of five or six possibilities, once you scroll past a load of science gobbledygook," Dave replied, spinning the wheel of his mouse. "Marine Gasoil, brackets, LCGO, whatever that means. They didn't get enough of a sample to be able to pin down exactly what the stuff is, but boat fuel deffo seems to be a possibility."

Logan regarded the photo on the Big Board. Lois and Ruby Mann stared back at him, challenging him to put everything together. To make sense of it all.

"Right. Good work," he said, turning back to Dave. "If you want to give DS Khaled a hand with Mumsnet, I'm sure he wouldn't object."

"You can say that again," Hamza said, jumping out of his seat and joining Dave at the Exhibits desk.

Ben's call came in a few moments later. Tyler took it, and quickly whipped open his notepad to start jotting down the information. From what Logan could gather from where he sat, though, the pen didn't touch the paper once.

"No joy?" he asked, once Tyler had hung up the phone.

"Nothing really, boss. Just that he doesn't think the owner was local, and that the company shut down soon after Lois and Ruby took their trip."

"But no name?"

The shake of the DC's neatly coiffured head said it all.

"Right, well, see if there's some other way to find out," Logan said, double-clicking on the next video in the sequence. "They owned a big boat. They'd have had to get safety certificates, that sort of thing. There'll be a record."

"Nessie Showboats," Sinead announced, drawing all the eyes in the room.

"What?" Tyler asked.

Sinead turned her computer monitor, revealing a short article from the *Highland News* website. The piece could only have been a couple of hundred words long, with a headline that read:

POOR REVIEWS FORCE CLOSURE OF LOCH NESS 'CRUISING THEATRE'.

"How the bloody hell did you find that so fast?" Tyler demanded.

"Google," Sinead told him. "Stuck in, 'Fort Augustus boat cruise company shut down' then clicked the News tab."

"Oh. Right. Aye," said Tyler, shoving his hands in the pockets of his trousers. "That's what I was going to do, too."

"My arse you were," Logan said. "Good work, Sinead. Is there a name of the owner?"

Sinead scanned the article. "No. Just mentions a spokesperson for the company, but doesn't give any more information."

"Right, well, get on it. Both of you," Logan said.

"Wait a minute, boss," Tyler interjected. "Poor reviews?"

"What about it?"

"It's just... DI Forde mentioned something else. Just offhand, like, when he was telling me what Reverend Mann said. He mentioned TripAdvisor."

Logan's brow became marked by creases. "TripAdvisor?"

"Aye. I didn't get much more than that, though. Want me to phone him back?"

"See what he says, aye," Logan instructed.

There was a flutter in his stomach. A tingling across his scalp. A buzzing in the room that suggested a breakthrough was imminent.

It'd do no good to get too excited yet, though. It could be nothing. It almost certainly was, in fact.

And yet, the very atoms in the air hummed with excitement around him.

He clicked play on the next video, and watched Reverend Mann stumbling around outside the car where the camera was housed. Lois was briefly visible in the window of the living room. There was nobody to been seen now at the window upstairs.

Logan watched the footage through to the end, then watched it again.

What was he missing?

What didn't he see?

"Um, sir?" said Sinead, and there was an urgency to it that made Logan turn all the way in his chair.

"What do we have?"

"I'm on TripAdvisor. Searched for 'Nessie's Showboats.' Reviews are fairly middling, but there are half a dozen absolutely brutal ones." Her eyes blazed with excitement. That thing that Logan was feeling, clearly she was feeling it, too. "Including one from Lois Mann that was particularly harsh about..." She sat so upright in her chair she almost jumped right out of it. "Oh! Shite! Sir! Sandra Atwood! Sandra Atwood one-starred it!"

Everyone—with the exception of Dave, for obvious reasons—was on their feet then.

"What? Fuck. You're kidding!" Logan blurted.

"No, sir. S. *Atwood*. 'High time the curtain came down on this absolute joke of a trip.'"

It hit Logan then, like a punch to the chest.

Oh, God.

It had been there. The whole time, it had been there.

Staring him in the face.

How could he have missed it? Had he really been away that long? Was he really that rusty?

"The curtains were closed," he announced, much to the confusion of everyone else in the room.

"Sorry, sir."

"At the house. On the video. Lois Mann shuts the curtains."

"Uh, yeah. That's right," Sinead confirmed.

Logan stormed back to his screen. "She *closed the curtains*. We see it, right there."

"Aye, we get that bit, boss," Tyler said. "What's the big deal."

"The big deal, Detective Constable, is that if she closed the curtains," Logan said, as slowly and deliberately as he could given the surge of adrenaline that had suddenly started to whoosh through him. "Then, how the *fuck* could that postman see her body through the living room window?"

CHAPTER THIRTY-SIX

IF THE CURTAINS WERE A GAME-CHANGER, IT WAS THE next discovery that blew the case wide open.

'Nessie's Showboats' was a Loch Ness Monster-themed kids' show that took place aboard a boat as it cruised Loch Ness itself.

And, according to most reviews, it was an arse-numbingly awful experience.

It had lasted just over six months—the business, not each individual show, although those who'd sat through one may have disagreed—before collapsing into administration and having its assets stripped.

There were just under forty reviews on TripAdvisor for the cruise, which was rated the second-worst experience for families with children in the Fort Augustus and Drumnadrochit area, narrowly beating six small stones in a field just off the A82.

The reviews ranged from 'apathetic' to 'brutal'. They were all three stars or below, with six one-stars that were so harsh and so cutting, that they made Logan physically wince as he read them.

All were posted by different accounts, but there were similarities between them, and they were all posted just a day or two apart.

The rest of the reviews were all largely negative, although markedly less brutal. The only exception was a five-star review so glowing in its praise that it could only have been written by the owner.

It was mention of the owner in one of the reviews that joined all the dots. It was buried halfway through a particularly lengthy, but reasonably balanced three-star write-up, and read as follows:

'The actors, for want of a better word, recite their lines like they're reading them from an autocue somewhere in the middle-distance, all under the watchful gaze of the desperately grinning Welsh captain."

It took under thirty seconds from there.

Prior to joining the fine men and women of the Royal Mail, Gwynn Dugdale had been co-owner of Nessie's Showboats with his wife, Judith. The collapse of the venture had ended both their business partnership and their romantic one, and cost them over a hundred thousand pounds.

She'd relocated back to Wales soon after, and almost immediately started divorce proceedings. Gwynn had moved into rented accommodation, taken the first job he could find, and hung around.

So far, all attempts to contact Judith had failed, but the local constabulary were on their way over to ask her some questions. The chief one being, 'Is your ex-husband a fucking psychopath?'

Once they had a connecting factor to search for, Hamza quickly found a post on Mumsnet in which Lois Mann, Sandra Atwood, and four other women, had agreed to vent their frustration at the awfulness of the showboat in a targeted assault.

Lois Mann had volunteered to help write the reviews, which explained the similarities between them. Sandra Atwood had supplied photographs she'd taken on her trip, showing dirty areas of the boat, disinterested performers, and two kids throwing up on the floor.

It had been a calculated attack. Not necessarily an undeserved one, granted, but calculating, all the same.

And two of them had now paid the ultimate price.

The Incident Room was abuzz with activity, Logan dishing out orders to his team, and them hurriedly relaying them to Uniform, either over the phone or to small groups who'd been dragged in from elsewhere in the station.

They'd managed to get Gwynn Dugdale's address from his employer, and Ben had turned around to check it out, with Uniform meeting him there.

The chances of finding him there were slim, though, Logan knew.

"He's here somewhere. The bastard's in Inverness. He told me to my bloody face."

"Got addresses through, boss," Tyler said. "For the other four women. Two in Inverness."

He recited them both. One wasn't a kick in the arse away from where Ben lived. The other was on Anderson Street in Merkinch.

Just around the corner.

Logan didn't waste time grabbing his coat as he jumped up and hurried to the door. "Get Uniform to all four addresses, and tell them to be careful. The bastard's probably armed and definitely dangerous."

"Right, sir," Hamza said, snatching up his phone's handset and hurriedly jabbing at the buttons.

"I'm taking Anderson Street. Tyler, Sinead, you take the other one. And for Christ's sake, no heroics."

"Same goes for you, boss," Tyler said, but he was saying the words to the doors as they swung shut at Logan's back.

THERE WAS a single uniformed officer in the street outside Gwynn Dugdale's house when DI Forde pulled up. He was a younger fella—mind you, they were all younger these days —and Ben recognised him from various call-outs over the last few years.

"Hello. Kevin, isn't it?"

"Kelvin, sir," the officer replied. He'd barely made a dent in his twenties, Ben reckoned. Good looking lad, too, with hair cropped close to the bone, and an open, honest sort of face. "Kelvin McGowan."

"Kelvin. Sorry. I think I've made that mistake before," Ben said. A vague memory of the man came back to him. "You were getting married, weren't you? Last time we spoke?"

"I was, sir," the constable confirmed, positively beaming that the DI had remembered. "February. Got a wee one on the way now and everything. Proper grown-up stuff."

"Good for you, son," Ben said. "Congratulations."

He looked both ways along the street. They were only a dozen yards off the main road, and he felt the wind buffet him as a truck went thundering around the bend heading north from Fort William.

"You on your own?" Ben asked.

"That I am, sir. I think we've got more coming down from Inverness, but I'm all there is for now, I'm afraid."

"Aye, well, between us I'm sure we'll be grand," Ben assured him. He gestured up at the house beside them. It was one of a block of three whose doors opened directly onto a street otherwise lined with large detached dwellings, all with big gardens. "This is him, then. You knocked yet?"

Kelvin shook his head. "Was told to hang fire until backup arrived, sir."

"Well, I guess that makes me the cavalry," Ben told him. He crossed to the door, raised a fist, and thumped out a machine-gun beat on the blue gloss-painted wood. "Mr Dugdale? Mr Dugdale, open up. Police."

The door did not open. The house remained silent and still.

Kelvin tried to peek in through the window, but the curtains were drawn, and what little of the room could be seen through the narrow gap between them was mostly in darkness.

There was a path at the side of the block that led to a small parking area out back. The door to Dugdale's house was locked, the blinds pulled closed over the kitchen window.

As Ben hammered on the frosted glass window that took up half the door, there was a *creak* from next door, and a woman with hair so dark it couldn't possibly be real, and skin so orange she looked like the citrus fruit of the same name, came charging out.

"You come take him away?" she demanded in broken

English, the finger of a pink rubber-gloved hand jabbing accusingly at Ben and the uniformed officer. "Finally. Sick of all noise."

"He's been making noise? What today?" Ben asked, shooting a look at the door.

"Not today. Last few days, silent. For once. For *once*," the woman spat. She was properly seething. Clearly, this had been building for some time. "But before that, *boom-boom-boom*, music. All day. Into night. Always *boom-boom-boom*. So much noise.Walls not thick. I tell landlord. I say, 'He play fucking music too loud again.' He does not care. Long as he gets his money, why does he care?"

Ben clicked his tongue against the back of his teeth, then turned to the neighbour again. "Landlord local?"

"Landlord?" the woman replied, stalling for time as she deciphered the abrupt phrasing of the question. "Ah. No. Manchester. Never see him, except when I move in."

"Don't suppose you've got a spare key for the place, do you?"

"Key? Of course, no key. If I have key, I go in and fucking shut up his music when he play it."

"Right, aye. Got you," Ben said. He flashed her a reassuring smile. "We're going to take care of it. If you could go back inside, we'll sort everything out."

"Huh." The neighbour gave them both a look that suggested she'd believe it when she saw it. "I not hold my breath."

Ben waited until she'd gone back in her house, and then held her gaze through the kitchen window until she became too uncomfortable to keep watching.

"Right, then, Kelvin. Still no sign of that backup. Any chance you've got a battering ram in the boot of your car?"

"Afraid not, sir," the constable replied. "But, there's one at the station, just around the corner. I could get it and be back in under five minutes."

"Go do that, then. I'll wait here and keep an eye," Ben instructed.

Kelvin stole a wary look at the house, then nodded. "Right, sir. I'll be back right away."

Ben watched until he was out of sight around the corner.

Listened until he heard the car door close and the engine start up.

The lad was young. He had a wee one on the way. Wasn't right for him to be put at risk.

Humming to himself, Ben returned to his car, opened the boot, and took out the wheel wrench.

"Right, then," he muttered, slamming the boot closed, and hefting the metal tool from hand to hand. "Let's see if you can still break a window, you old bugger."

CHAPTER THIRTY-SEVEN

LOGAN MOUNTED THE PAVEMENT AND SCREECHED TO A stop in his Ford Fiesta, right at the end of Waterloo Bridge.

The house on Anderson Street was a two-minute drive away, but a quick dash across the short pedestrian area would have him at the front door in thirty seconds.

Cursing his car, and the stiffness in his legs, Logan heaved himself out of the vehicle. Sirens screamed past him, Uniform racing to the scene.

"Bollocks!" he ejected. Why weren't they there already? Why hadn't they already cleared the house?

Still, from here, he'd get there before them. And that meant that, if the bastard was in the house, Logan would have first dibs.

Bunching his fist around his car keys, he dodged around the large concrete planter and bins that had prevented him powering the car all the way across the pavement. And then, with his whole body crying out in protest, he threw himself forward into a painful, stumbling run.

BREAKING a window with a metal bar was a bit like riding a bike, it turned out. A) You never forgot, and B) It was a risky bloody business at DI Forde's age.

The door was old, and the glass predated the mandatory safety variety that would've seen it shatter into tiny crystalline pieces. Instead, it broke into long, deadly slivers that almost took his hand off when he clattered the thing with the wheel wrench.

After a quick check to make sure he hadn't severed any major arteries, Ben reached inside and—to his immense relief—found the keys were still in the lock, therefore saving himself the indignity of having to clamber through the hole where the window had been.

Glass crunched into the faded lino as he opened the door and crept inside. He held his breath, an old trick he used to steady his nerves at times like these.

But the nerves didn't come. There was no rush of adrenaline, or surge of fear. No racing heart. No heightened senses.

He felt... nothing. The space in his gut where the low-graded panic used to form in moments of danger or stress was now empty.

Closing the door, he picked his way around the worst of the glass and headed across the kitchen. It was a large room, but sorely in need of renovation. The worktops and cabinets were different shades of green, with clear plastic handles designed to look like enormous diamonds.

A small Formica table sat against one wall, three padded chairs positioned around it, two with their seats ripped. There were a couple of dirty plates stacked one atop the other in the centre of the table, right beside a bundle of mail in sealed envelopes.

Ben checked the envelopes, and found a multitude of names and addresses on them, all local. The letters were addressed to men, women, businesses, and all from different senders. Clearly, Gwynn Dugdale made a better murderer than he did a postman.

There were other piles of letters and packages out in the hallway, and in the living room. Most of them were still sealed, but a few of the more interesting ones had been ripped open.

Birthday cards stood in haphazard ranks on almost every available surface in the darkened living room. Ben peeked inside some of the open ones, and read the messages inside.

To Mia, from Nan.

To Kyle, love Grandpa.

The money, which no doubt would've been included inside each card, was nowhere to be seen.

"Dirty robbing bastard," Ben muttered, although this was almost certainly the least of Dugdale's crimes.

After a quick check a through gap in the curtains to see if there was any sign of the constable returning in his patrol car, Ben returned to the hallway, and looked up the narrow flight of stairs to the windowless landing above.

"Right then, ye bugger," the DI whispered, clutching the wheel wrench down by his waist. "Let's see if you're home."

His pulse didn't race. His breath didn't falter.

Feeling nothing, DI Ben Forde *creaked* onto the first step, and made his way up the stairs.

Tyler and Sinead arrived at the other address in Inverness to find Uniform already swarming around the place. Two women and a toddler stood huddled together near one of the half-dozen polis vehicles that blocked the street. The women watched the house, while the child tucked himself in behind their legs, warily eyeing the assembled officers.

Judging by the way the Uniforms were moving, there was little to get excited about. Everyone was just sort of milling around in the street and the garden. A sergeant appeared in the front doorway, talking into the radio on her shoulder.

As she came down the steps, a couple of constables followed, the one at the back closing the door behind them.

Sinead was first out of the car. Her beat days weren't far behind her, and she knew most of the officers on the scene.

"Anything?" she asked the closest constable. Jason, his name was. Nice enough guy, if a bit on the sleazy side.

He turned and regarded her with something like suspicion for a moment, then broke into a broad smile. "Alright, Sinead? Gracing us with your presence, are you? How's life upstairs treating you?"

"Good, thanks." She gestured at the house and asked the question again. "Anything?"

The constable shrugged. "Nah, doesn't look like it. I mean, I don't know what we're looking for—since when did your lot tell us anything? But, whatever it is, pretty safe to say we didn't find it."

Sinead felt the 'you lot' jibe, but chose to ignore it.

"Right. OK. Thanks," she said.

"I'm good, by the way."

Sinead had started to bend down to talk to Tyler who was still in the passenger seat, but stopped. "Sorry."

"I asked how you were. You didn't ask how I was," the

constable said, his smile fixed in place. "So, I thought I'd tell you. I'm good."

"Uh. Right," Sinead said. "Right. I'm glad." She returned his smile, but hers was less certain. "Nice to see you."

"Always a pleasure," Jason replied, holding the DC's gaze until she'd bent all the way back into the car.

"No joy?" Tyler asked. He had his phone in his hand, a text message window open with Logan and Hamza's names at the top.

"No," Sinead said. She looked ahead through the windscreen. The constable was still smiling at her through the glass. "No joy."

"Shite," Tyler groaned. "Hopefully the boss is having more luck."

LOGAN STOOD WHEEZING on the front step of the house on Anderson Street, swallowing back saliva and trying desperately not to throw up.

He hammered on the door for the third time in thirty seconds, tried to listen over the racket of his own breathing, then stepped back and hoped he had the energy left to put the door in.

His shoulder had just taken aim when the door opened a crack, and a short-haired woman in oversized glasses peered out at him from just above the security chain.

"Can I help you?" she asked.

Logan didn't waste time addressing her by name. Chiefly because he hadn't waited around to take note of it. Instead, he thrust his ID into her hands and babbled out a breathless introduction.

"Detective Chief Inspector Logan. We need to get you and your children out of the house. Now."

The woman looked up from the warrant card, her cartoonishly large eyes blinking rapidly behind the thick lenses of her glasses. "What? What are you talking about?"

A wailing of sirens and the shriek of a skid heralded the arrival of Uniform.

The woman on the other side of the door looked from Logan to the car, then back again, like she was trying to figure out if they were there to arrest this sweating, red-faced maniac on her doorstep.

"They're with me," he snapped, reading the look, then he confirmed it by spinning and dishing out orders to the two officers who jumped out of the car. "Get around the back. No one goes in until I say so!"

"Sir," confirmed one of the Uniforms, then they both went dashing towards the alleyway at the side of the block, just as Logan spun around to face the woman beyond the door.

"You and your children are in danger. You need to let me in, *right now!*" he barked.

With a squeal, the woman slammed the door closed in his face. He was about to knock again when he heard the rattling of the security chain being undone, and the door was thrown open again.

"Sonia! Alex!" the woman shouted, her head angled up to the ceiling above.

Logan was past her in an instant, the pain in his legs and the tightness in his chest both forgotten.

"What room?" he demanded, already mounting the stairs.

"The one on the right!"

The DCI's toe caught the top step and he stumbled straight at the door. His weight collided with it, throwing it wide open and drawing screams from the two young children on the bunk bed.

"Go. Downstairs!" he barked at the girl on the bottom bunk, then he snatched the still-screaming girl from the top bed and practically threw her out of the room.

"Here, Mum's here, Mum's here," he heard the woman say, as four little feet went thumping down the steps.

There was no cupboard in this room. No wardrobe. No obvious place for someone to hide themselves away.

No obvious place except for one.

Dropping to his knees, Logan pulled up the valance sheet from the bottom bunk, and came face to face with a leering, dead-eyed face.

Grabbing for the clown doll, he tossed it aside, hoping Dugdale had been hiding behind it.

He wasn't.

Aside from a handful of toys, two odd shoes, and a pair of child's pants, the space below the bed was empty.

A text came through, and Logan grabbed for the phone in his pocket, hoping for good news.

It wasn't.

No joy here, Tyler's message read.

Dugdale wasn't at the other address in Inverness.

Logan jumped up and hammered on the window to summon the Uniforms inside. He could hear more of them pulling up out front, the frantic cries of the woman and her children, the reassuring tones of a female officer.

They were safe, that was the main thing.

But it wasn't the only thing. Dugdale—assuming, of course, that it *was* Dugdale—was still on the loose somewhere. And that would not do. That would not bloody do at all.

It took Logan and the Uniforms just a couple of minutes of searching to determine that the bastard wasn't hiding anywhere in the house. There was nothing to indicate he had ever been there.

Another text came through, this one from Hamza. The searches at the two other addresses had drawn blanks, too. The families were all safe, but there was no sign of Dugdale at any of them.

Which begged the question.

Where the hell was he?

THIRTY MILES AWAY, in a darkened house on an unremarkable street, Detective Inspector Ben Forde adjusted his grip on his makeshift weapon, and quietly nudged open a bedroom door.

CHAPTER THIRTY-EIGHT

THE ROOM WAS MOSTLY IN DARKNESS, THANKS TO THE tabloid newspaper pages that had been taped over most of the window, shutting out the light. *The Sun*, ironically enough.

Ben flicked the switch by the door, and an old incandescent bulb flickered into life in the grimy, dust-covered fitting on the ceiling.

His foot slipped on something as he stepped inside, forcing him to grab for the door to steady himself.

Once he had, he glanced down to see what he'd slipped on and found hundreds of letters and envelopes carpeting the floor, along with more newspaper pages. Local press, this time.

The walls, though, had caught his interest even more. There were dozens of photographs pinned to all four sides of the small room in seven distinct, densely packed clusters. Each cluster showed a different woman, each accompanied by a child or children, and most of them taken at a distance through a long lens.

He spotted Lois Mann almost immediately. She was standing by her car, sweeping a strand of hair behind her ear, a smile on her face. Little Ruby stood on tiptoes in front of her, her arms stretched out wide, like she was sharing the most exciting story in all the world.

The photograph beside it showed Lois in the supermarket. It was a little blurry, and was tilted at an angle, suggesting that the person taking it hadn't been looking through the viewfinder when they'd pressed the shutter release.

There were a dozen other photos, too. At church. Filling up at the petrol station. A couple taken on what must've been a day out in Inverness.

Most disturbingly, there were a few taken inside the house. One showed Lois while she slept. Another was snapped in the living room, while she watched TV. Dugdale must have been just a couple of feet behind her when he took it. Close enough to reach out and touch her.

Ben looked along the wall to the next cluster. He didn't know the woman or two children in this one, but the pictures were all of a similar candid nature. In the park. In the garden. In the kitchen, seen through the window.

One had been taken through a narrow crack, like a partially open cupboard door. It showed a blurry image of the woman lying naked, her legs wrapped around the man on top of her.

Sandra and Simon Atwood were in the next group of pictures, and...

Wait.

He returned to the previous photograph.

The man in the picture. The man with the legs wrapped around his back.

It was Reverend Mann.

"Jesus, is there anyone he wasn't at it with?" Ben muttered.

A thought came creeping in. He reached for his phone, punched in Logan's number, and waited for the DCI to answer.

"Hello? Hello? Is this...? Ben, can you hear me?"

Logan sounded like he was underwater.

"Yes. Just. Where are you? On the moon?"

"It's this bloody car," Logan spat. "I'm hearing my own voice echo back to me. Christ, do I really sound like that?"

"Afraid so," Ben told him.

"I'm on my way down to you," Logan said. "I'm about halfway. We've been checking out—hello?"

"Aye, I'm still here."

"We found addresses for the four other women we think Dugdale is going to target, but he's not at any of them."

"Four other women?" Ben said. He counted the clusters of photographs. Seven. Two already dead. Five left. He turned back to the group of pictures beside him, where the mystery woman lay entangled with Reverend Mann. "Quick question," he said. "What does Kerry Philip look like?"

"Eh, bit like an elf."

"What, three feet tall with a big bloody hat on?" Ben retorted. "Can you be a bit more specific, Jack? Hair colour."

"Red."

"Like ginger, or *red* red?"

"Red red. Dyed. Why?"

Ben's eyes flicked across the woman in the cluster of photographs.

The woman with the red red hair.

"Shite," he spat. "I think I know where Dugdale is."

THEY HAD LEFT the room now. He could hear them downstairs, clattering dishes and rattling cutlery as they stacked the dishwasher after lunch. They laughed. They sang. They went about their day, unaware of him. Blinkered and unknowing.

They would know him, though, soon enough.

He hadn't seen her name for himself, but he'd been told of her. Told of her lies, and her wicked tongue. Of her mocking laughter. Of her taunting words.

They had cackled, those witches, when his business had failed. When his marriage had ended. When his dreams had collapsed. They had ruined him, and they'd laughed while they'd done it. They had destroyed everything important to him. Everything he held dear.

Balance. That was all he was doing. Balancing the scales. An eye for an eye. A tooth for a tooth.

Their lives, for his.

The sound from the kitchen grew louder as a door was opened.

Chattering voices rose up.

Giggling.

Glee.

"Mum'll be up in a few minutes, OK? Just going to quickly phone Granny."

"OK!"

"Don't be long!"

And then... footsteps.

Four little feet on the stairs, hurrying upwards. Returning to the room.

Returning to him.

THE FIESTA's gearbox ejected a mangled cry of displeasure as Logan tried to force the stick into a slot it was never intended for. The engine *whirred*, the acceleration slowed, then he managed to crunch the gearstick into place and, with a raise of the clutch, lurched the car into the right-hand lane, furiously blasting the horn at the Renault Captur he'd just been forced to overtake.

"Get out of the bloody road!" he bellowed at the driver, the Fiesta emitting a pained scream of effort as he crept past the other car.

A horn blared up ahead. Logan swerved back into the left lane just in time to avoid a head-on with a braking Mazda. Both of the other drivers flashed their headlights at him, and at least one of them made what was almost certainly a rude hand gesture, although Logan was going too fast to be able to tell for sure.

"Ah, fuck off!" he shouted to them, his voice echoing around inside the Ford's cramped cabin.

He passed the turnoff to somewhere called 'Kerrow-down'. He'd never heard of it, but the vaguely familiar build-up of houses on the right, and boats down on the loch on the left, made him think he was almost to Drumnadrochit, and Kerry Philip's house.

Hamza was trying to get her on the phone to warn her. Uniform would be horsing down the road behind him with the lights and sirens on full tilt, but he was closer. Life was giving him another crack at nabbing this bastard.

He just prayed that he wasn't too late.

CHAPTER THIRTY-NINE

Cole Philip put down his Iron Man action figure, stood up from the bed, and solemnly announced that he needed a poo.

Sitting cross-legged on the bedroom floor, his sister, Sophie, groaned and slapped both hands against her forehead.

"You always take *aaages* to do a poo!"

"I do *not* take ages to do a poo," Cole said, visibly horrified by the very suggestion.

"You do! You take eleventy-hundred *hours* to do a poo! We're playing a game!"

Technically, this was true. They had agreed to play a game when they'd come upstairs, but had then jumped straight into playing it without establishing what the rules were, what the point was, or even vaguely what they were meant to be doing.

So far, it had involved Cole swinging a succession of six-inch plastic superheroes around by their legs, while Sophie turned all the toy cars upside down on their roofs.

"You're just saying you need a poo so you can take the iPad!" Sophie protested. She was a veteran of this strategy herself, but was none too impressed with it now that the shoe was on the other foot.

"I am *not!*" an indignant Cole countered, looking genuinely hurt by this slanderous accusation.

He picked up the iPad.

"Poo quick!" Sophie urged, realising the battle had been lost, but still working to minimise the delay. "Or I'll win the game."

"You'd better not win the game!" Cole told her.

"Then you'd better not take eleventy-hundred hours," his sister countered. She sniffed a sniff of victory, and turned her attention back to the cars as Cole went racing out of the room, his shorts already halfway to his ankles.

Sophie picked up a small hatchback spent a few seconds trying to balance it on her finger, then shot a furtive look over at the door that Cole had just disappeared through.

With a triumphant smirk, she flipped the car over and placed it down on the floor on its roof, its bonnet touching the boot of the one beside it.

"I'm going to wi-in, I'm going to wi-in," she sang in a whisper.

She was almost out of cars to flip over, but there were others under the bed, she knew. Bending forward on her knees, she peered into the shadowy space below the bunk beds.

Behind her, the door to the toy cupboard inched open, and a sliver of metal glinted in the gap.

THE UNIFORMED CONSTABLE, Kelvin, had returned with his battering ram to find the back door of the house standing open.

Ben shouted down a reply when Kelvin called out to him, telling him to set up a cordon around the house, and not to come inside. It was likely a treasure trove of evidence, and the DI had already compromised it more than enough.

"What the hell is he after Kerry Philip for?" That's what Logan had asked when Ben had told him about the pictures.

After snapping off a few pictures on his phone—a process that involved putting on his reading glasses and staring blankly at the app icons until his powers of recollection kicked in and he remembered how to go about opening the camera—Ben headed for the bedroom door, and nearly went on his arse when his foot found another newspaper page and skidded on a carpet of envelopes.

Once he'd successfully regained his balance, he shot the page a dirty look, like it had somehow been responsible for him almost dislocating his hip.

Two people smiled up at him from a black and white photograph on the page. Above the image, a headline announced the opening of a new theatre company with a difference. This one would be putting on its shows aboard a boat on Loch Ness.

Ben's eyes crept across all the mail on the floor until it found another newspaper page.

An identical newspaper page. Same edition. Same article. Same two people smiling up at him from the photograph.

The caption below it identified one of the people as Gwynn Dugdale. Ben didn't need the caption to identify the other person in the image.

"Oh, God," he whispered. "No."

Gwynn Dugdale was one step from stabbing distance when the shape hit him. Dugdale was a big man, but the one that slammed into him was bigger. The new arrival had been moving much faster, too, when his shoulder connected with Dugdale's ribcage, propelling them both towards the window.

Dugdale cried out in pain and in fright. He twisted his grip on the knife, but then his head hit the window with a loud, hollow *thonk*, and the room went into a spiralling spin.

He heard the girl scream. Heard her mother shouting for her from out on the landing.

"Sophie, Sophie, come here, quick!"

A hand grabbed Dugdale by the wrist, twisting, trying to force him to drop the knife. He found a bedside lamp, grabbed it, smashed it against the other man's head. It drew a hiss, and a snarled, "Bastard!" but the grip eased enough for him to yank his hand free.

The other man leapt back, narrowly avoiding a stabbing thrust. Dugdale recognised him immediately, went into a panic, and slashed frantically, driving the detective back.

The girl and her mother both screamed as he stumbled out into the hall, hurriedly retreating beyond the detective's reach.

He ran for the stairs, but could already hear the detective coming after him, his bear-like frame shaking the floor beneath him.

A door opened between Dugdale and the stairs. The boy stepped out, wide-eyed with curiosity, his iPad clutched under his arm.

Yes. Oh, God, yes!

"No!" the detective bellowed, but he was too late, too far away.

The boy stood frozen to the spot, his mother's screams echoing along the landing towards him, warning him to go back in the bathroom, to lock the door.

But Dugdale got to him first. A hand around his neck. A jerk into the air. A knife to his throat.

"Nobody fucking move!" he screeched, and Logan stumbled to a stop just a few feet from them. "Back off. Back off! Now!"

Logan didn't make a move other than to raise his hands in a show of surrender. "Easy, Gwynn."

"Fucking back off, or I'll kill him right now!"

"No, don't!" Sophie cried from her mother's arms. "He's my big brother!"

"Alright, Gwynn. I'm backing off. I'm backing off," Logan said, his voice a calming murmur. "You're in charge, son."

"I know I'm in fucking charge! Obviously, I'm in fucking charge! Look!" He tightened his grip on the boy, forcing a cry of pain from his lips.

"Cole!" Kerry sobbed. "Please, don't hurt him!"

"Like you hurt me, you mean?" Gwynn hissed, his face knotted up in rage. *"You ruined my life!"*

"Please, I don't know you. I don't know who you are!"

"You don't even remember? You just casually destroy everything I worked for, and you don't even *remember*?"

Cole let out a shrill sob as the knife was pressed tighter against his throat.

"Put the boy down, son, and let's talk," Logan said. "I know what this is about, and Kerry had nothing to do with it. We saw the reviews. She wasn't on the list."

"She was on the list! She was! She told me she was on the list!"

"I didn't tell you anything! I don't know who you are!" Kerry told him, her face shining with tears and snot.

Dugdale practically screamed at her along the hallway. "No, not you! Not *you*! I don't mean you!"

Sirens rang out somewhere in the distance. Dugdale glanced down the stairs, and Logan raised himself onto the balls of his feet. Pain roared through his leg muscles, but he ignored it, boxed it away. That was a problem for another time.

"Drop the boy, and you might be able to get away before they arrive," Logan said. "I won't even come after you."

"You will!" Dugdale said. It was his turn for the tears to start streaming now. He was coming apart right before Logan's eyes.

A rivulet of blood ran down Cole's throat from the tip of the knife.

"I won't. You have my word. And believe me, I'm in no fit state to run anywhere," Logan told him. The sirens were drawing closer now, their howling becoming more insistent, more urgent. "Drop him, and go. Make a run for it. You might make it. You might not. But, it's your only chance of getting out of here."

"Let go of my brother!" Sophie wailed. "Let him go!"

"Please," Kerry sobbed. "Please, let him go."

Dugdale's face contorted into a snarl like he was about to spit something back at them, but Logan intervened.

"Time's running out, Gwynn," the DCI said. "I'm trying to help you here, son. What's it to be?"

Another backwards glance. Another shuffled step towards the staircase.

Then, with a roar, Dugdale thrust his arms out, propelling the screaming boy along the landing in Logan's direction.

He spun around, stumbled down the steps, then ran out into the front garden just as two police cars skidded into the drive, spraying gravel up in the direction of the house.

"No, no, no," Dugdale whimpered, diverting at a right-angle and running along the front of the house, then hanging a left up the path at the side.

He vaulted the small gate at the far end, almost tripped over a yappy bastard of a dog in the back garden, and was halfway to the fence—halfway to freedom—when something hit him like a charging bull and he face-planted onto the grass.

His arm was twisted. The knife flew from his fingers and landed beyond his reach. A knee dug into his back, pinning him helplessly, as that yappy wee fucker of a dog yelped and snarled in his face.

"Well, would you look at that," wheezed the inordinately heavy man on his back. "Turns out I can still run, after all."

CHAPTER FORTY

THEY WERE LAUGHING WHEN BEN APPROACHED. Chatting away like old friends. It was the lightest and most relaxed the DI had ever seen the Reverend.

That would only make it all that much harder.

"Detective Inspector, you're back," Gareth said. Up close, he still looked happy, but it was evident that the smile was taking an effort to maintain. "If you've come to lend a hand, you're too late, I'm afraid. Elizabeth has worked wonders. See?"

He gestured to the now almost spotless door. There were still a couple of flecks of yellow that hadn't come off, but you'd have to be looking very closely to notice them.

"That's great. Much better," Ben said. He looked past the minister to the woman beside him. "I actually wanted a word with Mrs Strand."

Elizabeth pulled off a rubber glove with a *snap*, then set to work on the other one. "Right. Well, off you go, then."

"In private might be best," Ben told her.

She hesitated then, the remaining glove half on, half off.

Ben indicated the church with a tilt of his head.

"Mind if the two of us step inside for a wee minute, Reverend?"

Gareth frowned, but gave a nod of approval. "Uh, yes. Yes, of course. Help yourself."

He opened the door for them, and Ben motioned for Elizabeth to lead the way.

A look passed from the woman to the minister. Her eyes darted across his face as if trying to capture it, memorise it, exactly as it was in that moment.

And then, she disappeared inside.

"This shouldn't take long," DI Forde told the perplexed minister. He put a hand on the younger man's shoulder and squeezed. "It's all going to be alright, son. It's all going to be alright."

Elizabeth was waiting for him on a pew down at the very front of the church, her hands clasped lightly in her lap, her back straight like she was trying to get in the proprietor's good books.

Bit late for that, Ben reckoned.

"We've caught him," he said, and his voice echoed around in the cavernous space.

She didn't lie, or try to hide it. He'd say that for her, at least.

"Mentioned me, did he?" she asked, still facing front.

"No. But he will," Ben assured her. "The Reverend told us you'd lost your life savings on a bad investment. It was the boat, wasn't it? I saw the two of you in the paper. You put in money."

"Almost half a million pounds," Elizabeth said. "Everything I had. Even the house. I mean, we get to live in it until I die, but then that's gone, too. And for what?" She let out a little snort of disgust. "Some mouthy women talking rubbish on the internet?"

She turned then and looked back at Ben. There were no tears, no sorrow, not a flicker of remorse on her face. "*Reviews*. Libel, more like. 'Judge not, lest ye be judged.' Matthew, chapter seven, verse one. It's there. Black and white. They tried to judge us—they conspired, all of them, to judge us—and so they were judged in return."

"By you," Ben said.

"By their own actions!" Elizabeth countered, standing as quickly as she was able to and turning all the way to face the detective. "We did not find them guilty, the Bible itself found them guilty. Luke, chapter six: 'Judge not, and you will not be judged; condemn not, and you will not be condemned.' Romans, chapter two: 'For in passing judgement on another you condemn yourself.'"

She held her hands out imploringly.

"Don't you see? How could we be doing wrong, if we were simply doing God's work?"

"I do see, Mrs Strand, yes," Ben said. "And I could almost buy that you believe that. I think Gwynn Dugdale probably does. I think he was probably so broken after losing everything, that you managed to convince him that you're fighting the good fight. But me? I'm a cynical old bugger, and I can see clean through your shite." His eyes flitted to the image of Christ on the wall at the front. "Excuse the language, son."

"What are you talking about?" Elizabeth demanded. She'd been quick to confess to her involvement in the killings, but her body language was becoming evasive now that they were digging into motive.

"Kerry Philip was never on that cruise," Ben said. "You

just wanted her out of the way, so you could have the Reverend for yourself."

"How *dare* you?" the old woman yelped. "How *dare* you suggest such a thing?"

"That's why you sent Gwynn after Lois first," Ben reasoned. "That's probably why you made sure he went for Ruby, too. Really isolate him. Make him hurt so badly, he needed someone to turn to. Someone to hold onto him while he cried. Someone he knew. Someone he trusted."

The anger and indignation had left Elizabeth's face now, replaced by a vague sort of slackness that left her mouth drooping open and her eyes wide.

"That's why you waited outside for him every day. You wanted to be the first to give him a wee hug. Tell him everything was going to be OK. Tell him you'd be there for him, night or day, he just had to say the word."

"He's a good man. He deserved better," Elizabeth whispered. It sounded unnaturally loud in the empty church. "I love him."

"You didn't. You betrayed him. He was your victim *and* your thirty pieces of silver," Ben said. He took no pleasure in the next part. Quite the opposite. "And I'm arresting you on suspicion of murder."

KELVIN WAS STANDING by his squad car when Ben and Elizabeth stepped out of the church. On DI Forde's signal, he made his way over to join them.

"Everything OK?" Reverend Mann asked, drying his hands on a towel. He looked from Ben to Elizabeth and back again. "What is it?" he asked, his face falling. "What's happened?"

"Take Mrs Strand up the road, will you, Constable?" Ben asked, ignoring the minister's questions for the moment.

"Will do, sir," Kelvin replied. "Mrs Strand? This way, please."

"Elizabeth?" Gareth said. He half-laughed, but it was a nervous reaction, that was all. "What's going on?"

"I did it for us," she told him.

"Us? What do you...? Elizabeth?" His eyes were wide, almost to the point of bulging. They flicked from face to face, searching for an answer. "What's this about? What's going on?"

Without another word, Elizabeth turned and let herself be led over to Kelvin's waiting car.

"What's this about?" Mann asked again, this time aiming it at Ben.

"Come away inside and we'll have a chat, son," Ben replied, putting a hand on the younger man's arm and holding it. "I'm afraid there's a few things you need to know..."

CHAPTER FORTY-ONE

MacCallums Bar on Union Street was quiet for a Saturday evening. At least, it was until they turned up.

It wasn't the swankiest boozer in Inverness, but then that was part of the appeal. A swanky bar was a place best reserved for *metrosexuals*, Ben had said. Although, on further interrogation, he was forced to admit he had no idea what a metrosexual was, or what sort of pubs, if any, they might frequent.

MacCallums was a traditional Scottish pub, from the cheap and plentiful booze, to the withering put-downs from the bar staff when any of the punters started making too much of an arse of themselves.

There was even a big mirror on one of the walls, proudly displaying the lyrics to 'Flower of Scotland' and it was possible to while away many an hour watching someone with a few bevvies in them trying to read the words while their own reflection went out of its way to put them off.

The first round was on Logan. It was only right.

Pints for the three constables—detective and uniform—

fresh orange and lemonade for the detective sergeant, and a wee Lagavulin for DI Forde.

Logan ordered a Coke for himself, before deciding that, all things considered, the barman should probably, "Make it a Diet."

Back at the table, the drinks were passed around. Food was on the way, too, Logan announced, drawing a cheer from Dave, who was already clutching a fork in one hand, and a knife in the other, both pieces of cutlery held upright in anticipation of the grub.

"What's that you're drinking?" Ben asked, scowling at the black and red can that Logan had set down on the table.

"Coke Zero," Logan told him.

"What's that when it's at home?"

"It's Coke, but without the calories."

Ben picked the can up and turned it around, studying the design. "Is that no' just Diet Coke, then?"

"No, it's different, boss," Tyler said.

"How?"

There, Tyler's knowledge of the product fell short. He blew out his cheeks and shrugged, leaving Sinead to take up the reins.

"It tastes more like Coke than Diet Coke."

"But still has zero calories," Hamza added.

"Then why do we still need Diet Coke?" Ben asked, apparently genuinely annoyed by this duplication of effort. "Just say, 'Good news, we've made Diet Coke taste more like Coke than it used to.'"

"Look, I'm just telling you what the boy at the bar told me," Logan protested, but Ben wasn't finished yet.

"Or do away with Diet Coke. Just get rid of it, altogether.

Have one or the other, you don't need both. That's all I'm saying."

"I'll be sure to pass on your concerns to the Coca-Cola corporation next time I'm speaking to them," Logan said.

Gradually, talk turned, as it invariably did despite all their best efforts, to the case.

Both Gwynn Dugdale and Elizabeth Strand had confessed to planning the murders, with Dugdale owning up to being the one who carried them out.

Reverend Mann had not taken the news well. No great surprise there. Ben suspected the minister's ability to turn the other cheek was likely to be tested to its limits, but he'd insisted his faith would get him through.

Ben envied him that. He'd realised then that he didn't have that. His was a fake faith. His church was not a place of comfort, but a place to go to hear comforting words, and to nod and smile like they were helping, when deep down he knew otherwise.

He looked around at the others. Logan. Hamza. Tyler. Sinead. Hell, even Dave, though he barely knew the lad. He knew the type, and that was good enough.

This here? Now? Them?

That, he had faith in. This was his church.

And the bevvy was better, too.

"I think we should have a toast," Ben announced, half-raising his glass. "To Detective Chief Inspector Jack Logan. The man who returned to save us from Snecky."

The others, with the exception of Logan, reached for their glasses.

A voice intruded from a few feet away.

"Maybe we should save that one until we see if he passes the fitness test."

They all turned and immediately straightened in their seats when they saw Detective Superintendent Mitchell approaching their table, a frothy-headed pint in her hand.

With a glance from Mitchell, Tyler, Hamza, and Sinead all slid further along the padded bench they were sitting on, making room for her to take a seat beside Logan.

"Besides, Senior Investigating Officer should make the toast. Don't you think, Jack?" she asked him, very deliberately. "I'm sure you can think of something more... important to raise a glass to."

Damn it. Much as Logan hated to admit it, she was good. And she was right.

He picked up his glass. He met the gaze of his oldest friend across the cluttered table. "I'd like to propose a toast, to a woman we've loved and lost," he said, and he saw the pain behind Ben's eyes. "To Alice."

The others waited. Maybe they already knew, or maybe they picked up on the significance of the moment, but they waited, glasses poised, all eyes on DI Forde.

He sniffed. He nodded.

"To Alice," he said, then there was a chinking of glasses, a glugging of liquid, and the near-imperceptible sound of something broken becoming ever so slightly less so.

"THAT WAS A GOOD CALL, MA'AM," Logan said, joining the DSup at the bar.

The food had arrived, and everyone was getting stuck in. Especially Dave, who had wrapped one arm protectively around his plate and was shovelling chips into his mouth like a global ban was about to be announced.

"I'm ma'am in the office, Jack," she said, just as sternly as she'd said pretty much everything else to him. She held a hand out for him to shake. "Chuki Mitchell. Nice to meet you."

Logan smiled, and shook the hand. "Likewise."

"You did good," she said. "All of you."

"Aye. Aye, I suppose we did," Logan acknowledged.

"No suppose about it," she said. "Snecky has put in for the transfer to Aberdeen. I won't be sad to see the back of him."

"I can imagine."

"So, I hope you're ready for the bleep test on Monday. I'd hate to see you fall at the final hurdle."

Logan shifted his weight from one aching leg to another. "I was thinking, maybe we could push that back for—"

"You were thinking wrong then, Jack," Mitchell said. "We do things properly, or we don't do them at all. You're booked in for Monday. It's important you attend."

Logan groaned, but then nodded his understanding. "Aye, fair enough."

"I hear the pathologist from Raigmore has been helping you train."

"Nearly bloody killing me, more like."

"She not joining us tonight?"

"Uh, no. Not tonight," he said.

Mitchell watched him, her face completely immobile, until he gave in.

"But... She invited me round afterwards," he confessed. "I'm just heading there shortly."

The Detective Superintendent raised an eyebrow. "More fitness training?"

"I bloody hope not," Logan said. "But who knows where the night will take us?"

She nodded curtly. "Yes. It's good you're taking it seriously. And it's good that you have support. Someone to give us that little push. We all need it sometimes. *All* of us."

Logan glanced back at Ben. He was giving Tyler a bollocking for nicking one of his onion rings. "Aye, sometimes a wee nudge is all it takes, I suppose."

"Quite," Mitchell agreed. "But I wasn't talking about DI Forde."

"Fuck me, what now?"

Logan stood on the step, the collar of his coat pulled up to his ears, the rain rattling off the canopy above him.

"Alright, Bob?"

"Dandy as a fucking Highwayman until I clapped eyes on your girning bastard face," Bob Hoon spat back. His breath was a toxic blast of alcohol, stale smoke, and what might have been Pickled Onion *Space Raiders*. "Long fucking way to come to ask me that."

"Aye. Tell me about it," Logan said, before a snort of laughter from the former Detective Superintendent stopped him.

"Fuck me sideways, that's no' your car, is it?"

Logan didn't bother to turn. There was no doubting which vehicle Hoon was referring to.

"It is."

"That wee clown thing? Jesus Christ, what do you do, stick your feet out the bottom like Fred fucking Flintstone?"

"Something like that, aye," Logan said. He scratched his

head, unsure of how to phrase what he'd come to say, despite having rehearsed it in his head several times on the way over. "Listen, Bob, I just wanted to say... Last time I was here, you said you and me were alike."

"Did I? Fuck knows," Hoon said. He was leaning against the wall in the hallway, one hand still on the handle of the door. He didn't want Logan to come inside, which suited the DCI just fine. "What about it?"

"You're right. We are," Logan told him. "And... look, I know what it's like, alright? I've been there."

"What the fuck are you getting at here, Jack? I'm king of the fucking world, me. I'm Champion the fucking Wonder Horse." Hoon sneered at him through the gap in the door. "Maybe you couldn't fucking keep it together, but me? Robert fucking Hoon? I'm sorted. Fine. A-oh-fucking-kay."

Logan's mouth curved slightly into the faintest suggestion of a smile. "Good. That's great, Bob. But, eh... take this."

He held out a card with his number on it. Hoon regarded it with contempt and made no move to take it.

"The fuck would I want that for?" he demanded.

Logan shuffled forward, bringing the offered card closer. "Day or night," he said. "If you need me."

Hoon made a show of rolling his eyes and groaning, then snatched the card and thrust it into the pocket of his faded jeans.

"That it?"

Logan nodded. "That's it, Bob."

"Good. Then away climb into the Twatmobile there, and fuck the fuck off."

There was a faint *splash* as Logan stepped down onto the driveway, which was currently just one big puddle. The rain hammered a drumbeat on his coat as he turned back to the door.

"We all need a hand sometimes, Bob," he said. "Day or night. You know where I am."

And with that, he went marching through the rain and into the night.

LOGAN THOUGHT about parking out of sight of Shona Maguire's house, but the torrential rain put him off the idea. Besides, she'd have to see the car eventually. Best to just go ahead and get the jokes out of the way now.

He sat there behind the wheel for a moment, checking his reflection in the rearview mirror and breathing into his hand to make sure it was still the stench of Hoon's breath lingering in his nostrils, and not his own.

"Right then," he announced, to nobody in particular, then he jumped out of the car, scurried up the path in the pishing rain, and knocked on the door of Shona's cottage.

He heard footsteps approaching almost immediately. They were quick and eager, and he drew in a few quick breaths, steadying his nerves.

Nerves. Since when did he get *nerves*?

Jesus, this must be more serious than he'd let himself think.

He plastered a big smile on his face as the handle turned, and managed to dial it back to something less demented-looking before the door could swing open.

The smile fell off him completely when he saw who was standing on the other side of the threshold.

The fist of a pre-teen girl punched him in the stomach. It wasn't particularly hard, but it caught him off guard.

Olivia Maximuke, daughter of the Russian drug dealer he'd been instrumental in putting away for the next decade or more, glowered up at him.

"You got fat," she said, then she stepped aside and held the door wide. "You're late. The movie was supposed to start half an hour ago."

Logan looked past the girl, to where Shona stood leaning in the doorway of the living room, a mischievous smile playing across her face. "Sorry, didn't I mention...?" she asked.

Logan ducked in through the low front door. "No. Can't say you did."

"Must've slipped my mind."

They both jumped as the door was slammed shut at Logan's back.

"Don't even think about eating my popcorn," Olivia warned him.

Logan watched her go striding past into the living room. "I wouldn't dare, kid," he said. "I wouldn't bloody dare."

"Sorry, probably should've told you she'd be here," Shona said, stepping in closer. "But this is all your doing, after all."

"I suppose it is kind of my fault," Logan admitted.

"No 'kind of' about it. It's completely your fault," Shona said. "But, she's getting picked up at ten. You could... if you like, I mean... stay longer?"

"I'm going to start the film!" Olivia hollered, before Logan could formulate a reply. "I mean it, you're going to miss it. Ten-second warning."

Shona shut her eyes and groaned. Then, to Logan's

surprise, she raised herself onto her tiptoes and pecked him on the lips.

"I'm glad you came," she said.

Logan stood in the hall, his coat dripping onto the carpet, his heart hammering a drumbeat in his chest.

"Aye," he said to himself. "Me, too."

And then, he shrugged the coat off, hung it by the door, and braced himself for two hours of Roger bloody Moore.

CHAPTER FORTY-TWO

THE BASTARDS WERE WAITING FOR HIM IN THE CAR PARK on Monday morning.

"Looking good, Jack!" Ben hollered, when Logan emerged from the station, hoiking his shorts out of the crack of his arse.

"Nice legs, sir!" Sinead added.

"I'd give you one, boss!" Tyler said.

There was a heavy, awkward silence.

"I might've taken that too far," Tyler concluded, more quietly.

"The hell's all this?" Logan asked, storming over to them. "It's no' a spectator sport."

"Oh, really?" said Ben. He turned and looked up at the front of the station. Faces watched from almost every window.

"Oh, for f—" Logan began, then a woman with the air of an old hospital matron appeared beside him, a whistle around her neck, a clipboard balanced in the crook of one arm.

"Which one of you is DCI Logan?"

Dave held up a hand. "That would be me."

He grinned up at the woman as she stared at him in confusion.

"Nah, not really," he said.

"He's the one in the shorts," added Hamza.

"And what lovely shorts they are, boss," said Tyler. He winced as he felt everyone's eyes on him. "Shit. I did it again, didn't I?"

Logan made a variety of muttering sounds that never really came close to materialising as actual words, then sighed and turned to the woman in the tracksuit. "Aye. It's me. Where do you want me?"

"In a minute, I'll ask you to approach the first line, then I'll start the CD. You'll run on the first bleep. You must reach the second line before—"

"Aye. I've done it before," Logan said, wearily. "I know the score."

The trainer practically bared her teeth in contempt at having her spiel cut short, then headed off to set up the CD player.

"Raring to go, Jack?" Ben asked. He was bloody loving this, it was written all over his face.

"Oh aye. Can't wait," Logan said. He watched the trainer take out her measuring tape and double check the distance between the first and second lines marked out on the car park. "There must be some way out of this."

"Doubt it, sir," Sinead said.

"We're a bright bunch," Logan said, urging them on. "I bet, if we put our minds to it, we could figure out some way of me knocking this on the head."

"Problem with that, though, Jack, is that we don't want to,"

Ben said, his enjoyment of the moment now fully front and centre on his face. "In fact, it'd mean I'd wasted a lot of money."

Logan's eyes narrowed. "Money? What do you mean?"

With a nod from Ben, everyone unzipped their jackets, and Logan saw his own face staring back at him. They'd taken the photo from his file, added an 80s style headband, and blown it up to be printed at actual size.

Above the image, in Comic Sans font, were the words: 'Run, Fat Boy, Run.'

"To cheer you on," Ben explained. "Bit of motivation, and that."

Logan looked across their faces, slowly and solemnly, like he was marking them all for death.

"You're a shower of bastards," he remarked. "The lot of you."

"That's a horrible thing to say to your fan club, sir," Hamza told him, nostrils flaring as he tried to hold the laughter in.

It was Tyler who finally came through for him. "All joking aside, boss," he whispered, shooting a glance in the trainer's direction. "If you want out of it, I could get Sinead to call me before you start. We'll say it's something important that we need you for, and they'll have to call it off."

Logan pointed at the DC. "Yes. Yes. That's good. Fucking obvious, mind, but I'll take it. I always did like you, son."

"Please approach the starting line, DCI Logan," the trainer called over to him.

Logan kept his voice as an urgent whisper. "Right. Do it. Sinead."

Sinead reached into her pocket, subtly took out her

phone, and hid it behind DI Forde's back while she started to dial.

"Good. Great. Well done," Logan said, giving them a thumbs-up. He flicked a sneer in Ben's direction. "Looks like you wasted your money, after all, Benjamin."

His confidence bolstered, Logan approached the line, making a show of stretching and warming up. "Right, let's do this!" he boomed, safe in the knowledge that he wouldn't actually have to. "Let's get this done."

He stood by the line, jogged on the spot, swung his arms up over his head, then placed his toe on the strip of white tape.

"You'll run on the first bleep," the trainer reiterated. "You must reach the second line before the next bleep sounds. If you arrive before, then wait until you hear the bleep before you run back to the first line."

"Aye, aye," Logan said. "Bring it on."

He waited for the chiming of Tyler's phone.

And waited.

A horrible sinking feeling formed in his gut.

And then, just before the trainer could hit play on the CD player, the jangle of Tyler's phone cut across the sound of the dual carriageway traffic.

The trainer ignored it. "OK, so—"

"Hold on," Logan said, raising a hand. He turned in Tyler's direction. The DC tapped the answer button, then brought the phone to his ear.

"DC Neish," Tyler said. He opened his eyes wide, glanced in Logan's direction, then frowned like he'd been given bad news. "Uh-huh. Uh-huh."

"Go on, my son," Logan whispered.

"Right. Yes. Absolutely. No problem at all," Tyler concluded.

He hung up the phone and returned it to his pocket.

"Can we continue?" the trainer asked.

Logan side-eyed her, then turned his attention back to Tyler. "Problems, Detective Constable?" he asked.

Tyler smiled back at him. "Nah, boss," he said. "Just a wrong number."

Logan's face fell. His stomach flipped.

"Shower of absolute bast—" he began, then the CD player went *bleep*.

And on that, he ran.